KATE

"Sexy ramp on the
high seas…and all that jazz!"
Jina Bacarr, Author of
The Japanese Art of Sex

CRAZY FOR YOU

50599

0-505-52616-6

9 780505 526168

A WOMAN WITH RULES

He squeezed her hand. "Ready?"

She nodded. "Go slow."

Fast was not an option with the psychic. With every step, she paused, listened, ran her free hand along the wall. "Checking for termites?" he asked.

"Checking for cold spots."

Sex lifted one brow suggestively. "Hot spots are more fun."

She looked down her nose at him. "Not if you're seeking a wayward spirit."

No touching. No flirting. The woman had rules.

Sex wondered how many of her rules he could break on the five-day cruise.

Other *Love Spell* books by Kate Angell:

DRIVE ME CRAZY
CALDER'S ROSE

CRAZY FOR YOU

KATE ANGELL

LOVE SPELL

NEW YORK CITY

To Bobby

LOVE SPELL®

April 2005

Published by

Dorchester Publishing Co., Inc.
200 Madison Avenue
New York, NY 10016

ISBN 0-505-52616-6

The name "Love Spell" and its logo are trademarks of Dorchester Publishing Co., Inc.

Printed in the United States of America.

Visit us on the web at www.dorchesterpub.com.

ACKNOWLEDGMENTS

To those fellow authors and special friends who enhance my life. You are appreciated!

Marty Ambrose, Jina Bacarr, C. J. Barry, Dianne Castell, Marion Brown, Stella Brown, Maggie Davis, Emma Holly, Karen Kay, Angela Knight, Lora Leigh, Jean Lorenz, Deborah Anne MacGillivray, Tess Mallory, Jenna Mills, Angi Platt, Theresa Ragan, Debbie Roome, Leigh Smith, Catherine Spangler, Carol Stephenson, Heather Waters, Sue-Ellen Welfonder.

Prologue

June 3, 1925

"I'm crazy for you, Daisy."

Daisy Alton swayed, as much from the motion of the SS *Majestic* as from Randolph St. Croix's declaration of love. Her knees gave out and she dropped onto the narrow berth in her third-class cabin. Seated, she plucked nervously at the wrinkled skirt of her georgette frock. The hem drooped, in need of stitching; the peach hue was faded with wear. She looked a fright.

"I want to marry you," Randolph continued softly.

Daisy's heart ached with her need for him. From the moment she and Randolph had met on the boat deck, her gay and fickle heart embraced his calm reserve. She looked up at him now and slightly moistened her lips. "You're engaged."

"I broke my engagement to Eloise Hogue over afternoon tea," Randolph informed her as the pitch and roll of the luxury liner forced him to settle beside her on the narrow bunk. He collected her hands, absorbed her trembling with a squeeze to her fingers and a gentle smile.

"Eloise won't like being jilted."

Randolph shrugged. "She has threatened a breach-of-promise suit, or worse, to kill me. As far as I'm concerned, the only 'til death do us part' will be exchanged at our wedding."

Their marriage would cause a scandal. Society would never accept the heir to the St. Croix Cruise Line wedding a flapper who danced at backdoor clubs and speakeasies. Many considered her hedonistic and brash, with her short skirts and shorter hair. Most others found her distinctly common. A Dumb Dora without a red penny.

"I'd be a drag on you." Her throat closed on the words.

"Never, my dear," Randolph assured her as he drew her hands to his lips and kissed each palm. When he next spoke, his words were straightforward and fierce. "Gossip can't kill our love. We'll weather the storm."

Tears of happiness filled her eyes. "I am yours, forever."

Releasing her hands, he reached into the inner pocket of his herringbone jacket and removed a small square satin box. He flipped open the top with his thumb. Inside, a ring sparkled, brilliant and fiery. "A fire opal to reflect your spirit."

Daisy's eyes widened. A six-carat opal surrounded by diamonds. "Nice handcuff. Is it *real?*" she asked, then blushed at her blunder. Everything about Randolph was the Real McCoy, from his smile and his honesty to his pleasure in giving gifts.

Lifting her left hand, Randolph slipped the ring on her finger. "The opal is as real as our love," he declared.

Daisy loved him to the depth of her soul. Leaning into him, she brushed a light kiss on to his smoothly shaven cheek. Then, whispering near his ear, she repeated his vow, "Til death do us part, my darling."

One

"Door's open, I'm decent," Sexton St. Croix called to Bree Emery, who stood outside the owner's suite on the SS *Majestic*. A turn of the handle, and she entered his life of luxury.

The sitting room was large and lavishly furnished in black and gray and touches of turquoise. Sunshine slanted through the bay window, and the scent and sounds of the ocean rose from the open balcony. An oil painting of the *Majestic* hung on the wall above the wide-screen television. A mesmerizing portrait of elegance and opulence. Of heritage.

A stirring near the minibar drew Bree's eye to a half-naked man. St. Croix's idea of *decent* differed greatly from hers. As he turned, Bree took him in, every inch of him, all tall and tanned, and damp from his shower. He shook out his dark blond hair, then finger-combed it off his face. A Nordic sculpted face with sharp, angular cheekbones and a strong jaw that had just the

5

slightest hint of a dimple in the chin. His nose was straight, and his mouth full and sinful. Beneath dark eyebrows, the bluest eyes she'd ever seen stared back at her.

She eyed his bare chest, cut and defined, then checked out his brown silk boxers designed with tiny hamburgers, French fries, and bottles of Coke. *Supersized* ran the white strip on his fly. She lifted her gaze. "Interesting advertisement."

"The boxers were a gift."

"Some woman likes fast food."

"Constant craving." His smile curved, suggestively slow, unnerving her with its intimacy, as he took one step forward and extended his hand. The faint scent of Armani wafted from his skin. "Sexton St. Croix."

"Bree Emery." She took his hand and, to her surprise, trembled from his heat. Clairsentient, she *read* through her sense of touch. The mere brushing of palms produced feelings and experiences. St. Croix was definitely *experienced*.

"Pleasure before promises," she said, describing his lifestyle as emotions sifted through her. "Climaxes without commitment."

"All that from a handshake?" He threw back his head and laughed. A deep-from-the-gut laugh that made her fingers tingle before she withdrew her hand. The less contact she had with him, the better.

His smile broadened. Devastatingly slow, flashing white teeth and the tip of his tongue. Banked heat darkened his eyes.

Bree forgot to breathe.

The man was raw seduction in brown silk boxers and his supersized sex. She'd known the instant their hands touched that St. Croix was more player than partner, a man who walked the same path as her ex-boyfriend, Max Adkins.

Max . . . his memory left Bree weary of men. Two days prior to the cruise, she had wanted to surprise him with a catered deli lunch at his condo. The surprise, however, had been all hers. She'd caught Max in the dining room with his curvy brunette neighbor perched on the edge of the table, her legs splayed while he snacked on her edible panties.

Bree had lost her appetite. While Max had fallen over himself trying to protest his innocence, his guilt was proclaimed by the red food coloring from the panties that ringed his mouth like a clown's.

She didn't need another Bozo in her life.

It was well known that Sexton St. Croix changed women as often as he changed his bed sheets. She made it a policy to research her potential clientele, cracking closet doors for family skeletons. She'd read about his father, Byron, in *Forbes,* and Sexton in the *Enquirer.*

Affluent, charismatic, and wild, the supermarket tabloids had labeled him. They'd tracked Sexton through his misspent youth, when his life lay naked on the deck of his sailboat with a cold Corona and a hot date.

At sixteen, the tabloids had tagged him Sex, after the heir to the St. Croix Cruise Line had been photographed exiting a limousine and entering a convenience store to buy condoms. The tag had stuck for eighteen years.

Most recently, he'd celebrated his thirty-fourth birthday in Cancun. A photographer's wide-angle lens had captured Sex and his latest lover buck-naked on a private beach. As he stood in the surf, his broad shoulders, muscled back, and tight butt had glistened bronze against the setting sun, while his lover's breasts flashed like golden peaches for all of America.

Studying him now, his aura shimmered red, all male heat and sex appeal. A man ready to make love.

The very thought made her shiver.

"I'm here at your request, Mr. St. Croix—"

"Sex." He charmed her with a purely male grin.

"Sex." She allowed his name to roll over her tongue, tasted the full impact of the man. She licked her lips. "Tell me about the *Majestic.*"

"The St. Croix Line has always been known for its plush accommodations and polished service. Until recently, passengers disembarked and promptly booked another cruise." He reached for a pair of khakis tossed over the back of the black leather sofa. He stepped into them and pulled them up his long legs. After adjusting himself, he zipped and fastened his slacks.

The man had no modesty. At ease in his skin, he dressed in front of her as naturally as he drew breath. "Built in nineteen-o-five, the *Majestic* sailed for twenty-one years," he continued. "Tragedy at sea involving my great-great Uncle Randolph placed the luxury liner in dry dock. In celebration of our centennial, the ship's undergone extensive exterior reconfigurations and interior renovations before returning to sea. But it's a ship with a sordid past. A past that's returned to haunt us."

Bree had researched the strange occurrences both past and present. She'd scanned miles of microfilm at *The Miami Herald* until she'd located a small black-and-white photograph and a short article on the 1925 deaths of Daisy Alton and Randolph St. Croix.

The picture portrayed Daisy as sleek and fast. Her face was oval, her cheeks dimpled. The ends of her bobbed hair brushed the corners of her mouth. A pouty mouth with a playful smile. A long strand of pearls wrapped her neck, dipping into her cleavage.

The article confirmed her love of gin and a good time as she explored life through the Charleston and unfiltered cigarettes. Case files revealed her seduction of Randolph St. Croix, heir to the St. Croix Cruise Line. A man pledged to wed another woman.

At sea, and unable to resist the flapper, Randolph had presented Daisy with an expensive fire opal encircled by diamonds. A family heirloom meant for his fiancée, Eloise Hogue.

Catching wind of Randolph's gift, Eloise had confronted the couple, demanding St. Croix end his fling with the flapper. All accounts of the affair indicated that Randolph had returned to Eloise.

The story concluded that a devastated and brokenhearted Daisy Alton had lured St. Croix to her cabin one final time. Unwilling to live her life without him, and refusing to see him with another woman, Daisy had shot Randolph, then killed herself. Scotland Yard marked the case a crime of passion. A murder-suicide.

When the case closed, all fingers still pointed at Daisy. The gun and priceless opal were never found.

Transatlantic bookings fell off drastically following the tragedy. Within six months, the scent of death left the cabins as empty as the haunting memories that lingered on the ship.

Bree had sensed there was more to the story than the account in the newspaper. Following eighty years in dry dock, travelers were disembarking white-faced and demanding refunds. Over the past week, thirty crew members had quit the ship, all wide-eyed and spooked. National newspapers hyped several paranormal sightings on deck seven. The Death Deck.

Neither structural engineers nor sea dogs could explain the abnormal activity.

"This Caribbean holiday has been billed as a psychic cruise," Bree put in.

"More like a psychic circus," Sex ground out. "You're the only reputable psychic aboard. I've seen your television show, *Here and Beyond*. Very interesting."

"I enjoy my work." As cohost of a weekly show, Bree did readings for audience members. Any participant could place a piece of antique jewelry on a silver tray. Bree would then select a ring, brooch, necklace, or earring, and give the history behind the piece.

"After I'd hired you," Sex continued, "my sister, Cecelia, opened the bookings to anyone with tarot cards. My great-grandfather, Ramsay St. Croix, even hired Ouija master Zara Sage to track the ghost. I should never have offered a finder's fee."

The fee was enormous: a hundred thousand dollars to the psychic who rid the *Majestic* of the spirit.

"Do you believe in ghosts?" she asked. "Countless travelers claim the spirit on your ship is a woman. Specifically, Daisy Alton."

"Daisy, Daisy . . ." A muscle ticked in his jaw. "In life, she killed my great-great uncle. In death, she's costing me financially. If the rumors of her haunting the *Majestic* aren't put to rest, I'll be forced to auction the interior fittings to collectors and break up the ship for scrap."

Bree was about to defend the spirit's right to be aboard when the ship surged left, then dipped against a crosswave as it maneuvered the rough waters beyond the Port of Miami where the Gulf Stream crossed the Atlantic. In her mad grab for the back of a club chair bolted to the floor, she bumped Sex's arm. Pinpricks of heat jabbed her shoulder to wrist. A transference of energy made her aware of a redhead, pretty and persuasive, pleading with Sex to take her on the cruise.

"A woman wanted to travel with you," she noted.

His gaze narrowed sharply. "My friend, Heather, dropped me off two days ago."

Bree moved away from him. "I can still feel her on your skin."

One eyebrow spiked. "Even after my shower?"

"Soap and water can't remove desire. Heather wanted to travel with you."

"This isn't a pleasure cruise," he explained. "My concentration must be on the *Majestic*. I've booked you in Daisy Alton's cabin."

Bree nodded. "Am I the only one on deck seven?"

"One and only," he told her. "In honor of the centennial cruise, my great-grandfather Ramsay St. Croix is on board with his lifelong friend, Harlan Talmont. Ramsay recently turned ninety-eight and still hasn't lost his love for the *Majestic*. But to this day he refuses to go belowdecks. He can't face the memories of losing his brother."

Sex rubbed his hand along the back of his neck, suddenly uneasy. "You should know in advance that deck seven remains as it did in nineteen twenty-five."

She understood. "You didn't renovate those rooms?"

"The workmen refused to enter them after a few incidents. Same pattern in Randolph St. Croix's first-class cabin," Sex informed her. "It's all just as it was, from a copy of Agatha Christie's mystery, *The Man in the Brown Suit*, down to Randolph's argyle socks and wingtips. The cigar ashes are probably still in the ashtray."

"Time fixed in tragedy," Bree murmured. "Regrets or

11

recriminations. Lack of resolution. There's more to their deaths than meets—"

She bit her tongue on the next wild wave. The heave and plunge of the ship sent her to her knees. But she never hit the plush gray carpet. Sex grabbed her shoulders just in time. Flush against his bare chest, she felt his heart beat, the rise and fall of his chest. The contact scared Bree as no ghost ever had. She was swamped by touch-triggered images turned explicit and erotic. She closed her eyes against the carnal visions that flashed in rapid frames.

Sex's *friend*. "The brunette attired in leather and lace—" her words spilled over each other. "A slow striptease. A beauty mark on her right breast; a Tweety Bird tattoo on her left hip."

Bree's breathing quickened as the images grew more intimate. Stiffening against the visions, she vicariously relived St. Croix's most recent seduction.

So much wanting and willingness. Satin-cool sheets warmed by their bodies. The sampling of strawberries dipped in champagne, swirled in powdered sugar, then finger-fed between moist lips. Chocolate-covered blueberries. Raspberry caramels.

The lovemaking . . . long, deep kisses. Sex palming the woman's breast, the woman stroking his erection. His stiffness, her wetness. His entry and her acceptance as she wrapped her legs about his hips. The motion . . .

The grinding. Rocking. Rolling over rumpled sheets. Pillows falling to the floor.

Tongues laving, tasting. Lips sucking.

Love bites. Pale bruises.

The heat. The sweat.

The woman's gasp. St. Croix's deep moan.

Bree clutched Sex's back, dug her nails in, scoring his flesh as she shattered.

She wanted to die of embarrassment.

Sexton St. Croix stood as stunned as Bree. What the hell had just happened? An explosive dry hump? The woman had rocked his groin to a royal hard-on. Her breath still warmed his neck. His own hand shook as he stroked her back until she stopped trembling. Stiff-armed, he set her away from him.

An eternity of moments passed before she met his gaze, her color high, her expression pained. "Your sexual exploits overtook me," she softly confessed. "I sensed your lover. Your lovemaking."

"You climaxed, Bree." He grinned knowingly. "Was it as good for you as it was for me two nights ago?"

She wanted to wipe that self-satisfied grin off his face. "Please don't touch me again," she said evenly. "Next time I lose my balance, let me fall."

Sex studied her. White-blond hair, hazel eyes, her body blow-away-in-the-wind thin. A thick suede belt circled her pale yellow tunic, loosely draped over hips encased in white jeans. Tiny crystals dangled from her ears, and a larger pendant from a necklace. Cast in the late afternoon sunlight from the bay window, she glowed, ethereal, as the prisms danced rainbows across her chest.

She was incredible. A clairsentient whose curves absorbed his sexual heat. A psychic who climaxed in the aftermath of his pleasure with another woman.

Sensitive and insightful, Bree had sizzled. She would no doubt burn skin-to-skin. Combust from penetration.

Sexton St. Croix had pretty much seen and done it all, in every possible position. He hadn't, however, experienced a woman like Bree Emery. Her telling him not to touch her made his fingers itch. He fisted his hands to keep them still.

"I need to settle into my cabin." She broke the lengthy silence. "I've yet to unpack."

He snagged his blue Oxford shirt from the back of the sofa, slipped it on, tucked it in. Buttoned his cuffs. He threaded a brown leather belt through the belt loops. "I'll go with you," he said as he slid his bare feet into a pair of Topsiders.

"I can find my way below," she insisted.

"I'd feel better if I joined you."

"I'd feel better if you didn't."

He crossed his arms over his chest. "It's my ship."

She planted her hands on her hips. "It's my chance to view the cabin without interference."

The need to go with her was strong. "I promise not to get in your way."

"You'll stand in the passageway?"

"Right outside the door," he promised.

"You're pushy, St. Croix."

Pushy or protective? He wasn't certain. "After you." He motioned toward the door.

He followed her, admiring her backside as her hips swayed with the ship. Time and again, the luxury liner pitched, yet Bree refused to take his arm, choosing to stagger like a drunken sailor down the corridor ahead of him. She'd stepped out of her ring-toed sandals twice before she reached the glass elevator. Standing barefoot, she clutched her sandals to her chest.

A blend of the romantic past and a modernized present, the elevator was lit by blue neon illuminating the intricate grille surrounding the glass tube. Bree paled during the quick descent to the promenade deck. They then took the dramatic dual staircase that swept to the lower decks. When they were halfway down the staircase the ship lurched, knocking her against the hand railing. She nearly lost her footing. Sex lunged for her, only to fall back when her gaze warned him off.

"Headfirst down the stairs doesn't work for me." He moved to block her path. "Sit on the steps and go down on your bottom."

"I'm not five."

"Then take my hand."

She hesitated, leery of touching him.

"We've three decks to go." His lips twitched. "I'll try not to turn you on."

"No bare skin." She pulled the long sleeve on her tunic down over her right wrist to her fingertips and motioned him to do the same.

Now he felt like a five-year-old afraid of cooties.

Unbuttoning one cuff, he jerked the blue Oxford over his left hand. When their hands connected, it felt as if they were wearing mittens. The protective fabric made Bree smile.

He squeezed her hand. "Ready?"

She nodded. "Go slow."

Fast was not an option with the psychic. With every step she paused, listened, ran her free hand along the wall. "Checking for termites?" he asked.

"Checking for cold spots."

Sex lifted one brow suggestively. "Hot spots are more fun."

She looked down her nose at him. "Not if you're seeking a wayward spirit."

No touching. No flirting. The woman had rules.

Sex wondered how many of her rules he could break on the five-day cruise.

15

Smiling to himself, he watched her work. The constant touching of walls, windows, doorframes; the stroking of the aged teakwood hand railings as they traveled deeper into the ship. Deeper into the past.

The ocean had calmed by the time they reached deck seven. A deck that looked its age. The paneling and wood trim were now bowed and peeling. Sex hunched his shoulders in the low-ceilinged corridor. An eerie stillness quelled the vibration from the engines at the stern of the ship. The hair on his arms rose as they closed in on cabin 7001.

Bree's leather suitcase had been left outside the cabin door. "No computerized keycard," she murmured as she fingered the tarnished lock.

Sex retrieved a long brass key from above the doorframe. He inserted the key, then struggled with the lock. The key and lock rattled like a skeleton in a closet, yet the lock refused to give. "It's old and rusty."

"Let me try," Bree said softly.

She waited for him to step back before she placed her palm on the lock and lightly jiggled the key. "*Feel* anything?" he asked.

"A lock that won't open." She looked at him over her shoulder. "I'm not certain the cabin wants another passenger."

"Should I have one of the crew break down the door?"

"That would be trespassing." She continued to work the lock. "Daisy Alton died in this cabin. You can't rush into her past. When she wants visitors, Daisy will—"

The lock clicked open.

Bree smiled, relief evident in her hazel eyes. "—come to terms with my presence and let me enter."

Sex watched as she removed the key and the door

swung soundlessly open—*by itself.* Musty, stale air nearly stole his breath as he peered inside. The third-class cabin was the size of a walk-in closet. Rivets and pipes ran the length of the ceiling; the spartan confines consisted of a narrow bed with the frame built right into the wall and a miniature mirrored wardrobe.

No more than a hairsbreadth separated them now as he stood behind Bree in the doorway. She stood incredibly still, the rise and fall of her chest shallow and slow. The top of her head brushed his chin, her hair soft and silky and scented from apple shampoo.

He caught the expectant tilt of her head as she stepped into the cabin. "Places, like people, hold memories," she whispered, taking it all in.

Sex hung back. Leaning his shoulder against the doorframe, he contemplated the psychic. He hoped she could clear the *Majestic* of the sound of footsteps in the passageways, the flickering lights, the creaking doors.

He'd never believed in ghosts until he'd sat in the grand salon at an antique writing desk and the bottom desk drawer slid open and slammed him in the knee. He still had the bruise from the unexplainable phenomenon. Later that day, as he stood on the boat deck and watched his passengers board, he'd felt someone at his side. The presence was so tangible, in fact, he'd sworn he heard breathing. Turning slightly, he'd noted the deck was empty of all but the lifeboats.

With the sun in his eyes, its heat beating against his chest, Sex had taken a sip of bottled water. The rim of the bottle had barely touched his bottom lip when he felt his elbow nudged. Water splashed, leaving him damp from collar to belt. He'd been forced to change his shirt.

If the ghost was Daisy Alton, her pranks were wearing thin. Sex did not want her near him. The flapper had cut more than her initials in the family tree. She'd severed one of its branches. He despised Daisy for taking Randolph's life. He wanted her gone.

"Ready to unpack?" he finally asked Bree, glancing at her single suitcase. He'd never known a woman to travel so light. The ladies in his life couldn't leave the house without a dozen pieces of designer luggage and a trunk for their shoes. Hefting her bag, he set the case in the middle of her narrow bunk, then backed out once again.

He watched, curious, as she unhooked the strap and undid the zipper. He could tell a lot about a woman from what she packed. He hoped Bree had a little spank-me-daddy red or begging-for-it black in her panty drawer.

Catching the hint of a tune, he asked, " 'Five foot-two, eyes of blue'?"

She blushed. "You could hear me all the way in the corridor?"

"Interesting choice of music."

"I sense the spirit likes music," she said simply as she scooped up a stack of sleeveless tops and pastel-colored shorts.

Turning in a tight semicircle, she tugged on the teardrop pulls of the tiny wardrobe. Two tugs and the bottom drawer opened, knocking her in the shins. She settled her clothes inside, then filled the top drawer with sports bras, cotton panties, and long nightgowns. No satin, no lace, no dental-floss-thin thongs. Strictly Hanes Her Way.

After hanging a basic black dress from the mirror on the wardrobe, she looked around as if seeking more space.

Sex released a sharp breath. Bree shouldn't be forced to live out of her suitcase. He reached for her arm but let his hand fall short of taking her elbow. "I've changed my mind about your staying in Daisy's cabin. It's confined, so tight—"

"You'd have to butter your hips to get in."

Startled, Bree banged her hip against a fold-down chair. The female voice was light and giggly and playful. Flirty. Bree's face tickled from the sensation of someone whispering against her cheek.

She glanced at Sex, whose expression held concern for her welfare. Not the shocked look of someone who'd just heard a voice. "How about a deluxe outside stateroom?" he pressed. "My family reserves such a suite for cousins twice removed who book passage on the day we sail."

"No, I'm fine here. The cabin's cozy." She closed her suitcase and pushed it under the bunk. The suitcase didn't fit.

"Problem?" He bent to help her. On hands and knees they peeked under the bunk. Well hidden beneath decades of cobwebs and dust, they discovered a battered, dome-topped traveling trunk with a tarnished lock.

Together, they tugged the trunk from beneath the bunk. Bree immediately brushed off the dust for a better look. Sex watched as she reverently ran her hands over and around the trunk, as if it were a priceless treasure.

"Daisy's clothes and shoes," she guessed.

He tilted the trunk and searched the bottom. "No sign of a key."

"The trunk will open when Daisy is ready to reveal its contents," she assured him as she got to her feet.

Sex also stood. Jamming his hands in the pockets

19

of his khakis, he asked, "Do you have plans for the evening?"

"I'd wanted to absorb the cabin's atmosphere."

"I'd hoped you'd attend the cocktail party I'm hosting at seven for the psychic circus. Promenade deck, the grand salon."

"You're paying me to deal with the ghost," she reminded him. "I seldom mix with other psychics."

"Too much competition?"

"Too many dramatics."

He blew out a breath and came clean. "I don't want to face them alone."

"Your sister's on board."

"Cecelia doesn't think for herself," he confessed. "She depends on psychics for direction."

"She'll receive a lot of advice on this cruise."

"I don't want Cecelia unduly influenced," he confided. "Thirty minutes, Bree. That's all I'm asking."

"Thirty minutes can feel like a lifetime."

"We'll take a walk around the ship afterward." His slow smile offered the grand tour.

"I have a brochure in my purse."

"Pictures can't compete with moonlight and ocean breezes."

"Doesn't the heir to the cruise line have obligations on the *Majestic*?"

His smile faltered. "More obligations than I can count." No matter what his duties were, he felt compelled to spend his first night at sea with Bree Emery.

She glanced at her black dress. "How dressy is the cocktail party?"

"*Swanky!*" the female voice said gaily.

"Your dress is perfect," Sex assured her. "However, emeralds would bring out the green in your eyes.

Chandelier-style earrings and a choker, perhaps. I'll send Jackson Kyle, my right-hand man, with a selection of jewelry from the family safe."

"You're used to dressing women."

"Undressing them is my specialty."

"You're unbelievable."

"That's what my lovers say."

Bree shook her head. "I'll see you at seven."

"I'll watch for you," he said as he turned to leave. "The grand salon is my favorite room on the ship. It's got all the preserved grandeur of heritage and age."

"I'm crashing." Once again the female voice rose heedless and happy, announcing her intent to attend the party uninvited. *" 'In the meantime, in between time, ain't we got fun?' "*

21

Two

"I'm Jackson Kyle," said the tall, dark-haired man with the twenty-inch neck, introducing himself to Bree Emery. "I work for Mr. St. Croix. Your host would like to offer a selection of jewelry for the cocktail party this evening."

Two hundred and fifty pounds of man, casually dressed in a white knit shirt and broken-in jeans, eased past her and placed a locked attaché case on the tiny wardrobe. Once opened, the case revealed six black-velvet-lined jewelry boxes. Stepping aside, he looked about the cabin, seeking the ghost.

"Daisy's here," Bree informed him, feeling a brush of warm air at her side. The flapper had taken to Bree as if starved for company and conversation. "She's as interested in you as you are in her."

The man raised one eyebrow, skeptical, but curious.

"M-mmm, sparkly!" Daisy's excitement touched Bree. Bree took in the jewelry.

Brooches, earrings, bracelets.

Cameos, amethysts, rubies, diamonds.

23

Blinding and breathtaking and worth a fortune, Bree imagined as she traced her finger over an emerald choker. Exquisite. Generations of St. Croix women, pampered and privileged, rose to her touch. Women spoiled by their men.

Sex was not her man.

She cleared her throat. "I appreciate Mr. St. Croix's generosity," she said slowly. "These are lovely, but I'll have to pass."

Jackson shifted his stance, a man with thick thighs in a tight-ass cabin. "There are other pieces. Allow me thirty minutes and I will return—"

Bree shook her head. "The jewelry isn't me." She was as basic as her black dress.

A corner of Jackson's mouth curved slightly as he closed the lids of the satin boxes and returned them to the attaché case. "I've never known a woman to turn down diamonds. You're unique, Ms. Emery."

Curious about Jackson Kyle, Bree laid her hand lightly on his wrist. A man in the shadows. Aggressive, but kind. He took care of his own. "Are you a body-guard?" she asked.

"I have Sex's back."

"To fight off his women?"

Jackson smiled. "Only happened once. A story for a later date."

A hint of elegance lingered on Jackson's skin. A very wealthy lady. A lady whose clothing allowance was more than his annual salary.

Bree lowered her hand. "Wealth does not define the man."

He looked down at his wrist, then into her eyes. His mouth tightened. "Reading me, Ms. Emery?"

"Surface sensations only."

"What you *sense* could lose me my job."

The woman? Was she married? An affair? "It all stays in this cabin," she assured him.

He reached for the attaché case, then moved toward the door. "I trust only once, Ms. Emery. Don't betray me."

As he closed the door behind him, Bree silently vowed to stay on the man's good side.

"Hard Boiled has a crush," Daisy sang in her ear.

"The bigger they are, the harder they fall," Bree agreed.

"Time to ready myself for the cocktail party," Daisy announced. *"I need to arrange my hair, add a little brilliantine to make it glisten."*

Daisy at the party? No telling how the evening would end.

Debating how to dress up her black sheath, Bree entered the hip-wide bathroom. There was a toilet and a chipped pedestal sink. No shower. She washed her face with cold water. Brushed her teeth. She caught a flash of Daisy from the corner of her eye and swallowed cinnamon-flavored Crest. She turned so quickly she bumped her elbow against the wall.

Daisy giggled, finding humor in Bree's bruised funny bone.

Returning to the wardrobe, Bree found a strand of pearls wrapped around the hanger with her black dress. Glancing at the trunk, she found the padlock had been removed. Her heart warmed. A gift from Daisy. Respect for the ghost's privacy kept her from sifting through her belongings. All would be revealed in due time.

Looking in the mirror, Bree caught the flapper in profile. Bree could only stare at her swan-slender neck and soft white shoulders curving into a slinky silver gown cut to expose her stylish bare back. Her style was both slick and shocking. Overtly sensual.

"I plan to be danced tired." Daisy winked, blew Bree a kiss through scarlet lips, then dissolved into the light.

Bree couldn't help smiling. She'd never known a ghost to be so hauntingly beautiful. Most apparitions swirled in darkness or shades of gray. Daisy was pure Technicolor. Vibrant and vivacious.

Thirty minutes later, Bree ascended the grand staircase to the grand salon. Designed with posh furniture and hand-carved paneling, the room gave the ship the look of a more glamorous era. Rosewood salon chairs and spacious yellow brocade sofas with overstuffed cushions awaited lounging passengers. Hung above a leather-topped pedestal writing desk, a beveled mirror had once reflected the elegant penmanship of countless correspondents. Near the bow, oval stained-glass windows pictured nautical scenes, while high above, an enormous chandelier illuminated the steeply angled ceiling, casting prisms on passengers dressed to the nines.

A mahogany sideboard buffet hosted an assortment of seafood hors d'oeuvres and exotic fruit. An open bar offered champagne and island cocktails. Jackson Kyle was tending bar.

In this crowded room of socializing psychics, Bree felt like an outsider. She fingered the strand of pearls knotted around her neck. She wasn't good at small talk. She never sought the spotlight. Had never staked her reputation on outlandish predictions. Shaking hands oftentimes made her skin crawl.

Spotting Sexton St. Croix holding court on the far side of the salon, she watched him circulate, working the room like a politician. Conversation flowed around him as smoothly as champagne. Women flirted openly with him; men slapped him on the back.

Handsome in a dark suit and gray silk shirt, he'd forgone a tie. Dressed down amid a room of tuxedo-clad men, St. Croix exhibited a casual refinement inborn in the rich. He owned the room.

"Young Sexton has a beef with me." Daisy Alton pouted, reluctant to join the party.

Sex had every right to hold a grudge against Daisy. He believed she'd killed Randolph St. Croix. Bree was less certain of the flapper's guilt. Only hard evidence would clear Daisy's name.

Bree was focused so intently on Daisy, she started when Sex appeared at her side. He selected two flutes of champagne from the silver tray of a circulating waiter and handed one to Bree. She avoided touching his fingers. The look in his blue eyes asked if she was glad to see him. His knock-her-off-her-feet smile could land her flat on her back if she wasn't careful.

She refused to take pleasure in his company. "Nice party."

"Better now that you're here."

She gazed around the room. "You weren't hurting for company."

"I was waiting for you."

"Silver-tongued darb." Daisy tossed in her two cents.

Bree bit back her smile. "Sweet-talker, huh?"

Sex's gaze narrowed. "I'm not feeding you a line."

"Daisy's got your number."

He paled slightly, his tone cautious. "She's here? Now?"

"And in need of a little giggle water." The flapper's warmth disappeared with her words.

"What the—?" Sex muttered as he shifted his stance.

"Someone stepped on my foot." Awareness struck, slowly, yet with the strength to make him blink. He shook his head. "No, can't be . . ."

"Daisy's on the *Majestic*," Bree said confirming his worst nightmare.

He worked his jaw. "You're absolutely certain?"

Sex wasn't the first to question her credibility. Would not be the last. "I don't stage publicity stunts."

He scanned the room. "You've seen her?"

She nodded. "Her reflection in my mirror. She's quite chatty."

"Girl talk?" He ran one hand over his jaw. "Don't make her your new best friend."

"Daisy needs to trust me," Bree explained as she sipped her champagne. "She's graciously sharing her cabin."

"*My* cabin on *my* ship," he reminded her sharply.

"She's sweet and generous—"

"And she *murdered* Randolph St. Croix."

Sadness settled over Bree, so sudden and profound, her own heart ached with loss. A devastating loss of purest love. She closed her eyes and took slow, shallow breaths.

"Bree, what's wrong?"

She slowly opened her eyes. Sex stood so close, she inhaled Armani, his maleness, and sensed his concern.

"I'm fine, really." She clutched the long strand of pearls.

He eyed the strand. "You chose pearls over my emeralds?"

"Daisy's pearls," she confessed. "I prefer the past over the present. It's far less complicated."

He didn't look at all happy. His features relaxed

somewhat when a tall, willowy blonde in ivory satin took his arm, then kissed his cheek.

"My sister, Cecelia," he said. "Meet Bree Emery."

Cecelia's blue eyes were lighter than her brother's, her fine-boned features expressive. She captured Bree's free hand. "The amazing clairsentient. Welcome aboard."

Kind. Sincere. Not as gullible as her brother thought. The hint of a man sizzled on Cecelia's skin. A man who excited her sexually.

"I'm not all that amazing," Bree corrected as she withdrew her hand. "It's just that I don't fear what others see as strange or frightful."

"I suggested a no-trespassing sign on the ship to send Daisy on her way, but Sex vetoed my idea," Cecelia confided.

Bree forced back a smile. "Signs seldom divert spirits."

Cecelia shivered. "I haven't seen Daisy and I'm not certain I care to."

"There's no reason for you to see the ghost, my dear." A large woman draped in an amber-and-gold caftan joined the group. "You must seek out your future husband, not Daisy Alton."

"Zara Sage." Cecelia looked genuinely pleased to see the imposing woman. Six feet tall and buxom, she wore her silver-blond hair in a Grecian twist. Good genes or face-lifts defied her advancing years. "Do you know Bree Emery?"

"By reputation." Zara dismissed Bree with a nod.

Bree was familiar with Zara Sage. Revered for her "cosmic fingers," Zara used a Ouija board to communicate with the dead. Her readings were high priced and surprisingly accurate, her clientele both rich and famous.

Cecelia turned to Sex. "Daisy Alton spoke to Zara through Ouija. She predicted that my future husband is on this cruise."

The flapper playing matchmaker? Bree felt as skeptical as Sex now looked. "You've contacted Daisy?" she asked Zara.

The older woman sniffed. "Daisy contacted *me*. I'm her medium."

Sex's eyes narrowed. "Medium?"

"Daisy's earthly mouthpiece," Zara explained. "She speaks only through Ouija."

"Bushwa! The lady's beating her gums," Daisy muttered in disgust. *"I'd never talk to a wooden board."*

Bree swallowed her smile.

Zara waved toward the salon entrance. "Here come Harlan and Ramsay and his companion."

Bree took a sip of her champagne, then glanced their way. One man maneuvered well on a walker, the other was wheelchair-bound. Similarly dressed in pressed white shirts and dark slacks, the men looked remarkably spry, despite a few liver spots, slumped shoulders, and thinning white hair.

It was the woman pushing the wheelchair who caught Bree's eye, and held the gaze of every red-blooded male in the salon. With her wild red hair, melon-size breasts, and yard-long legs, she looked more centerfold than companion.

Off to Bree's left, Daisy hovered, agitated and flighty, in imminent retreat. The air cooled and Bree shivered, as if she'd walked over a grave.

The elderly man with the walker shuffled forward. Bree caught the quick, discreet look he cast at Zara Sage. As if they shared a secret. "Harlan Talmont," he

CRAZY FOR YOU

said in an age-cracked voice as he came to stand before Bree.

"Bree Emery," she returned.

Harlan peered at Bree from behind rimless glasses, his gaze obsidian dark. "You psychic, little missy?" he asked.

Bree nodded. "I sense the past through touch."

"Sorry, I can't shake hands," he said flatly. "Need both hands on my walker for balance."

Bree didn't need him falling over from a handshake.

Harlan cocked his head. "Do you penny ante?"

The man had a hobby. "Poker or whist?" she inquired.

He turned his walker to face the man in the wheelchair. The pleated corners of his mouth curved into a gap-toothed grin. "Our mark, Ram."

"You're falling in with cardsharps," Daisy's hushed whisper warned, once again outside the circle of people.

Bree frowned. Men in their late nineties hardly classified as dangerous gamblers.

"You'll need rolls of pennies," Sex advised with a chuckle. "Harlan and Ram took me for ten dollars last weekend."

He placed his hand on the shoulder of the elderly man in the wheelchair and made introductions. "You met Zara Sage when she boarded in Miami. Now meet Bree Emery. Bree, my great-grandfather, Ramsay St. Croix. Known as Ram to family and friends."

Ram's arm trembled as he shook her hand. "I feel as if I already know you." His voice was a raspy croak.

Bree clasped his blue-veined hand lightly. Sensations flowed through him and into her. His life was as thickly ringed as a giant redwood. Filled with confidence and pride, he held onto life with the aid of a pacemaker and the fawning attention of his companion.

31

"My pleasure, Mr. St. Croix," Bree returned.

"Ram," he corrected. Breaking the handshake, he turned slightly, soon capturing the hand of the redhead who stood behind him. "Mimi Rhaine, my companion."

Harlan chuckled, low and rusty. "She puts the *ass* in assisted living."

Mimi patted Harlan's cheek and cooed, "Such sweet talk, gumdrop. I'm also psychic," she informed Bree. "I get flashes of past lives. Laird Ram and I once lived in medieval Scotland. I was his mistress then, and I attend his golden years two centuries later." She glanced at Sex with man-eater eyes. "I'd know Sex in any lifetime."

At a loss for words, Sexton St. Croix stared at Mimi. He knew why Ram had hired her when his previous companion had retired. Thirty-year-old Mimi was an affirmation of life. A whole lot of life. She hovered, teased, cooed. Ram lived for her hugs, often needing oxygen when pressed too long to her full bosom. Sex couldn't fault his great-grandfather for employing a pretty woman to push his wheelchair.

Ram accepted Mimi's flirting, his gaze bright and amused whenever she made a play for Sex. Sex, however, never dallied with St. Croix employees. Especially one responsible for Ram's comfort and medication.

"You'll have to do a past life regression for Sex," Bree suggested to Mimi. "I'm certain you were intimate."

"Definitely intimate," Mimi agreed. "Perhaps Sex was once a pirate and I a captured wench, tied to the mast of his ship."

"I'd have taken Sex for a highwayman," Bree said thoughtfully, openly amused by Mimi's pursuit. "A titled lord out for sport, riding a black stallion, holding up carriages, stealing both a lady's jewels and her virginity."

Mimi's nostrils flared. "Mmm, a man as untamed as his stallion. And equally as well hung."

Ramsay slapped his thigh, snorting.

Sex nearly sprayed his last sip of champagne.

"Regress into the past on your own time," Zara Sage told Mimi. "Our concentration should be on Daisy Alton." Striking a theatrical pose, she pressed the back of her hand to her forehead. "The flapper's in this room. I can feel her. So very near."

"How near?" Sex asked.

Bree nodded toward the bar. "Near Jackson Kyle."

Sex shifted his gaze, sucked in a breath. One shelf above Jackson's head, a bottle of Tanqueray tilted, wobbled, then toppled onto a row of brandy snifters. Crystal splintered, the sound as sharp as spraying bullets.

There was a moment of horrified silence, quickly followed by screaming. Mimi Rhaine's high-pitched shriek left Sex deaf.

Zara Sage crossed herself before joining the mass exodus from the grand salon.

Bree moved with the speed of light, faster than Sex could track her in the retreating crowd. Depositing her flute of champagne on the buffet sideboard, she grabbed the bar on Harlan's walker and ushered him to the door. The man could shuffle in an emergency. Mimi followed with Ram, all wiggle and nervous giggle. Sex winced when Mimi bumped Bree with the wheelchair, then ran over Bree's foot in her hasty departure.

Close to being trampled, Cecelia fainted dead away.

Jackson was at Cecelia's side in a heartbeat. Hunkering down, he pulled her against his chest and patted her cheek with a gentleness that surprised Sex.

Cecelia soon came around. "Was anyone shot?" she

whispered, fisting her hand in the black satin lapel on Jackson's tux.

Jackson wrapped his arms protectively around Cecelia. "No gun was fired. Nothing but broken crystal."

"What did you drop?" Cecelia asked.

Jackson glanced up at Sex. "A bottle slipped off the shelf."

Sex understood. "Take care of my sister," he instructed Jackson. "Cut the lights and lock up the salon when you leave."

The man who had stood by his side for ten years nodded.

Sex strode toward the bar, where Bree studied the shelved bottles of liquor. "Daisy's doing?" he asked.

Bree nodded. "She accidentally tipped the Tanqueray."

"Her accident cleared the room," Sex growled. "Psychics shouldn't fear her." Mimi Rhaine had made his ears ring.

"The shattered glass was unexpected."

"What will Daisy do next?" he asked.

Bree shrugged. "She's unpredictable. An outrageous and rebellious flapper."

Stepping over the glass, Sex rounded the bar, poured himself two fingers of Johnny Walker Black. One long swallow and the whiskey burn ignited his anger. Slamming the shot glass on the counter, he ground out, "Go talk to her."

"And say what? Ask her to behave?" She met his gaze. "Daisy is a soul in limbo. When the time is right, she'll free herself from her past."

After witnessing the mad dash for the door, Sex despised Daisy even more. Invisible, she had him at a disadvantage. She created more chaos than a storm at sea. "Daisy must be gone by the end of the cruise. If she doesn't disembark with the passengers, the *Majestic* goes on the auction block."

"You can't compare loss of capital with a captive soul," Bree replied, defending the flapper.

Frustrated, he fisted his hands so tightly the muscles in his arms flexed. Bree didn't live in the real world. Profit over loss was the philosophy he lived by. "You have five days to pull the welcome mat," he said.

The look in her eyes almost had him retracting his words. He'd hurt her. She chewed her bottom lip in thought. A sweet, soft lip meant to stir passion, not sadness.

Bree's chest ached with the weight of the *Majestic*'s future. Sexton St. Croix's hatred of Daisy was blinding him to a possible alternate ending to the 1925 murder-suicide. It was up to Bree to prove Daisy's innocence.

Warmth and a giggle announced Daisy's return to Bree's side. Tipsy and silly, she hiccuped, *"Nothing but flat tires. Get a wiggle on. Let's ankle!"*

"The party's over," Bree agreed with the ghost. "Daisy and I are off for a walk."

Sex sidestepped, blocking her departure. "I promised you a tour of the ship. Mind if I tag along?"

She most certainly did mind. "You can't push Daisy overboard."

He shrugged. "Worth a try."

She eased around him. "See you tomorrow."

Outside on the promenade deck, Bree stargazed. The clear sky was filled with brilliant constellations. Stars to be shared with a lover.

"Butt me?" Daisy requested, materializing against the railing in full view of anyone who might pass by.

"Sorry, I don't smoke," Bree returned. "Bad for the lungs."

"I'm already dead." She pursed her scarlet lips. *"Rhatz on young Sexton."*

Bree sighed. "I'm not that disappointed."

"Tell it to Sweeney," Daisy said tartly before her energy waned.

Daisy didn't believe her. Strange how the flapper was in tune with Bree's feelings.

Bree found strolling the empty deck a letdown. Closing her eyes, she clutched the side railing and breathed deeply of the salt air. The night breeze ruffled her hair. A breeze far cooler than when she'd first stepped onto the open deck. So cool, in fact, she wished she had a Windbreaker.

Seconds, perhaps minutes passed, and the deck seemed to shift beneath her feet. She felt herself sliding. She hung onto the railing for dear life.

The rail became a conduit as a tingling current ran through her fingers, then charged into her chest. A surreal calm settled over her as her present faded into someone else's past.

Promenade Deck
May 25, 1925

In a world that barely acknowledged knees, Randolph St. Croix was suddenly taken by a pair of curvy gams. Gams in twisted and knotted silk stockings worn just above the knee, exposed when the ocean breeze blew up the young woman's skirt. She had great sea legs. Her demure, white cotton shirtwaist appeared too innocent for the bold look in her eyes. Her red lips were turned in a practiced Venus-surprised-at-the-bath sort of way.

Admiring her beauty, Randolph cleared his throat

and reminded himself that he was a respectable, soon-to-be married man.

"Got a ciggy?" The woman's question was carried on the breeze.

Randolph stepped closer. Although puffing a Havana, he slipped an engraved silver cigarette case from the inside pocket of his pin-striped suit and offered her a smoke. The woman didn't wait for his assistance. Withdrawing a Camel from the case, she tapped it on the back of her left hand, then slipped it between her lips. She surprised him by reaching over, taking his lighted cigar from his mouth, and using it to light her own cigarette. It was an intimate gesture, turning complete strangers into immediate acquaintances.

Pleasure shone in her blue eyes as she dragged in the unfiltered smoke. Exhaling, she blew airy rings out over the ocean. "Thank you," she finally said, squinting at him through the haze.

Randolph hesitated in closing the cigarette case. There was a restlessness to her spirit that held his gaze. Her face was powdered, her cheeks rouged, her eyes artificially darkened. Her mouth was painted and moist. No other lady of his acquaintance made love to a Camel with her lips as this young blonde was now doing.

"Randolph Ambrose," he introduced himself, purposely leaving off his last name and the fact that he owned the luxury liner. Gold diggers hunted him like a partridge.

The woman finished her cigarette before giving him her name. "Daisy Alton."

He looked about the deck. "Traveling alone?"

"No fire extinguisher."

No chaperone. "I'm crossing the North Atlantic with my fiancée and her family," he told her.

"Your fiancée prefers London to New York?" she politely inquired.

"Eloise is fond of the theater."

She tapped her toe. "I prefer jazz."

A flapper. Risky and fast-living, and all of nineteen. Randolph was instantly taken by her. "I have yet to see you in the garden lounge or the grand salon."

"You might yet see me in the smoking club."

A male-only preserve. Scandalous, yet fascinating. "Most daring, Miss Alton."

Daisy liked Randolph Ambrose. He was tall and strong and conventionally handsome. She pegged him close to thirty. The years had been kind. There was yet no gray in his dark brown hair and his eyes still shone with life. He looked swell in his tailored suit and black wingtips. When he brushed her arm on the side railing as he looked out to sea, the sleeves of his pin-striped suit coat slid up slightly, and the muted light of evening caught the gold-and-diamond links that impaled his cuffs.

They stood together in companionable silence, admiring the sparkling water and the racing clouds until the sun had set. In the haze of darkness, Randolph pulled out his pocket watch, noted the time. "Seven o'clock. You must ready yourself for supper," he said, a hint of disappointment in his voice. "And I must check on my Eloise. She suffers from *mal de mer.*"

Daisy couldn't bear to tell him that as a third-class passenger she'd already missed her evening meal to remain in his company. She'd sneaked up on the upper deck to see how the other half lived, only to be charmed by a man who believed her first class.

"Perhaps ginger tea and digestive biscuits would speed her recovery," Daisy suggested.

Randolph nodded. "I believe a tin of biscuits was delivered to her cabin along with a bon voyage basket."

Bon voyage baskets. Gifts for the passengers from those remaining in port. Daisy had seen the stewards rushing about with baskets piled high with fruit and jellies and shrouded in amber cellophane. No one had seen her off at the dock, and such a basket was too frivolous and expensive to purchase for herself.

"What can't be cured must be endured."

Randolph nodded. "Most philosophical." He paused, met her gaze. "Duty calls. Best of the evening, Miss Alton." He crossed the deck and disappeared into the grand salon.

A salon Daisy couldn't enter.

She suddenly felt alone in the world.

"Bree?" Sexton St. Croix's baritone carried across time, calling her back to him. A hollowness had collected about her soul, and despite his closeness, she felt utterly abandoned.

"Bree?" His hands were on her now, shaking her gently, the power of the man pulling her from the past. The sensation of countless women ran through his fingers and settled in her bones. Her body hummed with sexual tension.

Jerking back, she focused on Sex. Concern darkened his gaze as he snapped his fingers near her nose, slowly enunciating each word. "Are you with me?"

She snapped her fingers back at him. "Right here, right now."

"Where were you?" He stood so close his breath

fanned her lips, warm and tangy with a hint of champagne.

In need of breathing room, Bree edged back. Sex's hands dropped to his sides. "I witnessed Daisy and Randolph's first meeting," she told him.

One brow arched, but he didn't say a word, merely stared at her, unconvinced.

She stroked the rail with her fingertips as she related what had happened. "They met unexpectedly on the promenade deck. Randolph was traveling with his fiancée and her family. Daisy was alone. He showed interest and she flirted, just a little." Bree shivered, as much from the night breeze as from her peek into the past. "Randolph never revealed his last name, and Daisy kept her third-class status secret."

"Such innocence," he muttered darkly as he shrugged off his suit coat and draped it over her shoulders. The heat from his body warmed her. His scent enveloped her. "How far would you go to defend the flapper?" His tone was both curious and accusing.

She stiffened. "I'm not making this up. I saw what I saw."

He raised his left hand to stroke her cheek, hesitated, then decided against touching her. "Your trance left you quite pale."

"Slipping into the past takes a lot out of me."

"Can I get you a drink? Something to eat?"

Her stomach took that moment to growl. "A sandwich would be nice."

"The grill or the Crystal Dining Room?" he asked.

"Somewhere there aren't a lot of people."

One brow arched, sexy and suggestive. "My suite?"

"Nowhere quite so private."

A short silence was followed by his decision. "I know just the place."

Unfastening the button on his cuff, he proceeded to pull the sleeve of his gray silk dress shirt down over his hand. He waited for Bree to slide the sleeve of his suit coat over her palm, then took her hand.

Shadowed by moonlight, his blue eyes appeared dark, his voice serious. "Will I ever be able to touch you?"

His question surprised her. "Why would you want to?"

"Why does any man wish to touch a woman?"

"Nookie," Daisy whispered as she breezed by.

Whipped by the breeze, Bree tucked her hair behind her ears. "I don't do casual sex."

"I never take sex casually. I'm a serious and giving lover. I have references."

Previous lovers would sing his praises. "I don't do shipboard romance. My last relationship ran a year."

His breath hitched. "A whole year? Who called it quits?"

"Max Adkins cheated on me. I caught him sampling edible panties on another woman."

"Mmm, what flavor?"

Flavor! Max had circus-red lips."

"Cherrypicker stains the worst."

"Speaking from experience?"

His grin flashed, leaving her to imagine the worst. Then he scratched his head. "I'm confused. You're psychic, yet you didn't pick up on his affair."

"I cared for Max . . ." She chose her words carefully. "It became difficult to read him."

Sex was digesting this information when her stomach growled a second time. "Let's get you that sandwich," he suggested.

She followed him through the ship, down the grand staircase to the Crystal Dining Room. Sex nodded to the maître d', then stopped briefly at the captain's table to greet Ramsay, Harlan, and Mimi.

"Captain Nash, I'd like you to meet Bree Emery," he said to a man who appeared far too young to command the *Majestic*.

The captain immediately stood and shook her hand. *Solid, capable, ambitious. A man of good conscience.*

"Would you care to join us?" Captain Nash inquired. "We've been discussing the incident in the grand salon."

"The *ghostly* incident where we barely escaped with our lives." Mimi Rhaine took Ramsay's hand, placed it over her heart. "You were so brave, snicker-doodle. My heart's still racing."

Ram winked at Sex. "Pitter-patter. Pitter-patter."

Sex rolled his eyes. "Thanks for the dinner invitation," he addressed the captain, "but Bree and I have prior plans."

Skirting diners and uniformed waiters, Sex and Bree made their way to the galley. The backswing of the doors hit Bree in the bottom, bumping her forward. She slammed into Sex. Hard. She felt painted onto his back. Her pearls would leave a permanent impression on his spine. The points of her nipples dimpled the silk of his shirt. Her soft abdomen pressed his tight ass.

Within seconds heat curled in her belly as awareness of St. Croix's sex life flooded through her. So many women. So many positions. So much sex.

She sizzled.

Sex moved first. He stepped forward, and Bree caught herself before she fell flat on her face. Her cheeks burned as hotly as her body.

"Doggie-style?" he whispered near her ear. "The position works best reversed."

Bree wished herself as invisible as Daisy.

"Coming through." A waiter bore down on them, carrying a tray laden with lobster tails.

Sex pulled her out of the man's path. "Follow me."

Moments later, amid a galley filled with European chefs and international cuisine, Sex fixed Bree a turkey sandwich. Then he sliced prime rib for himself. Seated on short wooden stools pulled up to a butcherblock counter near the walk-in cooler, they dug in. Before long, milk mustaches whitened their upper lips.

All the while Bree was aware that Daisy Alton drifted about the *Majestic*, liberated and daring, and hauntingly beautiful.

Three

"You didn't drop the Tanqueray, did you?" Cecelia asked Jackson as they entered her two-deck deluxe suite.

"I was pouring drinks." Jackson glanced over his shoulder, scanning the corridor before closing the door behind them. "I might have bumped the shelf—"

"But you didn't," Cecelia stated with a certainty that surprised him. "Psychic fingers point to Daisy Alton. We were in the same room as the ghost."

"There's no proof—"

"Don't protect me from what I know to be true." Her voice shook ever so slightly. "Where is Daisy now?"

Jackson shrugged. "Your guess is as good as mine."

Cecelia settled onto a hunter green sofa. Sinking into the soft leather, she clutched a decorative throw pillow to her chest, then crossed her legs. The side slit in her ivory gown split across her stocking-clad thigh. The woman had great legs, Jackson had always thought. Sleek and supple. Legs a man wanted wrapped about his hips as she drew her pleasure from his desire.

Cecelia patted the cushion on her left. "Sit with me, Jax."

A man of action, Jackson unbuttoned his tux, ran his fingers along his black suspenders, yet didn't cross to the woman who lived in every fiber of his being. Cecelia was elegance and refinement. Utter sophistication. Jackson didn't fit into her world.

As he studied her now, wide-eyed, her expression expectant, she reminded him of the birthday girl he'd met ten years earlier on a hot July day. . . .

Summer of 1995

Twenty-four and ready to explore new avenues of employment, Jackson had arrived at the St. Croix estate in Coral Gables the afternoon of Cecelia's pool party. He'd been escorted to the back terrace and gardens overlooking the pool, tennis courts, and freshly mown lawn. Several peacocks wandered the grounds, fanning their iridescent plumage in vain displays. Jackson had located Sex on the courts, playing doubles with one set remaining.

A cold Guinness in hand, Jackson dropped onto a stone wall shaded by poinciana trees. From there he had an ideal view of those splashing and laughing in the turquoise-tiled pool with a golden dolphin pictured on the bottom. He watched as a leggy blonde in a lavender string bikini stood waist-deep in the shallow end, accepting hugs and air kisses from numerous guests.

He recognized her from a picture Sex carried in his wallet. Cecelia St. Croix was turning eighteen today.

In between the red-flowered branches, he caught her climb from the pool. Water sluiced off her maturing body. A body that would soon have men howling for her attention. A cabana attendant met her with a fluffy blue beach towel that she wrapped about herself, knotting the ends over her left breast.

Snagging a long white T-shirt from a lounge chair, she crossed the bronze keystone deck, a young woman aware of her beauty, wealth, and place in the world. She left a trail of wet footprints on the steps that brought her to the terrace.

"Happy birthday, Celia," Jackson said when she'd hit the top step.

Startled, she stubbed her toe. "You scared me." She bent to rub her big toe where the peach polish had scraped off.

He'd taken a long pull on his beer, looking her over as she straightened; the towel had slipped to her waist.

She stood so close now, he could see that her nose was sunburned and peeling. Faint tan lines from a different swimsuit banded her shoulders. Her breasts and abdomen were sunkissed a berry brown. Unbidden desire tightened his gut along with his groin.

He mentally groaned. Shifting on the stone wall, he settled the bottle of beer between his legs to hide his hard-on. Cecelia was his best friend's sister. The distance between wealth and working man stretched long and wide. She was sweet eighteen to his hardened and streetwise twenty-four.

"Do you always hide in the shadows?" she asked as the towel pooled at her feet. She slipped the oversized T-shirt over her head. The white cotton shimmied over her B cups, then caught on her prominent hipbones before skimming her knees. The hot pink inscription

MIRROR, MIRROR ON THE WALL, MAKE THEM BEG, MAKE THEM CRAWL, had him shaking his head. Her attitude alone would cut men to their knees. "Who are you?"

"Jackson Kyle," he finally told her. "I'm waiting for Sex."

His gaze narrowed as she took him in, thoroughly, knowingly. Smugly. She shook out her hair with elegant fingers tipped with peach polish. Droplets flew, spattering his blue-jeaned thighs.

"Six-foot-five. Two hundred and fifty pounds. You're fierce, formidable, and adapt to any situation." She spoke with the intimacy of knowing him longer than sixty seconds. "You attended Ohio State with Sex. You're as celibate as he is active. You don't smoke, seldom drink, and work out twice a day. You're as much brawn as businessman. You're leaving after one season at tackle with the Chicago Bears to protect my brother's finances and guard his back."

He rubbed his hands down his denimed thighs. He was a private person, and Cecelia had crossed more than one line. "You know a lot about me."

A touch of embarrassment pinkened her cheeks. "I overheard Sex and my father in the study discussing the terms of your employment," she confessed.

He lifted a brow. "Eavesdropping?"

"That's how I stay informed."

"It didn't cross your mind to join your brother and father?" he asked.

"The conversation would have ceased," she said on a sigh. "I'm considered pretty but clueless."

His gut told him differently. "You're smarter than they think."

"And twice as charming."

Charming and cheeky.

A clatter on the terrace turned their heads. A man in a starched white shirt and black slacks pushed a sterling-silver serving cart past tables draped with ecru cloths, settings of cranberry glass, and matching dessert plates. The cart carried a three-tiered cake lit with candles.

She smacked her lips. "Confetti cake with raspberry frosting."

Sweet. Maybe he could score a piece.

She edged closer, standing between his splayed legs. "It's time to make my birthday wish."

He rolled the bottle of beer between his palms. "Wish, huh?" He'd never had a birthday party. He couldn't comprehend the fuss over making a wish. What more could Cecelia St. Croix possibly want?

She leaned so near, his blue-jeaned thighs abraded the soft curve of her hips. Then she whispered, "A birthday kiss."

He pretended to misunderstand. Lifting his Guinness in a toast, he nodded toward the dozens of young men in the pool. "Who gets the honor? Freckles, Cannonball, or Surfer Dude?"

She ran one fingertip along his jaw, a sweet young thing testing her appeal on an older man. "The guy with the five o'clock shadow."

A tempting invitation, but unrealistic. He leaned back slightly. "Look, sweetheart, I'm not a guest. You should be kissing boys your own age."

"Boys my age are boring."

"You want experience?"

She flicked her pink tongue over her lips, her mouth moist, dewy. "Mm-hmm. Your kiss would be the best gift ever."

His jaw worked. "We've just met and talked all of ten minutes. I'm not your man."

Her blue eyes darkened as she inched nearer. Her pubic bone pressed his groin. "A kiss in the shadows or by the birthday cake in front of God and Sex."

Cecelia was persistent and pampered and used to getting her own way. Jackson, however, didn't give in under pressure. "Sorry, kid, no kiss."

He pushed off the stone wall, tall and intimidating, expecting Cecelia to jump back. She didn't budge an inch. Their bodies stood flush against each other: her breasts brushing his chest; the significant bulge behind his zipper pressed against her belly. He caught his reflection in her clear blue gaze as she rose on tiptoe and took his mouth. Her lips were sweet and pink and cupid soft.

Her kiss pressed tentatively, a mere exchange of breath. Jackson fought his response. Someone else would teach her the technique that deepened desire when tongues tangled, teeth bit, and lips reddened from passion.

Curling his hands over her shoulders, he set her aside. Their five-second kiss ended with him shifting his stance and her frustrated sigh.

She wrinkled her nose. "That's *all* you have?"

"That's all you're getting."

There was silence, a flicker of disappointment in her eyes, before a slow smile spread, sexy and secretive. "I'll see you when I'm twenty-one, Jackson Kyle," she said, turning away from him and toward the friends who came pushing and shoving up the steps to the terrace.

He watched her walk away, his personal honor forbidding him to pursue her. Three years was a long time to wait for a second kiss. . . .

* * *

Cecelia St. Croix caught every concern and hesitation that crossed Jackson Kyle's hard face. The way he clenched his jaw in thought. Her stomach sank. She wished he'd stop fighting their attraction and acknowledge her as a woman. A woman he could love.

Looking at her now, his dark brown gaze held a hunger that both excited and frustrated her. She wanted him to act on his attraction as he had the night of her twenty-first birthday, when a heated swimming pool and deep shadows hid their one and only time together. That one time had spoiled her for other men . . .

Summer of 1998

Cecelia awakened in her queen-size bed, her heart slamming in her chest, anticipation a living thing. The clock on her nightstand read a little after two in the morning. She was officially twenty-one.

A tangible calling pulled her from her bed, across the room to the French windows that faced the back of the house, overlooking the pool. Branches swayed in the breeze, and shadows shifted. It took her several seconds to locate the lone figure in the pool, swimming laps. She didn't need to see his face to recognize the man.

It was Jackson Kyle.

Not bothering to dress, she left her room at a run, in nothing more than her red silk chemise and matching tap pants. She reached the bronze keystone deck with her heart racing, praying he hadn't finished his laps and left her alone in the night.

The shadows of trees overhead had hidden him as he made his turn at the deep end of the pool and headed toward the shallow. His strong freestyle brought him within a foot of where she stood on the deck, watching him move through the water. He was graceful for such a big man.

Her slow smile was replaced by panic when Jackson suddenly shot out of the water, grabbed her by the calf, and pulled her into the pool. She thrashed, the water over her head, as he jerked her back against his chest, one large hand covering her mouth. "Don't scream, Celia," he whispered near her ear.

She gasped for air. "H-how did you know it was me?"

"Caught your reflection in the pool."

Her body relaxed against his. She was in his arms, right where she wanted to be. With his one strong arm wrapped around her waist, she tilted back her head, her hair fanning his shoulder. His hair-roughened chest felt slippery against her silken chemise. With her bottom to his groin, his erection pressed the back seam on her tap pants.

He wasn't wearing a suit.

Swallowing hard, she reached back, her hand grazing his naked thigh, his bare hip, his—

Jackson shoved her facedown into the water.

Cecelia bobbed up and down. When her feet touched the bottom, she stood at eye level with his massive and muscled chest. Water trickled over his shoulders, down his thick torso, and back into the pool. He reminded her of a granite statue in a fountain. "Skinny-dipping, Jax?"

The tree branches shifted, casting half his face in shadow as he slicked back his hair with his hands. "I seldom sleep more than four hours a night. Sex and I have recently spent sunup to sundown in boardrooms on business. I needed the exercise."

"You exercise *naked?*"

"I swim naked while others sleep and I have the pool to myself," he admitted.

"Doesn't a hard-on slow you down?"

"I wasn't stiff during my first fifty laps."

The yellow cast of the underwater lights illuminated his erection. He looked enormous.

Jackson tipped up her chin with one finger, drawing her gaze from his sex. "Why are you up so late? Where are MaeLee and Kia?"

"Sleeping with the sandman."

"Your bodyguards need to know where you are at all times."

" 'Wealth draws undue attention,' " she quoted her father. "You guard Sex. Watch over me now."

His jaw tightened. "Go back to bed."

Her arms outstretched, she spun around in the water. "I'm not tired."

"I am." He moved away from her, heading toward the steps. "See you in the morning."

Cecelia watched the water swirl about his waist, his firm hips and buttocks, his muscular thighs. Her heart died a little with his departure. "My birthday kiss," she called to his back.

He stopped, turned slightly, his profile pained. "Why me, Celia?"

She prayed the darkness hid her blush. "I want you," she confessed with a boldness drawn from her soul. Never had she begged a man to kiss her. To do *more* than kiss her.

His jaw clenched. "Don't you have a boyfriend?"

"Lots of male friends, but no one special."

He looked up at the black sky, blew out a breath. "Don't make me special."

He'd soon be out of sight, but not beyond her thoughts. "I'll be leaving for Paris at the end of the week. A college graduation gift from my parents." She held her breath. "I won't see you for six months."

"Stay a year."

Reality struck like a slap on the face. Every fantasy, every dream she'd had involving Jackson Kyle felt as crushed as a rose under a boot heel. He'd rebuffed her. Rejected her. Never given them a chance.

She hit the water with the flat of her hand. "I hate you." Her words broke the stillness, sharp with hurt.

He stared at her as if he couldn't believe his ears. "No, you don't."

"I hate you for not wanting me."

He returned to her, sloshing through the water, fire in his eyes. Teeth clamped, he stood so close she noticed the white scar at the corner of his eye; a small razor nick along his chin from a recent shave. Anger honed his features to sharp edges. A muscle ticked wildly in his jaw.

Looking deep into her eyes, he curved one hand over her shoulder; the other dug into the soft skin at her waist as he jerked her against him. Her chemise hugged her breasts; her tap pants were askew on her hips. Pressed flush against him, she felt his heat and naked strength. So big, so forceful, so male. His reaction to their closeness now pressed hard and hot against her abdomen. His eyes glittered like jet. "Don't hate me for what you want and what I can never give," he ground out.

Her lips parted. "A simple kiss?"

He shook his head. "Nothing is simple where you're concerned, Celia."

Her breasts rubbed against his chest, the nipples taut and aching. "I promise to leave after one kiss."

He growled in frustration, warning her off. "One kiss would lead to sex. I don't have a condom."

She didn't heed his warning. "I'm on the Pill." She lifted her mouth to his. Inexperienced but determined, she kissed him with every ounce of unrequited love that lived in her soul.

Jackson Kyle did not respond.

Humiliated, Cecelia closed her eyes and rested her forehead against his. A single tear escaped her eye. She'd wanted him so badly that she'd made a fool of herself.

Her lips trembled as the warmth of his mouth captured the tear on her upper lip. Slow and sweeping, he licked her lips. She sensed a shift in him, not only in plated muscles that rippled when he eased her even closer but in the predatory air that now emanated from him.

Suddenly, his sheer size overshadowed everything in his presence. Including her.

Slanting his mouth over hers, he kissed her deeply, drawing her tongue between his lips, sucking the very essence of woman into man. His taste was raw, hungry, moist tongue and nipping teeth.

Her nipples grew diamond hard against his kneading palms. He yanked her chemise over her head so his teeth could follow in the wake of his hand, nipping a trail of bites along her neck, the sensitive skin of her breast, the points of her nipples. Desire burned, curling and consuming, spreading along nerve endings that tingled for his touch.

She struggled to remain standing when his thigh slid

between her legs. No matter how she willed herself not to, she rode him, the urge to rub herself against his thigh too strong to resist. She arched her back as the friction built, only to have Jackson still her hips before she came.

Growing as aggressive as he, Cecelia slipped her hands between them. Heart thumping madly, she smoothed her palms over his thickly muscled chest, traced the dark hair that trailed down his stomach into a slim line at his navel, drawn toward his shaft. She skimmed his full length before cupping him, then savored his low groan as his sex pulsed against her hand.

The night throbbed with their lovemaking.

Hungry mouths and fast hands.

Light moans and darker growls.

Jackson Kyle had lost control.

And so had she.

His large hands traveled the outside of her pale thighs and cupped the roundness of her bottom. His fingers curved into the elastic at her waist and stripped the tap pants from her body.

Naked. Vulnerable. Needy. She swayed against him, focusing on his muscles now tight with tension, the tilt of his head as the moisture from his tongue evaporated from her skin.

Sliding one hand beneath her bottom, he lifted her slightly. She willingly wrapped her legs about his hips.

Anticipation spiked her need, the rush of excitement so intense it drove away judgment, common sense, all but her craving.

Longing pierced her, so sharp her chest hurt.

She'd waited years for this man.

"Admit you want me," she whispered, nuzzling his ear.

"Always wanted you." His breath was hot bursts against her cheek.

Nothing mattered then but the feel of his wet body, the desire etched on his face.

Her breath caught in her throat when he slipped a hand between their bodies, slowly stroked, every touch designed to satisfy her hunger. His erection soon filled her, stretching her flesh until she melted against him with a soft sob.

"Why didn't you tell me?" Jackson's ragged breath broke against her neck.

She tightened her thighs about his hips, felt him deep inside her. "That you were my first?"

"I would have taken more time."

"You were perfect."

When his gaze locked on hers, hot and intense, claiming her, she nearly drowned in the need she saw there. He was pure male, pure aggressor as he withdrew, then penetrated once again.

She surrendered, rocking against him with pure instinctual need. She wound her arms around his neck as the imminent, unstoppable spasms brought her first orgasm. Gasping, she abandoned herself to the sensation, coaxing his climax with a final grinding against his groin, drawing his thick heat even deeper.

Their sounds of passion resonated above the liquid stillness of the pool. Resonated along every nerve ending in her heated body.

Jackson Kyle was hers.

In that moment she lost herself in him. Body and soul.

Jackson shuddered, exploded, growled his release.

Time fell for endless moments before reality once

again took hold of their lives. She felt drained. Satisfied. Consumed.

Contentment settled in her bones as she possessively covered his mouth with her own and whispered, "Happy birthday to me."

Jackson heard Cecelia sigh. She'd revisited the same memory he held in his heart. Though he wanted her as badly as she wanted him, hopping into bed was not an option. He'd taken her virginity, then lost his heart to her those many years ago. He'd dodged all serious relationships since the day he'd met her.

The way she was looking at him now, both nervous and hopeful, had him feeling like a bad guy. He knew how much it hurt her to be held at arm's length, yet he couldn't draw her closer.

Sex was his best friend. His friend wanted Cecelia to marry well. Well meant millions. Jackson was not a millionaire.

"Can I interest you in dinner and drinks?" she asked.

Jax loosened his bow tie but remained by the door. "I'm not hungry."

"Then stand at attention and starve," she said as she rose and crossed to the wet bar. Her ivory gown shimmered in the muted light, drawing his eye to her shapely back. She selected a Portuguese vino verde. "More wine for me."

He was at her side in a heartbeat, taking the bottle out of her hand and returning it to the refrigerator. "You don't drink, Celia."

"Socially I do."

"Who's being sociable?" he asked. "You never drink alone."

She edged around him, picked up a portable phone

from the top shelf of a curio cabinet. She tapped in several numbers, her red nails bright against the white plastic. She unclipped a ruby earring encircled by diamonds, then drew the receiver to her ear.

"Cecelia St. Croix." Her rich, cultured voice was as low and smooth as cream. "I know you're serving dinner and I apologize for the inconvenience, but I'd like an order of French toast sent to my suite." A brief pause, followed by a smile. "Thank you, Lawrence," she said, then hung up the phone.

"Still eating breakfast for dinner?" Jackson asked, amused.

A small smile played across her lips. "I had beef tips for breakfast."

"Interesting cravings." He wondered what she'd crave when she was pregnant. Pregnant with another man's child.

She stepped within his private space, so close, in fact, that the pointed toes on her white satin pumps brushed his black dress shoes. He locked his jaw. "You're stealing my air."

She laid her hand on his chest. "Wish I could steal your heart," she murmured, straightforward and honest as always.

He'd expect nothing less from her. "Don't go there."

She lowered her hand to her side. "Can't blame a girl for trying."

He prayed she'd never quit trying. Maybe someday . . .

Cecelia bit down on her bottom lip. "Zara Sage predicts I'll meet my husband on this cruise."

That didn't please him one damn bit. He hated psychics and their predictions. "Perhaps you will."

"I'm just one night in a pool from being a virgin," she said. "Most men appreciate experience."

His insides tightened. "Some men get turned on by innocence."

Stepping left, she began pacing the length of her suite, her expression pensive. "A fling might be fun before I settle down."

A fling? Not on his shift. "Sex would never approve."

She strolled back toward him, slowly, seductively, her breasts swaying along with her hips. "Sex need not know."

"You couldn't hide an affair on the ship."

"Two people who were discreet could dodge the public eye. Sex is too busy dealing with Daisy Alton to think twice about me." She pursed her lips. "Now to find a man."

"Choose wisely," Jackson said as he turned on his heel and headed toward the door.

"I choose you." Her soft words caught him from behind and brought him to a halt. Cecelia St. Croix smiled to herself. She had him cornered.

A knock on the door cut off his reply. Swinging it wide, Jax stepped aside as one of the waiters wheeled in her dinner, displayed her meal, then departed quickly.

He met her gaze across the room, his eyes dark and dangerous, and slightly dilated. He desired her, no matter how he fought it. He had only to admit it.

Stepping to the cart, Cecelia dipped her fingertips in a small bowl of warm maple syrup. Bringing her fingers to her lips, she slowly licked them clean. "Care to lick maple syrup off my thigh?" she asked.

He caved. On a low, defeated groan, Jackson Kyle tugged off his bow tie, shrugged off his tux, and approached her, stripping her with his eyes.

Four

Sexton St. Croix hit the sun deck at six A.M. It was his favorite hour to jog, when the world still slept and he was alone with his thoughts. He'd stretched, caught the hint of sunrise on the horizon, before setting off at a warm-up pace.

Three laps around the perimeter of the ship and his body felt loose and limber. He kicked it up a notch. Clearing the stern, he rounded Café Sol, where early risers could enjoy a selection of gourmet coffees and teas, blueberry muffins, and cinnamon Danish. That was when he caught a glimpse of a slender woman with white-blond hair, dressed in a teal blue tank top and matching shorts.

Bree Emery. Her body moved with practiced ease. She was fit and firm, ahead of him by half a ship's length.

His heart quickened along with his pace.

He wanted to catch her.

As if sensing his presence, Bree glanced over her

shoulder. He was close enough now to catch the flash of challenge in her hazel eyes, the hint of a smile that said she'd leave him in the dust. He'd endure a groin pull to prove her wrong.

It became an all-out race. Sex couldn't remember the last time he'd chased a woman. On foot. Running, twisting, and dodging the crew as they set out sun loungers by the pool. His muscles burned as he gained on the psychic.

She was damn fast. Sex's heart rate exceeded the beat of a rising orgasm. He was hot and determined to run her down. He thought about cheating—cutting across the deck instead of running the perimeter—but decided to catch her fair and square.

Bree was in fabulous shape. She ran like a track star, all strength and endurance and lean female sinew.

He closed in on her, enjoying the surprise on her face and the hitch in her breath when he reached her side. She slowed and stopped, bending at the waist, breathing heavily. Her eyes shone brightly, her skin glowing from her exertion.

The corners of her mouth curved ever so slightly. "You give good chase, St. Croix."

He watched the rise and fall of her chest beneath her tank top, caught the points of her nipples against the teal blue satin. Her body was in peak condition, like his own. She'd be superb in bed, a woman to match his stamina.

Thoughts of sleeping with Bree Emery heated rather than cooled him down. He motioned to her. "Let's walk."

She hesitated, and his heart clenched. Most women jumped at the chance to be in his company. Even for thirty seconds. Not so Bree. He could almost hear her mental debate as she looked up at the sky, then down at her light blue Adidas. She wasn't playing hard to get. She merely preferred her own company over his. Or the company of a ghost.

Sex breathed a sigh of relief when she shrugged and said, "Once around the ship couldn't hurt."

He had the perimeter of the sun deck to talk her into coffee, maybe even breakfast. "Did you and Daisy sleep well?" he asked.

"*I* slept like the dead."

"No midnight chat?"

"I never heard her enter the cabin," Bree told him. "I figured she'd be out late, so I turned in early."

Early and alone. Following their dinner in the galley, Sex had tried to lure her to his suite. Bree, however, had refused. Flat out. Without hesitation, without a second thought. He'd walked her to her cabin, turned, and left without a peck on the cheek. When he'd reached the stairs, he remembered Bree still had his suit coat.

After a brief mental debate, he'd gone back for it. One knock drew her to the door. She'd stood before him in a lavender cotton nightshirt with a box of chocolates pictured over her breasts along with the inscription CHOCO-LATE OR SEX? TRUFFLES LAST LONGER THAN SIXTY SECONDS.

Her lovers had been swifties.

Looking at her now, all warm skin and well-toned muscle, he wanted her bad. Slowing his pace, he asked, "When will Daisy contact you again?"

"In due time."

"Can't you contact her?"

Bree stopped on the track, facing him. With her blond hair making a halo in the first rays of sunlight, she looked ethereal. "No one can push a ghost to confession."

He slapped his hands against his thighs. "Have you had any more visions?" His skepticism was evident, no matter how hard he tried to believe Bree had entered Daisy's past.

She shook her head, explaining, "I can't call them at will. I've been up less than an hour, have jogged three miles, and am now walking and talking with you." She lifted her chin. "I will, however, try to work in a vision before noon."

"Work in the vision around eleven, so we can discuss it over lunch."

She rolled her eyes. "You're incredible."

"In bed."

"I sleep alone," Bree returned. "What I need most is a shower. Since my cabin has only a porcelain sink and a water closet, where can I clean up?"

"My cabin?"

"I'll be ripe by the end of the trip if that's my only option."

"Nemo's Spa is on deck three, along with the gym and indoor swimming pool," he informed her.

Bree fisted her hands. "I could go a few rounds on the bag before I shower."

He would enjoy watching her box.

Motioning toward the companionway, he followed her to the promenade deck. The blue neon surrounding the glass elevator blinked its availability. Arriving first, Bree depressed the brass disk and the door slid open.

"After you," Sex said as he came up behind her.

Bree couldn't have moved if her life depended on it. Nor could she remove her finger from the depressed disk. Her lips formed words without sound. Shivers skimmed her spine and her vision turned hazy. Her personal space ceased to exist as Daisy Alton's world unfolded before her.

Promenade Deck
May 26, 1925

Daisy held her breath as she depressed the ivory disk within its handsome bronze rosette, summoning the elevator. She tapped her toe, her breathing rapid. Surely Harland and Wolff could have installed an electric elevator that would move a little faster. She had no business being on the upper deck, but at such an early hour, she couldn't resist a quick peek at the deluxe accommodations available to the first-class passengers.

She'd wanted to see where Randolph Ambrose had dined the previous evening. On tiptoe, she'd crossed the reception room outside the Crystal Dining Room, where the elite collected for aperitifs prior to supper. Against the far wall, lavish gilt swags dipped between the great Bechstein and the fireplace. Daisy imagined the quality of the notes that would be played on the grand piano. To her right, crescent arrangements of wing chairs done in rich rose satin and flowery chintz invited conversation. She wondered what topics Randolph had discussed with his well-educated companions.

Holding her breath, Daisy cracked the double doors leading into the formal dining room. As dawn filtered through etched-glass panels and twin skylights, the massive room gleamed with rich, dark paneling suitable to an English castle. Off to one side a wine cellar boasted aging wines. The high domed ceiling was painted with silver clouds and golden-winged cherubs. The floor was carpeted in rich blue wool.

Daisy had taken one step, then two, into the elegant room, just to feel her feet sink into the carpet. Just to feel she belonged, if only for a moment. The dining room with its proper tables and comfortable armchairs was far more refined than the communal long tables used by the third-class passengers.

The tables for six had been reset for the evening meal. Cut-crystal stemmed glassware, silver utensils, a single white candle, and linen as starched as a nurse's cap awaited men in coats and ties and bejeweled women gowned by the House of Worth.

A supper menu had been left beside a crystal goblet, and Daisy fingered the scalloped edge of the expensive parchment. Six courses were listed, from consommé Olga and roast duckling to peaches in Chartreuse jelly. Food Daisy had never tasted. Food she could barely pronounce. She wished she could savor one night of fine dining amid the rich and cultured.

Her stomach growled, reminding her that she hadn't eaten since yesterday noon. Sighing heavily, she retraced her steps. Breakfast would be served below in less than an hour. Porridge and milk would suffice until dinner. She couldn't live on wishes.

"Going down, Miss Alton?" A man's deep voice rose from behind her right shoulder.

Daisy knew the voice without turning around. Randolph Ambrose made her tummy flutter. She glanced back, pleased that she'd worn her best dropwaist spring dress of robin's-egg blue batiste, even if it was three years old and the style slightly out of fashion. A blue mesh cloche covered her hair.

Randolph, on the other hand, was the bee's knees. He was casually dressed in a fawn shirt and brown herringbone pants, his hair neatly combed, his jaw freshly shaved. When he shifted his stance, she caught a glimpse of his argyle socks and dark brown oxfords.

Moistening her lips with the tip of her tongue, Daisy finally answered, "The elevator is moving slowly. I'd hoped to catch the sunrise but fear I'm too late."

Ambrose plucked his pocket watch from his pants pocket. "It's almost eight."

Daisy waved her hand in a breezy fashion. "I'll rise earlier tomorrow."

She breathed easier when the elevator finally arrived. The grille doors swung open, and an interior steel gate slid aside. A red-jacketed lift attendant ushered Daisy and Randolph in, closed both gate and grille, then rotated the half-round control. With a gentle hum of its motor, the elevator descended to the upper deck, the lowest deck for first-class passengers.

Stepping off the lift, Daisy heard her stomach rumble a second time. "Good day, Mr. Ambrose," she said, hating to leave but knowing she must. Travelers had begun milling about. Several members of the crew cast curious glances her way. She didn't need the bum's rush to get her belowdeck.

Turned around, and a bit disoriented by Randolph's strong presence, Daisy searched the long corridor for the main staircase.

From behind a long mahogany counter, the bespectacled purser caught her eye. "In need of assistance, ma'am?"

Daisy felt her cheeks heat. Any young woman of breeding would be traveling with her parents or a chaperone, not wandering the decks unescorted. Just then she spotted the staircase that led to the lower decks. Her body quivered with relief. "I'm fine, thank you. I was momentarily confused—"

"As to the location of the Palm Court." Randolph came to her rescue. "Miss Alton will be joining me for breakfast."

The purser looked at Ambrose over the rim of his glasses. Curiosity glinted in his eyes. "Will the Hogues be joining you also?"

"My fiancée suffers from *mal de mer*," Randolph informed the overly inquisitive man. "Eloise's parents greet the day nearer to noon."

"Very well, sir." The purser nodded, returning to his duties.

Randolph looked at Daisy Alton. The young flapper was wide-eyed, her painted lips parted in surprise. "Shall we?" He extended his arm, which she hesitantly took. He liked the way her slender fingers rested in the crook of his arm as they continued down the long galley toward the bow of the ship.

The Palm Court was a bower of greenery and wicker, a glass-enclosed meeting place and tearoom between open deck and closed public room. Palm-bedecked, with baskets of ferns and latticework woven with ivy, the room was suffused in sunshine.

Only one other couple sat facing the sea, arguing over mint tea and cinnamon scones, their words sharp, their expressions tight and unflattering.

"Milquetoast and a face stretcher," Daisy said softly once Randolph had seated her at a small table for two.

He glanced at the twosome. Daisy had pegged them correctly. The man was indeed hen-pecked, while the older woman was trying to look younger, her face heavily powdered, her rouge overly red.

Silence and sunshine surrounded them, comfortable and warming. "You've grown quiet," he noted.

"You'd rather I beat my gums?" she asked, her spunk returning.

"I'd like to get to know you," he said.

She started. "Know me? Why? You're engaged."

Yes, he was engaged. Yet in her company, he felt alive and unencumbered of responsibility. He cleared his throat. "I find you delightful, Miss Alton."

Daisy picked up a menu from the wicker table. "I'd delight in breakfast," she returned saucily.

He motioned to a server hovering near an ivy trellis. The man approached them. "Your order, sir?"

Randolph caught Daisy's expectant look. She looked thin, as if good meals came far and few between. "Tomato omelets, grilled ham, jacket potatoes—"

The waiter grew visibly uneasy. "We serve tea and scones in the Palm Court. Full-course breakfasts are served—"

"Baked apples and biscuits with black currant jam." Randolph was not about to sit down in the crowded Commodore's Grill.

The server's lips pinched. "Very well, sir."

Once the man had departed, Randolph smiled at Daisy. "I hope you're hungry."

"Starving, actually. I missed—" she began before catching herself.

"Supper?" he supplied.

Daisy looked everywhere but at him.

"You could have had food delivered to your cabin," he said. "Unless such service isn't provided on your deck."

She slid to the edge of her wicker chair, leaned toward him, whispered, "I'm not a first-class passenger."

He rubbed his knuckles along his jaw. "Hmm, truly?"

"Not even second class." The admittance drew a blush.

"I see . . ."

She started to rise. "In fact, I'm not proper company for a gentleman like yourself. I'll leave now—"

"Sit down, Miss Alton," Randolph said firmly.

She settled back on the wicker, her hands shaking as she laced them on her lap. "You wish me to stay?"

"I can't possibly eat everything I've ordered."

Her blue eyes grew as soft as her voice. "You're too kind, sir."

"Kindness comes with your willingness to join me."

"*Please*, Bree, come back to me." Sexton St. Croix sounded miles away. Desperation had him shaking her shoulders and even smacking her cheek.

"Bree!" His voice seemed nearer now, stronger, sharper, and raw with concern.

"Don't shout and *never* slap me," she finally managed, her vision slow to clear.

"It was a revival tap," he ground out, unnerved. "This is twice you've faded out on me now."

"And twice I've returned."

He blew out a breath. "Tell me how best to help."

"Allow me ten to fifteen minutes to experience the vision, then talk me back, slowly and quietly."

"Do you always come around?"

She rubbed her forehead. "I've never been stuck in someone else's past."

"But it could happen."

"Possibly," she admitted. "Fortunately, I've always been able to pull myself free."

His eyes narrowed. "What did you see?"

Bree relayed her vision. "I wonder when Randolph

will reveal his wealth and power. His St. Croix heritage."

"Daisy knew about Eloise Hogue," Sex concluded. "Yet she disregarded convention, flaunting herself, engaging the affection of a man soon to marry."

"She was neither flirting nor flaunting," Bree corrected him. "There was an innocence to their intimacy; they were two souls who found themselves at sea."

"Don't romanticize murder." His voice was as taut as his expression. "Daisy's *love* killed Randolph St. Croix."

"So you constantly remind me."

"Facts are facts." He ran his hand through his hair. "No more arguing; let's get physical. Care to work out?"

"Why not? Exercise clears my head."

The elevator arrived within seconds. They descended to the promenade deck, then took the staircase to Nemo's Spa.

Sunlight shot through the window walls across the stationary bikes, treadmills, StairMaster, and free weights. Nearing the glass, Sex pointed east, toward the faint outline of the Bahamas, an island that rose like an emerald against the aqua sea. "We dock at Prince George Wharf early this afternoon. Can I give you the tour?"

"We'll see." Bree wouldn't commit to spending time with him. "It all depends on Daisy."

"Perhaps your flapper would enjoy the Straw Market, shopping on Bay Street, gambling at the Paradise Island Casino," he suggested. "Perhaps enjoy it so much she'd leave the *Majestic* for the island."

"Daisy's too connected to the ship to play tourist."

"Then play tourist with me for an hour or two."

"As long as tourist is all we play."

He grinned. "I'm a great island guide. I can take you places not marked in any guidebook."

Secluded places. Intimate, and designed for seduction. Bree was certain he'd charmed many lovers in the Bahamas.

Heading for a stationary bike, she pedaled for thirty minutes while Sex worked out with free weights. She watched as he lifted and pressed, his body lean and tight, his muscles stretched to the max. The front of his gray T-shirt dampened from his exertions. The bulge beneath his black jogging shorts was evident when he bench-pressed two hundred pounds. Impressively evident.

"You've stopped spinning," he called to her, his breathing deep, his tone husky. "Tired?"

Bree blushed. She'd been so busy studying the flex and flow of his body, she'd paused in her pedaling.

Burying her face in a white fluffy towel, she blotted her hot cheeks. Then she slipped off the stationary bike and moved to the punching bags. Sex joined her there. With practiced ease, he helped her pull on a pair of lightweight gloves that would protect her knuckles.

"I'm surprised there aren't more people taking advantage of the facilities," she noted. The room was empty.

"Owner's privilege," Sex said simply. "I reserved the spa for us."

Did he think himself irresistible? "You're pretty sure of yourself."

"You're here, aren't you?"

She scrunched up her nose. "I hate being a foregone conclusion."

"Never that," Sex assured her. "I can't read you nearly as well as you read me."

Thank goodness. Bree relaxed.

Once he'd tightened the laces on her right glove, he

released her hand, then stepped back. "Speed or heavy bag?"

She eyed the balloon-shaped leather bag. "I'm not fast enough for the speed bag," she confessed. "I always take it on the chin."

He pointed toward the heavy bag. "Punch your heart out."

She punched and pounded until her arms grew heavy and her lungs burned. Perspiration glistened on her bare arms and legs. She felt tired, yet powerful. Euphoric. She held out her hands for him to untie her gloves.

"A great workout." Her mind felt clear and her body satisfied. "As good as chocolate. Far better than sex."

He slipped off her left glove. "If punching a bag leaves you sated, you haven't been properly loved."

With her free hand, she removed the remaining glove. "Sex is overrated."

"Me or the act?"

"No doubt both."

He wiped the back of his hand across his damp forehead. "You're hard on a man's ego."

"Better me hard on you than you hard on me."

"I tend to disagree."

"A shower?" Bree needed to change the subject and clean up.

Sex motioned her to follow him. "Ladies' locker room this way."

They passed through a set of golden doors. Polished hardwood floors led them down a corridor wallpapered in sand tones and seashell pink. Steam seeped beneath a door at the far end of the hall. Sex cracked the door, revealing a dozen hot tubs, all marbled and bubbly. "By early evening you'll need a shoehorn to wedge yourself into one of those tubs."

Bree could envision him there, surrounded by busty, giggly, adoring women. And loving every minute.

Sex nodded right. "Nemo's Spa offers salt-glow rubs and aromatherapy wraps."

He motioned left, to a door marked MERMAIDS. "Lockers and showers. I'll locate an attendant and have her bring you towels and a change of clothes."

Sexton St. Croix was a gracious host.

"While you shower, I'll do the same." He paused. "Breakfast in an hour?"

She licked her lips, hesitating. "We're spending a lot of time together."

"Daylight hours, nothing after dark."

"I'll think about it."

"Think long and hard."

Her thoughts went south. Shaking herself, she entered Mermaids.

Twenty minutes later, hot water had pinkened her skin, and the steam was so thick she could barely see the shower dial. Cracking the diamond-shaped door, she discovered a stack of soft lilac towels, a terry-cloth robe, and a selection of toiletries, along with a hairdryer and cosmetic bag. A small metallic blue gift bag sat atop a silver-foil package.

Bree quickly dried off and combed out her damp hair. Wrapped in her robe, she peeked into the gift bag. Wisps of satin lay amid the sheer tissue paper. Her heart raced as she slowly withdrew a butterfly-shaped strapless bra and matching black thong.

She found a card tucked between the cups of the bra. *Selected by Sex.* It was the perfect size, a sinful color. Meant for a lover.

Her fingers trembled as she stroked the black satin, envisioning the decadent fit of the bra and thong without trying them on. Her body would curve into the wings of the butterflies. Sheer and sparkling with jet black beads, the wings would fan each breast. Her stomach would flutter when the thong spanned her hipbones. Here were butterflies meant to take sexual flight when slipped from a woman's body.

A sigh of resignation escaped as she realized she couldn't accept St. Croix's intimate gift. She returned the lingerie to the bag, along with his card. Curiosity overcame her, and she was all thumbs opening the silver-foil gift box. Brushing aside the ivory tissue paper, she found a strapless sundress. As she eased it over her head, the ink-black silk decorated with red hibiscus flirted with her skin, slinking along her curves, swinging high on her thighs.

Bree tingled. She felt spoiled and pretty.

Unfortunately, the sundress must also be returned.

The dress came off slowly, as if wanting to be worn. Bree folded it back amid the tissue paper and resealed the tape on the foil. Retrieving her robe, she slipped it back on. Turning to a white wall phone, she punched in the attendant's number. A short time later, an Asian woman in indigo sweats delivered the items Bree had requested in a blue batik tote bag.

"You wish to exchange Mr. St. Croix's gifts?" the attendant asked, her gaze sharp with disapproval.

Bree nodded. "His selections aren't my style."

"His selections please many women."

Bree was not one of many. She couldn't live with herself if she accepted his gifts. "Please charge the T-shirt and shorts to my cabin. Cabin seventy-o-one."

All argument left the attendant. "The ghost's cabin?"

Bree's lips twitched. "Daisy doesn't carry much cash, so I'll use plastic."

White-faced, the attendant edged toward the door. "Anything further, Ms. Emery?"

"I'm all set," Bree assured the woman, who retreated as quickly as she'd arrived.

Forgoing bra and panties, she dressed in a tide-blue T-shirt embossed with an indigo *Majestic,* navy walking shorts, and her running shoes. Stuffing her worn jogging togs in the tote bag, she found her way to the main workout room. Sex was nowhere to be found. Only Mimi Rhaine strolled the treadmill.

A devil of an idea nudged Bree toward Ramsay St. Croix's companion. Bree had always believed once a gift was given, the giver had no further say as to how it was used.

She crossed the room, called, "Hello, Mimi."

Mimi's face was flushed, her body wrapped in plum spandex. Her breath came in short little pants. "Two miles. My heart's pounding and my legs feel like rubber. God, I'm worn out."

The woman was barely walking. "Where's Ram?" Bree inquired.

"My tall drink of Maalox sleeps until noon, eats a light snack, plays cards with Harlan, takes a nap, and then we go out for a nice dinner." Mimi stopped walking altogether. "I have a lot of free time on my hands. Working out and shopping usually fill my day."

"Shopping came to you today," Bree informed her. "There were gift boxes left in Mermaids. Perhaps left for you."

"*Expensive* gifts?" Mimi nearly fell off the treadmill.

"They're prettily wrapped. Perhaps from Ram or—"

"Sexton St. Croix," Mimi said with assurance. "He's hot for me."

"Wouldn't surprise me in the least." Bree bit back a smile. "Be sure to thank Sex for the gifts."

"Trust me, I plan to show my appreciation over and over again," Mimi shot over her shoulder as she wiggled down the hallway.

Relief settled over Bree. Mimi's pursuit of Sex would allow her time alone with Daisy. She needed to clear the flapper's name.

Sex leaned against the reception desk in the workout room and waited for Bree. What was taking her so long? Three emergency phone calls taken in the locker room had delayed his return. Surely that had given her enough time to slip on her butterflies and sundress.

Footsteps, soft, light, and feminine drew his attention to the hallway. His jaw dropped when Mimi Rhaine— not Bree—appeared in the black-and-red sundress. Once spotting him, Mimi approached, her walk slow and seductive.

She came on strong. Easing up to him, she licked her lips, as red and glossy as a magazine cover. "Love the dress." Her nostrils flared. "No net needed to catch this butterfly."

Sex wanted to drop a net over Bree Emery. Her decision to give his gifts to Mimi deserved an explanation. Perhaps retribution.

He'd find a way to make her squirm.

Preferably under him.

"My cabin or yours?" Mimi whispered in his ear. "I love to role play. How about you?"

Mimi already looked like a street walker. She was several inches taller than Bree, and the sundress exposed more of Mimi than Sex wished to see. The bodice barely covered her breasts and the hem stopped just short of being indecent.

Mimi traced his cheek with a blunt red nail and suggested, "You could work for UPS and deliver me a *big* package. Or how about firefighter and little match girl?"

Sex preferred coyote and roadrunner. How fast could he run? Not fast enough to escape her hungry eyes.

Out of respect to Ram, he'd never made a move on Mimi. And role playing held little appeal for him. Mimi wanted to dress up to be stripped down. She'd tempt and tease and have sex toys. He was only interested in knowing why Bree Emery had an aversion to butterflies.

"No role playing; I've a prior commitment." Forcing a smile, he stepped around her. "I've hired transportation to take Ram and Harlan to lunch at the Purple Parrot around one. You'll enjoy the conch chowder."

Mimi sighed. "I'd have enjoyed you more. So much time, so little sex." Her take-me-anytime gaze burned his back all the way to the door.

Sex paged Jackson Kyle to help him track down Bree. The *Majestic* would be docking in under an hour and he didn't want her leaving the ship without him.

"Any luck?" he asked Jackson when they met on the sun deck.

Jackson shook his head. "I put out an all-call. No one has seen her."

"She's hanging with her invisible friend."

"Rubs you the wrong way?"

"Damn straight. Daisy's as abrasive as sand in my shorts."

"Psychic's got you by the short and curlies."

"I'm interested," Sex admitted. "Unfortunately, I can't touch her, and she won't touch me. Whenever we collide, she senses my past lovers."

Jax cocked a brow. "Eighteen years of intimacy?"

"Only my most recent relationship," Sex explained.

"Was it good for her?"

"Riding the heat of Heather was a total turn-off."

"Sorry, man."

Sex dragged a hand down his face. "So am I."

Jackson nodded toward the stern, where sun loungers were pressed together like sardines, the metaphysical advisers slick with tanning lotion. "Let's check out the psychic circus."

Sex wove among the loungers. He stopped beside Rainbow's deck chair and watched as the lady in the pink, yellow, and blue tie-dyed T-shirt shuffled, then laid out her tarot cards. Her mouth pinched into a frown. "Death, always the death card."

Death. Daisy. How coincidental.

Sex slowed near Zara Sage, who was working her Ouija board. The alphabet curved across the top of the board and numbers one through ten were formed across the bottom. YES and NO, HELLO, and GOOD-BYE were spelled out on opposite sides.

Head bowed, Zara spoke, her voice clear and demanding. "I wish to enter the twilight—"

Zone? Sex anticipated.

"—world of all Ouija. Open your portal to the spirit realm. Talk to me!" Zara placed the tips of her fingers on a triangular planchette. Within seconds, the triangle moved, flying from letter to letter, spelling out words.

"D-a-i-s-y s-e-n-d-s a m-e-s-s-a-g-e," Zara said, her voice as spaced out as the letters. "S-h-e i-s s-e-a-s-i-c-k."

79

Seasick or hung over? One of his emergency phone calls at the spa had been from the bartender at Oasis. Three bottles of Tanqueray had come up missing during his morning inventory. Sex had an idea as to who had been drinking well into the night.

"Tell Daisy to take two aspirin and lay off the gin," Sex returned.

Zara shot him a withering look.

A tug on his right hand drew him around. Moriah with the dark hair and gypsy-gray eyes turned over his palm and traced several marks on his little finger with her fingertip. "Your psychic lines are well defined. You are one of us."

Definitely one of them.

She ran the tip of her finger along the right angle between his forefinger and thumb. "You are a take-charge man." She pulled on the tip of his forefinger. "Nice long finger. You hold great power."

She returned to his palm, tracking several lines that ran its width. "Strong heart, a man of stamina. Long life, longer . . ." Moriah's gaze drifted to the zipper on his black slacks. "You make women smile."

"Sex is the original happy-face sticker." Jackson's voice rose over Sex's shoulder.

Sex shot him a silencing look as he pulled his hand from the psychic's grasp. "Anything on Daisy?"

Moriah shrugged. "She's a ghost. No lines on her palm."

"Keep walking." Jackson nudged him forward.

At the back of the psychic pack, they found Shay gazing into a crystal ball. Her burgundy hair was short and stiff as a whisk broom. She looked more punk rocker than psychic. Eyes wide, she appeared to be in a trance. Or stoned. She didn't blink for a full minute.

Sex peered into the quartz crystal, which sparkled as if Windexed. "See anything?"

She looked up, met his gaze. "Daisy Alton."

"Ghost in ball?" Jackson's question drew Sex's smile.

Shay, however, sent both men a dirty look. "Will you laugh in Death's face, Mr. St. Croix? Or will you beg for mercy?"

Sex stiffened. A prediction of death? *His* death?

"Daisy Alton will kill again," Shay stated with a dark assuredness that made Sex's skin crawl. She curled her hand into a gun, pointed one finger at his heart. "Bang-bang. You're dead."

Five

"Psychic psycho," Jackson growled as he lifted Shay from her sun lounger and set her on her feet. He wrapped his big hand around her arm, just below her shoulder. "You've threatened Mr. St. Croix's life. I'm taking you to Security."

"It's not a threat, it's the truth," Shay shouted at Jackson. "I saw his death."

Jackson snagged the quartz crystal. "Evidence."

"Evidence based on a prediction won't hold up in court." Bree Emery strolled toward them in a green, beaded palm tree T-shirt and lavender capris. Plumtone shades were tucked just behind her bangs. Her icicle crystal pendant hung around her neck, and a solitary amethyst claimed her ring finger. She looked cool and serene and brought a calmness to the chaos resulting from the death threat.

"Shay said Daisy would kill me," Sex repeated to Bree.

"And you believed her?" Bree looked amazed.

"If Daisy's killed once, she can do it again." Shay raised her voice to be heard above the whispering of the gathering crowd.

"You've seen Daisy?" Bree asked.

"Big as life," Shay stated. "I'll never forget her face. Her terrible sneer when she held her gun to St. Croix's head."

Bree blinked against the sun and Shay's tall tale. She had yet to see Daisy today but found it unlikely the flapper would pop up in a crystal ball. Daisy was flirty and fun, not threatening and malicious.

She didn't want Shay's prediction to turn into a spectacle. She turned to Sex. "Can we discuss this privately?"

Sex looked at Jackson, who nodded agreement. "The Security Center has a small conference room."

Bree trailed Jackson and Shay, and Sex brought up the rear. He walked so closely behind her, his heat warmed her back. Sexual heat that sifted to her bones and left her liquid.

Security was located on deck five, a windowless room with an oval table and six metal chairs. The room was small, and Bree leaned her shoulder against the teak door frame until Jackson and Shay were seated.

The ship shifted, and before her eyes, the space suddenly appeared smaller, miniature, like a room in a dollhouse. Bree shook her head, breathed deeply, and staggered forward on wobbly legs. One step, then two. She fought against her fading consciousness. Before she could reach the table, the bright lighting flickered, then dimmed.

"Bree?" Sex's voice sounded miles away.

Within seconds, the heavy scent of cigar smoke drove her to her knees. . . .

84

Deck Five
May 27, 1925

Through a fine sea mist, Daisy Alton caught sight of Randolph Ambrose on the upper deck as he conversed with a man with sleek black hair and gangster looks. Whether from the stiff breeze or animated conversation, Randolph's cheeks reddened with each word spoken. He gestured wildly, openly agitated, unusual for a man of calm reserve. Throughout their exchange, the gangster's expression registered cold indifference. So cold, Daisy shivered.

Unprotected from the wind, she clutched the skirt of her floral shirtwaist and ducked behind a stack of steamer chairs no more than twenty feet from where the men argued. She knew better than to approach Randolph; their friendship was too new, tenuous at best, and she didn't want to embarrass him. Third-class passengers didn't converse with the privileged.

Her nerves shredded when she saw the gangster stick one hand in the pocket of his great coat and motion Randolph off the deck. It wasn't the man's finger that jabbed Randolph in the ribs. The impression of a gun was distinctly visible through the tweed.

A torpedo! Where was the hired gun taking Randolph?

Daisy's throat constricted. Cautiously, she followed the men, hunching her shoulders and remaining as inconspicuous as possible. Randolph walked with a limp, a limp Daisy had never noticed before.

She moved in closer as they descended the staircase to deck five. Her bare arms were damp from the humidity captured deep within the ship. Her nostrils filled with must and decay. She breathed through her mouth to prevent sneezing.

Her back against the wall, she inched down the corridor toward a tiny room at the bow of the ship. The heels of her beige-and-white, two-toned pumps were worn, as flat as slippers, enabling her to move along quickly and quietly amid the ship's creaks and groans. With starch in her backbone, she squinted into the slice of light from the cracked door.

Thick cigar smoke obscured one of the two men already seated. Shoved hard by the gangster, Randolph bumped his thighs against the table. The motion overturned a chrome flask. No one moved to set it upright.

"Here's your man, boss," the gangster said.

"Talk to me, Ramsay St. Croix." The man in the dark suit and fedora spoke with a thick Brooklyn accent. He was built like a baby grand. A fat cigar hung from one corner of his mouth, the rolled tobacco damp to the Havana band. A long white scar ran from forehead to chin, as if someone had halved his face like a melon.

Ramsay St. Croix? Daisy pressed her ear to the teak door. Had she mistakenly followed a man who resembled Randolph Ambrose? Resembled him so closely they looked like brothers?

Breathing shallowly, she lingered a moment longer.

"I'll loosen his tongue." The gangster slammed his fist into Ramsay's jaw.

Ramsay reeled backward, nearly hitting the door. Daisy heard his neck snap, followed by an agonizing groan. Her own scream rose, and she bit her tongue so hard her eyes watered.

The man in the fedora rested his hands on the table. Hands square and strong, with short-cut nails. A thick, gold wedding band flashed as he motioned the man off Ramsay. "Enough, Louie."

"A-ah, boss." Louie curled his lip. "A broken jaw would get across our message."

"Hit him again and you're back as pinboy in the bowling alley." The boss flicked cigar ashes onto the floor. "My money, Ramsay?"

"You promised to pay today," said the second man, his face still blurred by smoke. He clutched his hands behind his neck, relaxed in a room filled with tension. Daisy caught a flash of navy, an epaulet, a single brass button. *A ship's uniform?*

"Tomorrow." Daisy heard Ramsay swallow. "I'll have your money tomorrow."

The boss looked bored and dangerous, his tolerance waning. "Same promise, different day."

"I'm good for the dough." Ramsay's whine became a whimper as Louie pulled his gun from the pocket of his great coat and put it to Ramsay's skull.

"That's what you said the night before we sailed," the boss reminded him. "But I've yet to see a dime."

Louie released the safety on his gun, the click loud in a room gone utterly still. Daisy could smell Ramsay St. Croix's fear.

The boss eyed Louie once again. "Croaking him won't pay his debt."

Sweat now dampened Ramsay's forehead and the soft collar of his shirt. "My family's good for—"

The boss tipped back his fedora, suddenly interested. "You'll go to Randolph?"

"Yeah, sure, whatever you want," Ramsay was quick to agree.

Randolph? Daisy sucked in air. Surely not *her* Randolph!

"Randolph will not be pleased," the boss said bluntly.

"This is the third time you've asked him for money. Your brother doesn't approve of your gambling."

Brother? Daisy's knees nearly gave out.

"Randolph would rather have me alive than dead." Ramsay's voice sounded hoarse, as if his throat had gone dry.

"Randolph is a businessman and you, Ramsay, are a liability." The boss drummed his fingers on the metal tabletop, the rat-a-tat as rapid as machine-gun fire. "Out of respect for your brother, I extend repayment by two days."

Ramsay St. Croix blubbered his gratitude.

"Come to me, Ramsay," the boss instructed, "or I will send my collector."

The way the man said *collector* turned Daisy cold.

At this mention of him, the second man sat a little straighter. Obscured by the Havana haze, he laid his forearms on the table. Blue wool, impregnated with coal smoke and shiny at the elbows. The *Majestic* buttons at each wrist were oxidized by continual Atlantic damp. *An insider on the ship?*

"I run my quarry to earth, or in your case, to sea," the collector warned Ramsay before pulling out his pocket-knife and flipping open the blade. Then he pierced his palm with its point. Droplets of blood speckled his skin. "The slightest cut, blood in the water, stirs a shark frenzy."

Sharks! Daisy's stomach rolled.

"Beat it," commanded the boss, suddenly ordering Ramsay from the room.

There was no time for Daisy to flee. A split second and the door flew open. Shoved into the hallway, Ramsay bounced off the far wall, then into Daisy. The door slammed on his coattails.

Daisy's eyes widened and Ramsay gaped, his face deadly white. He swore softly, yet vehemently, as he grabbed her by the arm and hustled her down the corridor. She nearly fell on the stairs.

Reaching the next deck, Ramsay spotted a storage closet and pushed her inside ahead of him. His arm brushed her shoulder as he reached overhead and searched for the light pull. A dim bulb soon cast them in more shadow than light.

The room closed in around them, small and filled with brooms, mops, buckets, and shelves of lemon oil.

"Who the hell are you?" Ramsay demanded.

"Someone *not* to be bumped off," Daisy shot back, not the least bit afraid of the man doomed to be chum.

"Spill," he pressed. "What did you hear?"

She stuck out her chin. "Don't know from nothing."

He jabbed a finger near her nose. "You eavesdropped."

"I wasn't out to spy." Daisy picked her words carefully. "I believed you were someone else when I followed you below."

His eyes narrowed. "Someone you wanted to protect?"

She held his gaze. "Maybe."

He pursed his lips until understanding dawned. A smug smile spread over his face. "You thought I was Randolph."

"I didn't know he had a brother."

"*Half* brother," Ramsay corrected. "Randolph's father married my mother after his first wife died in childbirth. Twelve years separate us."

"I don't understand. Ambrose? St. Croix?"

Ramsay studied her for several seconds.

Daisy studied him right back. Up close, she found him shorter than Randolph, narrower in the shoulders,

89

his eyes a lighter brown. He looked rough around the edges, where Randolph appeared refined.

"Gold diggers sometimes prompt him to substitute his middle name for his last," he finally explained. "The heir to the St. Croix Cruise Line can't be too careful."

She felt oddly winded. "The heir . . ."

"You stuck on him?"

"You're off your rocker!"

At the moment, Daisy was more hurt than infatuated. Randolph *Ambrose* St. Croix hadn't trusted her to see the man behind the millions. Daisy suddenly needed to get out of this tight space and into the fresh air. "Pardon me." She tried to push past Ramsay.

He blocked her path, warned, "Randolph has a fiancée."

"Eloise Hogue." She waved him off. "I'm aware he's engaged."

"Were you also aware the *boss* is her father?" he shot back. "Thomas 'Tommygun' Hogue."

She lost all ability to speak.

"Hogue is a businessman by day and a mobster by night," Ramsay explained. "Randolph has no idea he's marrying into the Family."

"Bunk! Your brother seems smarter—"

Ramsay snorted. "Thomas Hogue buries his gangster roots alongside those he's had killed. He employs people to keep his name clean. He never dirties his hands."

Daisy took it all in. "Hogue's association with Randolph legitimizes the man."

"Smart cookie." He tapped her temple with his finger. "Hogue owns every nightclub in the Bronx. Bootlegged gin, gambling, prostitution. Once Randolph and Eloise are married, Hogue plans to launder money on the *Majestic*."

She licked dry lips. "You need to warn Randolph."

Ramsay shook his head. "Can't. Randolph believes I'm in New York, working in the cruise ship office. He doesn't even know I'm on board."

"Then I must—"

Ramsay shook his head, warned, "Don't rat me out like a mob stoolie. If you say one word to Randolph about Thomas Hogue, I'll spread a rumor."

Daisy cringed. News of any kind traveled like lightning aboard an ocean liner. If Ramsay should exchange a confidence on the bow, then run to the stern, that same secret, somewhat embellished, might be whispered to him on his arrival. In little time, rumors of Randolph's association with Daisy would reach Eloise Hogue. The indiscretion could prove disastrous.

"Randolph has not been unfaithful to his fiancée," Daisy said softly.

"You're a choice bit." Ramsay looked her up and down. His lip curled and his tone lowered, deep and dark. "You've a sweet kisser, nice bubs, and great stilts. My brother's no saint."

Daisy wanted to bash Ramsay St. Croix's head with a mop bucket.

"Bree!" Large hands wrapped around her shoulders, shaking her hard enough to make her teeth rattle.

"Is she still breathing?" A second male voice rose, anxious and concerned.

"Holy shit! Has Daisy hurt her?" A young girl spoke now, her tone piercing and frightened. "Is she dead?"

Ever so slowly, the present filtered through the past. Bree fought the final seconds that held her captive in 1925, finding it difficult to pull herself from the vision.

Tommygun Hogue, Louie, the collector. Men who killed for money and pleasure. The image of the blood on the collector's palm remained vivid in her mind.

"Get her some water," she heard Sexton St. Croix say.

Shortly thereafter the icy coolness of a plastic bottle pressed against her cheek, her forehead, the side of her neck. Her eyelids fluttered, and she regained her bearings.

Her focus centered on Sex. She was cradled on his lap, and the heat and passion of past lovers singed her hip, her bottom, between her inner thighs. Reached her very soul. Her sexually deprived body absorbed his prowess, intent and potent. She tingled. Sweet, sweet torture. She was so drawn into Sex, she nearly forgot herself.

Security, however, was not the place to climax.

With the last of her strength, she struggled off his lap, clutched the rim of the table, and pulled herself up.

Her dry throat made her voice crack. "Water, please."

Sex also stood, and offered her a sip of bottled water. She drank deeply. "Much better," she finally managed.

"Where were you?" Sex asked.

"In this very room eighty years ago," Bree told him. "I want to sort out the images before I discuss them. There's a lot of information to absorb."

Visibly stunned, Shay stood uneasily beside Bree, pale, the burgundy spikes now flattened from running her hands nervously through her hair. "You weren't faking it, were you?"

Bree cleared her throat and softly replied, "Not faking it the way you were earlier."

"Damn," the young girl muttered. "Busted."

"Busted?" Tall, broad, his expression dark and intimidating, Jackson Kyle jabbed a finger toward a chair. "Sit and explain," he ordered Shay.

"Let's all have a seat," Sex suggested as he pulled out a chair for Bree.

Seated between two men about to take the young girl apart, Bree took the initiative and reached out to Shay. "I'm Bree Emery."

"The clairsentient," Shay acknowledged. "I've seen you on *Here and Beyond.* Awesome show. Wish I'd been born psychic."

"When did you discover your talent?" Bree inquired.

Shay slouched on her chair. "Prior to boarding the *Majestic.*"

"Two days ago?" Jackson stood with such force that his chair tipped over. The crystal ball positioned on the table before him rolled to the right. Bree stopped it with her forearm. Slamming his hands on the table, Jackson leaned toward the young woman. "Don't play me, Shay."

Shay looked up at the big man. "I've worked at Crystals on South Beach for four years," she stated, as if she'd absorbed psychic powers from her work environment. "I watched other psychics give readings. Some flat-out lied, while others padded the truth. Most told customers exactly what they wanted to hear."

Bree blinked. "You felt Mr. St. Croix wanted to die?"

Shay screwed up her nose. "I thought I had a sure thing. Tradition and tragedy. St. Croix following in his great-great-uncle's footsteps."

"St. Croix men seek old age," Sex informed her stiffly.

Jackson straightened his chair, sat once again. Resting his elbows on the tabletop, he steepled his fingers. "Your prediction was a play for attention?"

"I'm one of five hundred psychics on board ship," Shay said grimly. "I had to make my move to be noticed."

Jackson blew out a breath. "You're after the finder's fee." He shot Sex a look. "I warned you about weirdos—"

"I'm not a weirdo," Shay retorted. "The fee would have paid my college tuition."

"You want to go to college?" Bree took a closer look at the girl. "What did you plan to study?"

"Veterinary medicine."

Bree hadn't planned to touch Shay, yet she felt drawn to do so. Uncertain as to what she would learn, Bree lightly pressed her forearm to Shay's own. Images flashed, fast and furious. Anger. The pain of loss. Her twelfth birthday had brought the death of her parents, victims of a hit-and-run driver. The candles on her cake had burned out, snuffing her dreams. She'd grown up quickly, broody and rebellious.

"Your aunt?" Bree touched on the girl's guardian.

And Shay exploded. "She's old and cranky. Aunt Margaret lives in nineteen-fifty. She has more rules than St. Mary's."

Sex spiked a brow. "You went to Catholic school?"

Bree noted the girl's torn black T-shirt, the dark Gothic webbing that ran up both her arms. "Your days of starched white blouses, pleated plaid skirts, and saddle shoes were short-lived."

Shay shrugged. "I don't conform."

"Yet you graduated," Bree said.

"My aunt fought for me to take the final exams," Shay admitted. "She believed a high school diploma was important."

Bree broke contact with Shay. She massaged her forearm, removing the girl's sadness and sorrow from her own soul. "You're smart enough to go to college. What about scholarships?"

"I applied, once." Shay plucked lint from her torn black T, then patted her spiked burgundy hair. "I'm not your All-American scholar. Interviewers see me as the campus freak."

"You'll find success outside the paranormal," Bree assured her. "Give yourself time."

Shay looked at Bree as if she wanted to believe her.

In the ensuing silence, Bree caught Sex looking at Jackson with a raised brow. Jackson tilted his head slightly, shrugged. The silent communication spoke louder than words. Close friends read each other's minds.

Sex shifted on his chair, pointedly turned to Shay. "Jackson and I have a mutual friend, Alex McIntyre, who runs the McIntyre Foundation—"

Shay glared. "I'm not a charity case."

Sex continued as if Shay hadn't cut in. "—that funds grants and scholarships. Are you interested?"

Shay looked confused. "You'd put in a good word for me even after my false prediction?"

"McIntyre believes in second chances," Sex assured her.

Jackson extracted a business card from his wallet. "Call me after the cruise. I'll schedule an interview."

"Thanks, man." Shay snagged the card, then shoved off her chair. She cast one final glance at the crystal ball. "No more predictions. I leave Daisy Alton to you, Bree Emery." She departed, her steps light.

Jackson scooped the crystal ball off the table. "Need me today, boss?"

Sex shook his head. "Go tell fortunes."

Jackson tossed the quartz crystal into the air, caught

it by the door. "Might be my true calling," he said as he left the room.

Alone in Security, Bree absorbed the shift of events. Sex and Jackson had gifted Shay with a golden opportunity. The men were well connected.

"Thank you for giving Shay a chance," Bree finally said.

"It's McIntyre, not me, giving her the chance," Sex quickly corrected.

Bree refused to let the good deed pass without notice. "A chance is still a chance."

"Speaking of chances," he said ruefully, "what do you have against butterflies?"

She fingered the crystal pendant on its silver chain. "Your gifts are too intimate."

"Women love sexy underwear."

"I prefer comfort."

"And I make you uncomfortable?"

The man was perceptive. "Acquainted just one day, and already you're adding to my underwear drawer."

"At least they weren't edible."

She rolled her eyes. "How very thoughtful."

His gaze warmed. "The butterflies would have looked great on you."

She dipped her head. "I'm sure Mimi did them justice."

"I'll never know." With daring slowness, Sex tipped up her chin with his forefinger. "Accept my apology?"

His touch rendered her speechless. She couldn't fight the sunbursts of sexual heat that sizzled along her jaw, shot down her neck and into her chest. Her breasts prickled and her nipples puckered as if gently pinched. Desire poured into her belly and curled her toes. She pulled back before she started to pant.

He took in her flushed cheeks, the taut peaks tenting her green beaded T. "You're excited."

"Not me, Mimi. I sensed her on you, so strongly in fact, I, um—"

"Was turned on?"

"A little."

"A lot."

"Mimi wants you bad," Bree told him.

"I want to take you on a tour of Nassau."

She hesitated. "I'm not certain that's a good idea."

He cocked his head. "You don't look like the type who fears fun, so you must be afraid of me."

"Hardly," she scoffed.

"Prove it," he challenged.

She gave in. "A *short* tour of the island."

"With or without Daisy?" he asked.

"She'll remain on board," Bree said.

"You and me. I like it." He paused, took a deep breath. "When you're able, I want to discuss your vision."

"It involved Daisy and—" she hesitated "—Ramsay St. Croix."

Surprise flickered across his face. "My great-grandfather? Ramsay wasn't listed on the liner's manifest."

Bree knew differently. She'd witnessed Ramsay aboard the ill-fated cruise.

"I saw him, Sex." She met his gaze, dark with apprehension. "It was assumed Ramsay remained at the ship's offices, but he sailed on the *Majestic*."

"Sneaked on the ship?" He shook his head. "Impossible."

"He might have booked under an assumed name," she said slowly. "Perhaps he found himself in some kind of trouble—"

"Ramsay St. Croix has always lived a sterling life."

A sterling life didn't include an association with

Tommygun Hogue. "Ramsay never gambled?"

Sex's laugh was tight. "The words bookish, intelligent, and honorable best describe the man."

Bree might have gone with thoughtless, reckless, and daring. A man didn't cross the mob and live long to tell about it. "Just the same, I'd like to ask him a few questions."

"Impossible. I won't have you upsetting an old man." His expression was dark and forbidding, and she realized he was closed to further discussion.

She backed off.

A scuffle outside Security drew Sex from his chair. Bree followed. The door opened, and twin boys charged inside, wet from swimming. Dripping swim trunks left puddles at their feet.

Blond, blue-eyed, and all of five, the twins softly shut the door. On seeing Sex, one of the boys put his finger to his lips conspiratorially. "S-shh, Mr. Sex Toy."

Recognizing the Wainscott twins, Sex grimaced. Stuart had a slight lisp and St. Croix always came out Sex Toy.

Sex was well acquainted with the twins' parents, Hugh and Andrea Wainscott. They were regular passengers on the St. Croix Line. The couple had reached their forties before ever having children. Just when they'd considered adoption, Andrea became pregnant. They now had two small terrors, adored, but spoiled rotten.

"Stevie, Stuart, where are you?" the panicky voice of Camp Majestic's coordinator, Cynthia Duff, echoed down the corridor.

Sex nudge the boys aside and cracked the door. "In here, Cyn."

"Aw, man, you spoiled our fun," Stevie whined.

Cynthia stepped into Security. One look at Sex and her smile slipped. "My apologies, Mr. St. Croix. The Wainscott boys got away from me."

"Looks like you could use some help." Sex scooped up the twins before they could protest. Their swim trunks squished into his gray pullover and water ran down his black slacks as the young ones wiggled and tried to escape. His eyebrows drew together as he gripped them even tighter.

"You look like Oscar the Grouch who lives in the garbage can," Stevie laughed.

He couldn't help chuckling along with the twins. "Where to, Cyn?" he asked.

"Back to the pool!" Stevie stopped squirming long enough to shout.

"They've been in the pool for two hours," Cynthia told Sex. "When the other children tired and chose to return to the virtual reality center for rides and games, Stevie and Stuart took off."

"Pool, pool," the twins chanted.

"Camp Majestic now, the pool later with your parents," Sex announced, holding the wiggleworms tight. He turned to Bree and motioned her to follow with a jerk of his head.

Located at the stern of the promenade deck, the kiddie camp offered a variety of activities for those youngsters who ran their parents ragged. Supervised activity programs involved Circus at Sea, clowns, face painting, and juggling, along with treasure hunts and outdoor play centers. The sandbox and swimming pool produced the most excitement.

At the entrance to the camp, Sex released the twins.

"Bye, Mr. Sex Toy." Stuart hugged Sex's leg before bounding off.

"Thank you, Mr. St. Croix," Cynthia Duff cast over her shoulder as she dashed after the twins.

Taking a moment, he leaned against the door frame and watched the scurry of activity. So much noise. So much fun. Even at his age, there had been times aboard ship when he couldn't sleep and had sneaked down to Camp Majestic and challenged the virtual reality games until his eyelids drooped. His initials, SSC, ranked number one on many of the high-scoring games.

"Sex Toy?" Bree stood beside him now, fighting a smile.

"Hopefully his speech will improve with age."

"Cute boys." Had he heard a wistful sigh in her voice? "Do you like kids?" she asked.

"Other people's kids," he admitted. "Those you can tickle, spoil, baby-sit on occasion. Full-time parenting scares the hell out of me."

"You *baby-sit?*" She looked astounded.

"For two of my college buddies and their wives. Three-hour shifts. That's my limit."

She studied him. "Bet you're the biggest kid of all."

Sex wouldn't bet against her. Checkers, Chutes and Ladders, Clue; he played to win.

He shifted his stance, and his wet slacks clung to his thighs. The twins had left their mark. "I need dry clothes before we hit Nassau. Come with me to my suite?"

Hesitancy darkened her green eyes. "I could wait at reception."

He shook his head. "I want you with me when I change."

100

Six

Go with him to change his clothes . . .

The idea left Bree Emery as hot as the Caribbean sun. She trailed him to his suite. One step into the room, and Sex had stripped off his shirt and slacks before she'd settled on the black leather sofa.

Standing in his boxers at the bedroom door, he said, "Ten minutes; make yourself comfortable."

Bree bit down on her lip and forced a nod as her gaze drifted from his sharp Nordic features to his broad chest with sun-hardened muscles and tawny hair trailing down his stomach into a thin line at his navel. Then, lower still, to his pale blue boxers with tiny wide-bed trucks. BUILT FORD TOUGH ran the length of his fly.

Her stare made him twitch, just the slightest stirring of his sex, before he turned and sought dry clothing. Sliding frosted glass doors separated the living area from his bedroom. He left the slider cracked, just enough for her to see the tight curve of his flank, the shadow of his erection, when he dropped his boxers and crossed to his dresser.

The man had one fine body. He lived well in his skin. He radiated sensuality, his body created for the sole purpose of pleasure. From the brief times their bodies had brushed, Bree knew his effect on women. Handsome, wealthy, incredibly hot, *Sex Toy* had only to smile and women threw themselves on his bed.

His experience frightened her. His timeless appeal would charm women to their graves.

"Ready to hit the island?" Sex asked as he entered the room. A white-and-navy pin-stripe collared shirt now hugged his chest, the sleeves casually rolled to his elbows. Navy chino shorts had replaced his black slacks. He had the undeniable edge of looking casual yet one cut above most men.

"I'd like to snag a brochure at reception," Bree requested.

"No trust in your Bahamian host?"

"We have different historical interests."

"I can do ancient stone forts."

"I can do more than forts."

He winked. "I'll gladly show you more."

Disembarking, they sauntered along Prince George Wharf. Six other cruise ships had docked, and the cruise terminal hummed with tourists.

Old Nassau's character was epitomized in the sunshine, the Straw Market, and the street vendors' smiles. A brass sign over the doorway of a gift shop described the island well: SUN-KISSED AND FOREVER FROST-FREE. The weather was as perfect as nature would allow.

Even the most buttoned-down tourist found the laidback lifestyle to his liking as he strolled along the pink sidewalks on Bay Street. Spilling from inside shops and restaurants, Goombay and calypso music captivated the crowds.

The tropical flair entered Bree's very bones. She became one with the island. So much so that with a little nudge from Sex, she braved Hairbraider's Centre and had her hair braided and beaded like Bo Derek in *Ten*. With each turn of her head, the crystal and lavender beads tickled her neck, making her smile.

Sex admired her new look with hot eyes and an approving smile. Peeking at him now from the corner of her eye, Bree watched as he shook hands with native musicians and barefoot islanders. The locals knew and loved him. "Sex *mon*" was chanted throughout the Straw Market.

Involuntarily, her mind strayed, and her gaze shifted below his belt. What image emblazoned the boxers he was now wearing? Bright red lips, chili peppers, or lightning bolts? All hot and shocking. With her mind on his boxers and not on the sidewalk, she walked straight into a stack of straw baskets.

"Caught up in *mon* thoughts?" the vendor's *Conch* accent lilted on the island breeze.

Bree blushed as the dark-skinned woman's knowing gaze slid to Sex, then back to her. She smiled, woman to woman, as she sat on a stool in a red blouse and flared orange skirt and slowly wove a palmetto plait into a broad-brimmed hat.

Sex stopped beside Bree. "You're so fair." He lifted his hand as if to stroke her cheek, then thought better of it. "A hat would prevent sunburn."

Bree agreed. "How much?" she asked the woman.

The vendor stood and selected a straw hat with a green ribbon around its brim to match Bree's beaded T. "For Sex *mon's* pretty lady, no charge."

The very thought of her being St. Croix's woman sent a sharp thrust of lust through Bree's body. Anticipation burned between her legs. She reached for a colorful straw fan and whipped the heat from her cheeks.

"Bree Emery, meet Samana Rolle, vendor of straw hats, voodoo curses, and the best conch fritters on the island," Sex said.

Bree cocked her head, intrigued. "Voodoo curses?"

"I cast both love and hate," Samana said with a devious smile. "A recent female tourist wished her husband impotent. The man was having an affair. A pin to the doll's genitals and he lost his sex drive."

"Ouch," Sex muttered as he shifted his stance.

Bree's gaze strayed to the zipper on his navy shorts.

"Don't even think it," he softly growled.

"Many women want Sex *mon* to love them, to marry them, yet you not like them, Ms. Bree." The vendor had astute insight. "This time Sex *mon* need to cast spell."

"No spells." Sex shook his head. "My charm will win her over."

"Cocky son of a bitch," Samana stated with the fondness of familiarity. "Put him in his place, Ms. Emery."

"My place is to show Bree a good time." Accepting the straw hat on her behalf, Sex dropped it on her head.

Bree straightened the brim so that it dipped over her eyes. Touching the freshly woven palmetto, she sensed the arthritis that claimed the vendor's fingers, the pain that would soon cripple and steal her craft.

Bree reached for her purse. "Please, Samana, I insist, let me pay."

Sex covered her hand with his own. "No," he said under his breath as his open palm pressed the back of her hand with the intimacy of naked bodies spooning in bed. "You're most generous, Samana," he said. Then, craning his neck, he looked deep within her shop. "Your grandsons, are they in?"

"They be diving for conch." She sighed. "No help today."

Sex squeezed, then released Bree's hand. The squeeze shot up her arm and straight to her breasts. Her nipples stood at attention.

Her arousal drew his grin, then his whisper, "Nice tents." Turning back to Samana, he withdrew his wallet from the pocket of his shorts. "Dinner at the Pink Conch?" he asked.

Samana nodded. "I cook for you, Sex *mon.*"

After removing several large bills, he handed them to the vendor, then repocketed his wallet. "Back room, candlelight, so I can cast my voodoo on Bree Emery."

"Fool man, you need more than voodoo to win this woman's heart," Samana said as she waved them on their way. "Show her our island, Sex *mon.* Scooters be at Jacaranda House."

The bed-and-breakfast was on East Bay Street, a pale yellow colonial with a wide veranda and peach shutters. Wicker rockers welcomed guests to relax in the shade cast by the Jacaranda trees covered with blue blooms.

Though Sex would have loved to reserve a room and initiate Bree Emery to the island seduction of naked bodies on cool sheets, windows wide open, and sea air stirred by bamboo ceiling fans, he opted instead for motorized scooters and a tour of Nassau.

"Scooters are in the back." He motioned Bree to follow him along a narrow fishbone walkway.

Parked behind a white gazebo, green scooters awaited island visitors. He walked to a group tagged for the *Majestic*'s passengers. "You'll need to wear a helmet," he told Bree, then watched as she removed her straw hat and shook out her beaded braids. After arranging the straw hat in a white basket attached to the handlebars, she secured her helmet. Not quite biker babe, but sweet scooter mama, nonetheless. She started the scooter, and it putted to life.

"We drive on the left," he called to her as he climbed on his own scooter and edged into traffic.

Bree motored close behind him as they played tourist, rounding Rawson Square with its flamingo-pink government buildings, stopping off briefly at the Junkanoo Expo to view the display of vivid island costumes worn to celebrate both Boxing and New Year's Day. Following the Expo, they headed down West Bay Street to Fort Charlotte.

Together, they climbed from the dark and dank dungeon to the open, weather-beaten battlements. Sex kept his eye on Bree as she took in the view. He saw Nassau through her eyes. A light breeze tugged at the ends of her beaded hair, and even with the protection of her hat, the sun pinkened the tip of her nose.

He leaned against a cannon while Bree ran her hand over the ancient rock wall. She closed her eyes. "Memories locked in stone. I can almost hear the cannonfire, the chilling laughter of marauding pirates above the splashes of the waves." She peeked at him through lowered lashes, and a teasing smile spread. "Perhaps you once lived as a pirate, as Mimi Rhaine believes. You might have been the infamous Calico Jack Rackham and she, Anne Bonny."

He pushed himself off the cannon. "Ho-ho-ho and a bottle of rum." After meeting Bree, his attention hadn't strayed. Although she was a hands-off woman, he had no desire to seek out Mimi or any of the Nassau women who gave great island pleasure.

Beside him, Bree shook out the travel brochure. "Where to next?" she asked. "The Botanical Gardens?"

He looked down into her face, alight with interest in the island, and wished half her interest would shift to him.

"We're headed to Caribe Bleu," he informed her.

She studied the brochure. "I don't see it on the map."

"It's a bit off the beaten path."

Way off the path. Caribe Bleu wasn't a typical tourist attraction. Only the rich, the royal, and the famous knew the spa existed. Those who paid well for anonymity and privacy.

Bree folded the brochure, looking at him warily. "Where are you taking me, Sexton St. Croix?"

"Call it a surprise."

She shook her head. "I don't do surprises."

"Just this once? Indulge me." He jammed his hands into the side pockets of his chino shorts. If he told her more, she'd hop on her scooter and putt back to Bay Street. "I promise you pampering and relaxation."

She released a breath. "Without touching?"

He held up his hands, all innocence. "Not by me."

He headed toward his scooter before she could change her mind. Bree hesitantly followed him. Hearing the putt-putt of her scooter, he maneuvered to a maintenance road behind the fort. The pavement soon ended and they drove on packed earth, cutting across the island. The sun warmed his back, the sky so clear and bright it was nearly opaque. The scent of the ocean rose sharp and tangy.

They passed a short airstrip and a heliport. Steering his scooter over a rise, he cut the engine. The view below always hit him hard. It was the only place on earth where heaven and earth meshed seamlessly.

Beside him, Bree's breath escaped on an appreciative gasp. "The edge of Eden."

Colored by red hibiscus and purple bougainvillea, Caribe Bleu curved along Mango Bay. Palm-fringed and fenced for security, the shoreline spa blended beautifully with nature. Leaving their scooters on the rise, they descended a stone footpath until they reached the gatehouse.

Recognizing Sex, the dark-skinned man in the brown suit and flashy tie pressed several buttons and the gate swung wide, allowing them entrance. "Welcome, Mr. St. Croix," the man greeted.

"Good to see you again, Adjulle," Sex returned.

Walking ahead of him now, Bree turned full circle, taking pleasure in the tropical gardens and terraced stairs that led down to the arched entrance. With the lapping ocean at her back and cool shadows urging her onward, she no longer felt wary.

He motioned toward the golden doors. "Join me?"

She released a breath, nodded.

As they stepped inside, floor-to-ceiling windows cast sunshine on pink marble floors. Angled for the best view, teal-cushioned chairs invited guests to sit and absorb a stunning view of white sand and the calm Caribbean. Beneath an aerial color photograph of Mango Bay, a small brass plaque dedicated the spa to health and wellness and Alex McIntyre.

"Your friend?" Bree pointed to the plaque.

Sex nodded. "Alex is one of the prime investors. He saw the potential of an island spa and supported it."

"Smart man," Bree said as she preceded him down

the hallway. Just beyond the windows, outdoor steam baths and bathing pools offered relaxation before therapeutic massages.

A flash of skin made her blink as she caught sight of a couple sunning themselves on a raised deck beside an open cabana. They reclined, all buff and beautiful, and *naked.*

"You brought me to a nudist colony?" Bree could barely voice the question.

Sex shrugged. "The spa promotes freedom of both body and spirit. Clothing is optional."

Bree glanced once again at the man and woman, all tanned and glistening. The man shifted on his chaise—stretched—and lifted more than his arms toward the sun.

"People are more than their bodies," Sex said over her shoulder. "Spend enough time here and you hardly notice."

"Do you come here often?"

"I've a standing appointment whenever I visit Nassau."

"Do you bring all your women here?"

"You're my first female guest," he admitted. "I wanted to make you feel good."

"*How* good?"

"Let me spoil you with a couples' massage."

Her body tingled with nervous anticipation.

"Mr. St. Croix?" An elegant woman in a yellow linen sheath seemed to appear out of thin air. Her professional tone held both warmth and intimacy. She welcomed him with a light kiss to each cheek, then a lingering one on his lips. "We've been expecting you."

"Helene, head of client relations, meet Bree Emery, my guest for the afternoon."

"My pleasure." Helene's smile tightened fractionally as she extended her slender hand, and Bree hesitantly shook it.

The woman's love of business and Sexton St. Croix scored Bree's palm. Helene had filled his bed.

"Your regular suite?" Helene inquired.

"Not this trip." He turned thoughtful. "A key to Mango Shores East. We'll find our own way."

Bree caught Helene's surprised blink before she composed herself. Disappearing, Helene quickly returned with a plastic room key. Instead of handing it directly to him, she slid the key along his palm in a slow, sensual slide. "Let me know if I can be of further assistance."

"I'm sure we'll be fine," Sex assured her. "I've scheduled Emile and Filomena. Please inform them that we've arrived."

Helene turned to leave. "As you wish."

Once out of earshot, Bree turned to Sex. "Helene's quite taken by you."

"She's been taken by me once, and I'm not interested in an island affair," he said flatly. "I'm here to enjoy you, Bree Emery. Only you."

The desire in his gaze stroked her as boldly as a full-body massage. Her heart stuttered, nearly stopped.

"I won't touch you," he said reassuringly. "We're here to relax. Let's make the most of our day."

Privacy and intimacy imbued their suite on the eastern tip of Caribe Bleu. Decorated in sea blues, island greens, and snatches of sun yellow, the room seduced with its king-size bed and cozy love seats. Carved into the antique wooden headboard, an illustration from the Kama Sutra depicted lovers in an amorous embrace. It was tastefully done, yet distractingly erotic.

Facing east and south, sliding glass doors opened onto the beach, admitting a cross breeze that cooled the room. Just outside, a canopied cabana of terra-cotta canvas sat on a deck surrounded by royal palms.

Beneath the cabana, two padded massage tables were pressed together like a double bed. Very shortly, Bree would be stretched out beside Sex, naked beneath a towel, with mere inches separating them.

He snatched a list of scrubs, wraps, and massage treatments from the nightstand and handed it to her. "Pick your pleasure?"

Their fingers brushed for no more than a second, yet the charge of sexual heat forced her back a step. A second jolt rose from the list of spa resources. Countless couples had handled this menu. Couples on their honeymoon.

No wonder Helene had given him the eye. This suite was reserved for newlyweds, two people deeply in love and starting a life together. Whereas she and Sex were no more than two ships passing in the night. She wasn't into a shipboard romance.

She forced her attention back to the treatment list: a Couples' Chocolate Swedish Massage, as good for the soul as it was for the tastebuds. Or a Peaches and Ground Pecan Body Scrub, guaranteed to leave the skin as soft and sweet-smelling as ripe fruit.

These were sensual treatments, designed to leave the body pliant and primed for sex.

Reaching the bottom of the list, she scrunched up her nose. "A Seaweed Wrap?"

Sex smiled. "The wrap has enough juniper and lemon so it won't leave you smelling like a beach at high tide."

She wouldn't mind smelling like high tide if it kept

Sex at a distance. Not certain which treatment to pick, she said, "Any suggestions?"

He would make this easy on her, Sex decided. They would begin with a simple yet pleasurable steam and soak. "A eucalyptus steam, followed by a hibiscus bath."

"This is done . . . ?"

"Nude." He caught her glance toward the door. He wasn't about to let her leave. "Wrap yourself in a towel for the steam. The bath is best taken naked to enjoy the full-body experience."

She licked her lips. "Where can I slip into my towel?"

"There's a changing room down the hall on the right. The steam and bath are at the back of the suite, just beyond the walk-in closet."

She looked amazed. "Everything's right at our fingertips."

"Most couples never leave their suites."

Actually, within the first hour of their arrival, most couples hit the bed and climaxed twice, if only to get the fire out of their blood, so they could enjoy the slower burn of leisurely lovemaking.

"I'll meet you in the steam room," she said.

Fifteen minutes later, they sat across from each other on low benches, banked in thick swirls of steam. Sweat dripped from his brow and beaded his chest. Bree's face was flushed, her skin slick, hot silk. He watched as she dabbed her forehead with a plush white towel.

Sex tightened the towel at his waist, then draped a second over his groin. The very sight of this woman had him rising with the steam.

"Can it get any hotter in here?" Her voice drifted to him, thick and lazy.

He could make it a whole lot hotter; one kiss, a

brush of her breast, one stroke up her thigh, and steam would come out of her ears. "Ready for the hibiscus soak?"

She rose slowly, the damp towel clinging like a second skin. She fanned her face. "Time to cool off."

Two deep enamel tubs offered cleansing from the steam. Red and pink hibiscus floated on the surface, camouflage for their naked bodies. Sex allowed Bree to submerge before he entered the room. Her sharp exhale sent ripples across the flowered surface when he dropped his towel and stepped into the tub.

A tray of sliced fruit sat on a glass table between their tubs, along with iced glasses of fresh pineapple juice. The skilled staff worked behind the scenes, silent yet ready to meet every guest's need. He indulged in a bite of passion fruit, then sipped his juice.

Beside him, Bree reached for a cluster of red grapes. The beads in her braids clinked against the enamel as she slid deeper into the water.

Stretching his arms along the side of the tub, he caught a glimpse of her full, firm, bouyant breasts, her nipples as pale as the pink hibiscus. Sex wished himself the icicle crystal that lay in her cleavage.

"Relaxed?" he asked.

She popped a grape into her mouth, peeked at him through hooded lids. "This could prove addictive."

"Me or the spa?"

"You're neither eucalyptus nor hibiscus."

He wiggled his fingers. "Magic hands, better than any quarter-fed vibrating bed."

"I'll stick with the massuese."

"You'll like Filomena. She's a known healer."

She reached for a slice of peach. "What are you known for, Sexton St. Croix?"

He hesitated. His reputation preceded him. Everywhere. The image he portrayed to the press was not really him, though. Only Jackson Kyle knew his life beyond the women. "Most people associate me with the cruise line, my love of travel, my skills in bed."

"This is my first cruise," she softly admitted.

"I grew up on cruise ships," he told her. "I'd sailed around the world twice by age seven. Monaco, Tahiti, Los Cabos, and Paradise Island were the playgrounds of my youth."

"Travel broadens the mind."

And the selection of bedmates. Strangely enough, there was something special about Bree that nudged him from nooners and one-night stands toward a five-day commitment.

A part of him truly admired her modesty, her directness, her self-sufficiency. Most women clung to him as if he were a lifeline. Bree would never be engulfed by his life. She preferred things that went bump in the night to his brushing against her.

"I hope to make your cruise memorable," he said with a sincerity that surprised him.

Bree flicked the tip of her tongue to capture the peach juice left at the corner of her mouth. Sex felt the sweep of her moist, pink tongue all the way to his groin. He groaned low in his throat.

A groan Bree ignored. "My connection to Daisy has been the highlight of this trip thus far. There's a mystery behind her haunting the *Majestic*."

Mystery? More like mayhem on Daisy's part. The ghost would be the death of his cruise line.

Finishing off his pineapple juice, he asked, "Ready for your massage?"

"I'll . . . give it a try."

He knew she was hesitant to be touched. Sex had faith Filomena would not cause her discomfort. The woman was a skilled therapist.

"I'm getting out," he warned, and Bree averted her gaze.

Walking to the linen closet, he selected two plush robes. He left one robe and a pair of spa slippers on the counter by the sink. "Meet me at the cabana," he directed.

She did in a very short time. On bamboo stands filled with oils, countless tea candles flickered in amethyst clusters, lavender and tangerine scents rising on the flames.

After introducing Bree to Emile and Filomena, Sex turned his back while Filomena helped Bree disrobe, then lie on her stomach upon the massage bed draped in pale green terry cloth. Filomena spread a soft towel over Bree's backside.

With Bree's face angled away from him, Sex slipped off his robe and slid onto the table. He nodded to Emile, who covered his buttocks with a towel.

"A Swedish massage, Shea Butter Soufflé Wrap followed by the Honey Body Polish for the lady," he instructed Filomena.

Bree lifted her head slightly. "Sounds good enough to eat."

"Let me know when you're ready to be tasted."

She blushed to the roots of her hair.

He nestled his face on the lavender-scented headrest, welcomed the power of Emile's hands. "Citrus oil and a Deep Tissue Massage."

Two hours passed, the serenity absolute. As a solitary activity, Sex found a massage an unbeatable experience. But sharing the process with a beautiful woman was spellbinding.

Within the privacy of the pavilion, he'd watched Filomena wrap, polish, and work the kinks on Bree's body, knowing she was being well-cared for. Oddly enough, her pleasure brought him peace. He listened to her breathe, so slow, so even. So into the massage. When she released her appreciation on a soft moan, his chest warmed. When she yawned, he wanted to take a late afternoon nap beside her.

Relaxed beyond reason, Bree felt as liquid as sea grass. Lying on her back now, she stared up at the terracotta canvas, a woman well massaged.

"Would you like tan-glow body glitter to add sparkle to your skin, or would you prefer a Henna tattoo?" Filomena offered Bree in a soft, soothing voice as she opened a leather-bound folder with an assortment of washable tattoos.

After scanning the tattoos, Bree met Sex's gaze. "The butterfly with the blue wings." Wings so blue they matched his eyes.

His approval spread in a slow smile. He had possibly the finest mouth ever to form words. "Place it where I can't see it when you're dressed."

On the side facing away from Sex, she peeled back her towel, exposing the curve of her hip, the concave dip of her abdomen. She tapped her finger near her navel. "Right here, please."

She heard his groan, caught his nostrils flare, as he pushed up on one elbow and watched Filomena apply the butterfly. He patted his chest with the flat of his hand. "Be still my heart."

"Enjoy the remainder of your day." Filomena bowed, departing behind Emile.

Alone beneath the cabana, Sex whispered near her ear, "How do you feel?"

She cast a glance his way. "Like melted butter."

He tugged on his towel, which refused to lie flat. "I was about to take a nap before your tattoo."

Clutching her towel to her breast, she sat up, to see the butterfly more clearly. She swayed, suddenly light-headed.

Sex jackknifed, caught her by the shoulder. "Easy, Bree. Move slowly. Allow your blood to circulate."

She looked down at his hand, long-fingered and strong, around her shoulder. She flinched, waiting for the sexual jolt that would leave her hot and tense. Utterly stimulated.

Time slowed as seconds became a minute. She felt nothing but his concern, along with the warmth of his oil-slicked palm. His fingers flexed, but he didn't release her.

His brows spiked in amazement. "You haven't come out of your skin."

"No . . . no, I haven't."

Taking a chance, he touched her beaded braids, then ran one finger over her jaw, across her lips, tapped the tip of her nose. "You're not running for your life."

"It has to be the oils," Bree quickly concluded. "The Shea Butter and Honey Polish penetrated my skin, making a buffer against my sensitivity to your touch."

"Promise me you'll never shower."

"A promise you wouldn't want kept after two days in the Caribbean sun."

117

"We could always reapply the oils." he offered.

Bree shook her head. "I wasn't hired to play with hot oils. Daisy Alton is my primary concern."

"Our concern when we return to the ship."

She licked her lips. "It's getting late—"

"Not that late." His gaze flicked to her mouth, blue fire and desire, and her heart quickened.

His kiss was imminent. Unstoppable, yet welcome. Her resistance was as weak as her body from the massage. Her throat went so dry, she couldn't draw a decent breath as he slanted his head to cover her mouth.

The man ought to have a warning label. He had to be the best kisser on the planet. Meltingly slow, he made love to her mouth as if he knew exactly what she needed, and how badly she needed it.

She yielded, receptive and willing, when he bit her bottom lip, then nipped each corner of her mouth.

Give and take. She slid her tongue over his.

Needing and receiving. He sucked her tongue deep into his mouth.

Rhythmic and heady. His mouth mated wickedly with hers.

No other women preceded her this time. She sensed only his need and the heated rush of her own blood.

Exchanging no more than breath, he smiled against her mouth. "You taste like honey."

He tasted of citrus and hungry heat.

A second, deeper kiss. Sensations twisted and spiraled, detonating a need so deep he touched her soul. Desire tugged them close. Naked desire if her towel slipped any farther down her breasts.

She blinked. It was too soon. Too fast. Yet it was Sex

who broke the kiss. He appeared dazed, his expression suddenly closed. Her gaze drifted to his towel, which lay flat against his hips. No bulge, not a hint of an erection.

Confusion sifted through her. Her shoulders rose and fell with each tight breath. "You don't want me?"

For the longest time, Sexton St. Croix just looked at her. Deeply. Intently. He felt frozen in time, out of body and gripped by emotion, much as Bree must feel during one of her visions.

He couldn't take his eyes off the blush that covered her stark cheekbones, the fragile curve of her chin. Her mouth was red and erotically swollen from his kisses. Her hazel eyes were dilated, her eyelids heavy.

Their first kiss had left him so hard he hurt. His heart had raced at just the thought of touching her. Desire had grabbed him, a sharpening hunger. He'd been eager for her, had craved more contact.

Then something inside him stirred, shifted. Something beyond hot tongues, her pebbled nipples, and his rigid shaft. Something hard and fast, and as jolting as any orgasm.

Her body next to his had felt right. *Too right.* Family, home, and hearth right. His lust had been deflected, replaced by an unrecognizable sensitivity that surpassed his passion.

He liked Bree Emery. His feelings scared him.

Scared him so badly, performance anxiety left him one limp noodle.

Judging by the way she looked at him now, all wide-eyed and flustered, she believed he'd blown her off. Dipping his head, he shot her a self-deprecating smile. "The massage relaxed *every* muscle."

"I'm pretty played out myself."

A breeze picked up as the sun reached the horizon, casting orange and pink along the shoreline.

Straightening, he swung his long legs over the edge of the massage bed and slid off. After knotting his towel at his hip, he helped Bree into her robe. He avoided touching the sweet curve of her shoulder, her soft upper arms. "It's time to leave."

They walked side by side back to the suite. He kept his distance, not wanting her to sense the change in him.

As he stepped into their suite, the coziness and Kama Sutra depictions closed in around him. The bed would remain made, the countless positions untried. He couldn't wait to leave.

"Dress, and we'll depart," he said. "We have dinner reservations at the Pink Conch in an hour."

Legs wobbly, Bree moved unsteadily down the hallway. Watching her, Sex doubted she had the balance to ride the scooter back to Jacaranda House. He made a quick call to Jackson, declaring his whereabouts and the approximate time he'd be returning to the *Majestic*. A second call to the front desk, and new transportation was provided: a Suzuki Crotch Rocket.

The downward slant of the motor bike's seat brought Bree flush against his back. She hugged his waist as he revved the engine. He prayed the massage oils continued to buffer her ability to read him.

Zero to sixty wasn't fast enough to rid him of her touch.

Seven

"Touch me, Jax." Propped against the lacy headboard of her queen-size bed and half-hidden by big, fluffy pillows, Cecelia St. Croix crooked a finger, inviting him closer.

Jackson Kyle planted both feet by her bedroom door, stood firm with the crystal ball clutched in one hand. "My hands were all over you last night and you still want more?"

Her smile seduced him. "A lifetime of more."

His gut tightened. "One night does not make a lifetime," he reminded her, his voice firm. "We're too damn different."

"Different is good. We bring variety to the bedroom."

Variety had spiced their night. He'd taken her with his hands, his mouth, his sex. They'd rolled from the head to the foot of the bed, then gotten rug burn from the carpet. His knees remained as red and raspberried as her back and bottom.

He wouldn't be wearing shorts anytime soon. Neither would Celia don a cocktail dress cut low on her spine. The soothing lotion he'd applied led to a lot of slipping and sliding, and the sheets were soon slick from aloe vera.

He couldn't get enough of this woman.

He tapped the face on his watch. "You've slept the day away."

"All because of you," she reminded him. "You kept me up all night."

And into the dawn. Her bedside clock had read five A.M. when he'd slipped from beneath the covers and into his clothes and departed for his own cabin.

"I woke up and you were gone," she lightly accused.

"I woke up for work. I've duties on the *Majestic.*"

"I'd rather you saw to my needs than to Sex's."

"Sex is my boss," he reminded her.

"He treats you like a brother."

But never a brother-in-law. Jax knew he should resist her. Guilt from going behind his best friend's back branded like a hot poker. Sexton had trusted him to protect Celia. Jackson's protection had come in practicing safe sex. His box of condoms was now nearly depleted.

His time with Celia was short and excruciatingly painful. They had a history, but not a destiny. As he looked at her now, his blood warmed and his entire body hummed. His fingers moved against one palm as if his hand itched. He scratched his ankle with the heel of his black boot.

He was two hundred and fifty pounds of pulsing muscle. With no relief in sight. He shifted, and the light from the portal glanced off the quartz, casting reflections across the carpet.

"What's in your hand?" she asked.

"Confiscated crystal ball. The fortune teller tried to

pull a fast one," he told her. "Bree Emery saw right through her."

"Bree's an amazing lady." Celia snuggled deeper into the satin bedding. Her golden hair curled wildly about her face and pillow; her lush mouth was full and pouty.

Jackson knew how quickly pouty could turn passionate. He'd kissed her so hard and hungrily, he'd been afraid he'd bruised her lips. There was nothing gentle in his taking of this woman. After years of keeping his distance, after years of playing the gentleman, his inner animal had mated with a fierceness that scared even him. Yet Celia's need was equally strong. She came to him, her eyes bright, her body burning. She blurred his rough edges. Tamed his beast. Fulfilled his every fantasy.

He thanked God for their night together.

"Sex gave Bree the tour of Nassau," Jax relayed. "He phoned from Caribe Bleu. They'll be returning to the ship after dinner at the Pink Conch."

She arched a delicate brow. "My brother took Bree to his sacred spa? Then on to Samana Rolle's?"

"Couples' massage, then the best conch dinner on the island."

She pushed herself up on one elbow, her expression thoughtful. "He's sharing his life with Bree. A first for my brother. Sex's interest in the psychic leaves me in your *very* capable hands."

Too much temptation. White-hot and consuming. Delivering him deeper into this relationship than he could handle. "I'm a busy man," he reminded her. "You don't need a baby-sitter on board."

"I want you, Jax."

"How often do you get what you want?"

"Not nearly enough where you're concerned." She sounded wistful. "But a girl's got to try."

She never had to try very hard. He wanted nothing more than to strip and slip beneath her satin sheets. To feel her lithe body slide against, then over his own. She liked being on top. He loved watching her expression tighten in passion, her breasts bounce, her thigh muscles flex. The way his big hands cupped her buttocks, then lifted and settled her over his shaft, drove him to madness.

He snatched his last shred of resistance. "Get dressed and I'll escort you to the dining room."

She frowned. "I won't be dumped at the captain's table."

She'd read his mind. "Where did you want to dine?"

"Anywhere with you."

He'd planned to grab a drink at the Zoo, then eat when hunger growled. Taking Cecelia St. Croix to the wildest, noisiest bar on West Bay Street was out of the question.

The nightclub entrance greeted guests with the sounds of animals and made no apology for having the most bars in a single location. Over the years, he and Sex had beat their chests with the gorillas and roared with the lions. They'd raised hell with the island rowdies. Not tonight, however. Tonight he went tame.

"How about the Green Turtle?" he suggested. The café was close to the docks, noted for its seafood and smooth island cocktails.

"Too touristy." Celia shot down his idea. "How about Bahama Heat?"

A couples-only club. The astronomical cover charge discouraged most patrons. Guests paid well for the dark and intimate atmosphere that encouraged surrender. The evening would prove pure torture.

The stubborn tilt of her chin forced his hand. He gave in. "We'll go for one drink."

"Three drinks, dinner, and four dances."

"Two drinks, dinner, and one dance," he countered.

"Two dances," she insisted.

"I don't fast dance."

"All the better. I prefer slow."

Touching her in public would bring him to his knees. He blew out a breath. "Agreed."

Flashing him a smile, she tossed back the covers, stretched. A languid stretch, all flushed skin and bed-tumbled woman. Her mauve satin gown molded to her breasts, outlining her nipples, tucking against the flatness of her belly. She rose gracefully, enticing him with each sensuous step to her dresser.

He forced himself to remain by the door as she selected a bra, thong, and matching garter belt, all in gray mist and threaded with silver. La Perla. Filmy and ultra-feminine. He'd shopped with her so often, he knew her preferences.

He was also aware of the designers who dressed her in linen and cashmere, along with the price tags on every dress and pant suit in her closet.

Cecelia St. Croix didn't do sales or blue-light specials. She never followed fashion trends. Casual elegance was her style. She turned her clothing into a walking art form. Designers fought over her for charity fashion shows. She had the body of a model and the air of knowing she belonged. She lived the fairy-tale life of Grace Kelly. Bore the sophistication of a young Jackie O.

She ripped the breath from his lungs, the air hissing through his teeth, when she slipped the thin straps on her nightgown over her shoulders and the satin shimmied down her body, exposing petal-soft skin.

In profile, her breasts jutted, high and firm, while her mauve nipples tightened from the brush of the gown. They didn't, however, pucker as tightly as when grazed by the pads of his thumbs. The revelation stroked his ego.

His mind ordered him to leave, to wait in the living room until she'd fully dressed. His feet, however, refused to take that first step. Fighting temptation, he clenched his jaw. He was caught between the door and his hard-on.

He hungered for her. Had been hungering for her ever since the cocktail party last evening. Which proved damn embarrassing when his concentration failed behind the bar and he'd handed Zara Sage a Miller Lite instead of an Apple Martini. The psychic had cast him a withering look.

His gaze now hooded, he watched Celia slip on her thong, then hook her garter belt. Bending slightly, she slowly unrolled, then smoothed her nylons from toe to thigh, then fastened them to her garter.

Being a leg man, Jackson almost whistled. He loved garters. He'd always enjoyed the erotic slide of the clasp when he separated garter from nylon and stroked soft skin. Celia had the softest skin in memory.

In a show of modesty, she gave him her back as she hooked her strapless bra, then adjusted the creamy swells beneath the filmy strip of lace. That's when he noticed the bruise high on her left buttock. His love bite. In the heat of the night, he'd kissed her all over, nipping and sucking along her spine, her hip, and finally her bottom. A baby-soft bottom with the toned firmness of a woman pushed by her personal trainer.

"Hmm, what to wear?" Celia walked toward her closet. She shifted through two racks before selecting a soft gray halter dress by Escada. "You like?" she asked Jackson.

"A T-shirt and jeans work best for me."

"I don't own a pair of jeans."

She preferred to play dress-up. Always stylish, never a hair out of place. He liked her best with her hair wild, her expression wanton, her body loose and giving in sex.

She slipped the dress over her head, and it slid down her body with the same tremor Jackson's hands had stirred on her skin during the night. Black Jimmy Choo stiletto sandals added to her height, bringing her gaze level with his mouth.

Licking her own lips, she returned to the dresser and selected her jewelry. Diamonds soon studded each ear, and a choker with a seven-carat solitaire flashed at the pulse point of her throat. She slipped a ruby ring the size of a radish onto her forefinger.

"Fasten my ankle bracelet?" She dangled a delicate gold chain from her fingertips. Then inching up her dress, she lifted one Jimmy Choo onto the vanity stool.

Jackson's gut grew as tight as his breathing. Pushing himself away from the door, he approached her. Her fingers brushed his wrist as she dropped the ankle bracelet onto his palm. Gold against calluses. The heiress and the hired help. The fact stared him in the face a dozen times a day.

Yet, at that very moment, he faced garters and stockings, and stilettos. His eyes focused on her painted toenails, her trim ankle, the curve of her calf. His gaze skimmed higher, over her knee, following the hem of her dress as the material pulled to mid-thigh. He knew her skin burned, begging for his fingers to explore her firm and shadowed flesh.

With what little coherent thought remained, he tossed the crystal ball on her bed and quickly wrapped her ankle in gold links. Patting her calf, he drew back before he ventured into the shadows.

Nodding toward the door, he asked, "Ready?"

"As soon as I fix my hair."

She took her sweet time combing and securing the strands with ruby clips. He studied her reflection in the mirror. "What, no tiara?"

She stuck out her tongue at him. "We're going clubbing, not to a ball."

Jackson wanted her tongue in his mouth. Moist and hot, and tangling with his own. Her sweet taste lingering long after their kisses came to an end.

"How do I look?" She patted her hair one last time.

Too beautiful for words. "Take—" *Out those hair clips*, he wanted to say, and let your hair fall free.

He cleared his throat, tried again. "Take—" *Off that dress*. He liked her best naked, all flushed and wet and ready for him.

He sounded like an idiot. "Take—" *Yourself back to bed. Let me make love to you until we're both spent*.

Damn, he couldn't form a sentence that didn't end with her naked and passionate.

He forced himself to focus on the round portal above her head. "Take a last look in the mirror before—" *Before I change my mind about taking you to dinner*. He doubted he'd survive the meal.

Cecelia St. Croix caught Jax grinding his back teeth, watched as tension-drawn lines cut deeply at the corners of his eyes and mouth. Dread settled heavily in her stomach. She recognized his expression immediately. Countless times she'd witnessed his struggle, his ethical debate between his loyalty to Sex and his attraction to her.

Jax's resistance to her was strong. She'd raided her female arsenal to hold his interest. Moments earlier, she'd stripped, strutted naked across the room, and he hadn't batted an eye. If not for the significant bulge beneath his black slacks, she'd have believed him stone.

She took one step toward him, then a second. "I look just fine. You, however, look pained."

He dipped his head, and a dark blush rose up his neck, flagging his tanned cheeks red.

Her sigh became a hiss of frustration. She knew that look. Hated that look. She held out her hands imploringly. "Don't you dare withdraw, Jackson Kyle," she ordered. "Don't go all noble on me."

He looked up then, and met her gaze squarely. "I know what's right for you, and it isn't me."

"We're going to dinner, Jax, not for a marriage license."

He didn't blink, didn't flex a muscle. She wanted to shake him silly. "Consider it a duty-date, if you must. Sex expects you to protect me. Feed me, then return me to the ship."

He rubbed the back of his neck, rationalized. "I am responsible for your safety."

Celia wondered who would keep Jax safe from her when she felt restlessly hot and unbelievably wild? When her need grew as great as his. When control was lost to touch.

As if getting down to business, Jax rolled up the sleeves of his starched white shirt, then held out his hand. "Stay close to me tonight."

She didn't need to be asked twice. Lacing her fingers with his, she followed him, breathing in his scent, admiring every inch of his broad shoulders and tight butt. He emanated power and male energy. She absorbed the aura of the man she loved.

Bahama Heat swung its doors wide to Celia St. Croix and Jackson Kyle. The doorman recognized Jax and, after welcoming him like family, led them to the best booth in the club.

Her stiletto heels clicked against the black, white, and red tiles as she crossed the dance floor to a black leather booth. Red-hot flames licked the walls, painted with flecks of orange and gold, depicting the rising heat that burned between couples.

Cast in more shadow than candlelight, the booth curved into one corner of the room, private and intimate. Deliciously intimate. Cecelia slid onto the leather, settled in at the middle of the booth.

Jackson moved in beside her, leaving enough room between them for a third person. She wanted him closer. She patted the seat, but he ignored her. She decided to inch closer. Two inches, and he cut her a sharp, stop-right-there look.

"You're near enough." His voice was as stiff as the set of his shoulders.

"Not nearly close enough," she whispered near his ear.

"We're in public," he reminded her.

Public meant no hand-holding, no heated looks, no signs of affection. She clutched the edge of the leather booth, curled her fingers into its posh softness. She'd wanted their night out to be hot and arousing. So much so that when they returned to the *Majestic,* Jax would release his inner beast on her in bed. A beast so hungry and devouring, so satisfying and exciting, that she grew wet imagining his hands and mouth on her. All over her.

"Wipe those thoughts from your mind." Jackson's expression was as dangerous as her need for him.

"What thoughts?" she asked, looking innocent.

He visibly fought for control. "Thoughts that make your eyes dilate and your lips part."

She flicked the tip of her tongue over her upper lip. "Thoughts of undress and indecency."

"*Damn* . . ." His nostrils flared, and the muscles in his neck pulled taut. The air surrounding him vibrated with a sensual force that skittered over her skin as powerfully as any touch.

Celia knew the images they shared. From the flicks of her tongue on his flesh to feeling him long and thick and eager for her.

Before she could tantalize him further, a tall, thin man in a black tuxedo approached their table, infusing reality into a memory of naked bodies and erotic pleasure.

"My name is Vincent," he greeted in a baritone as deep as a bass drum. "This evening, our specialty drinks include Bahama Mama, Goombay Smash, and, in honor of the *Majestic,* a St. Croix Cocktail, a mixture of banana rum, strawberry puree, and pineapple juice."

"The lady will have a Casablanca, and I'll have Cougar Black on the rocks," Jax ordered for them both.

Celia smiled to herself. Jackson remembered her favorite drink. She softly hummed "As Time Goes By."

"Bogart and Bergman?" he asked.

"*Casablanca* is one of my favorite movies." She loved stories of self-sacrifice and bittersweet romance but didn't wish to live one.

" 'Here's looking at you, kid,' " Jackson toasted her when Vincent delivered their drinks.

"Dinner, Mr. Kyle?" Vincent inquired.

Again Jax took charge and placed their order. "Scrambled eggs and an English muffin for Ms. St. Croix, and I'll have the mahi-mahi and steamed vegetables."

Vincent shifted uneasily. "Breakfast for dinner, sir?"

Jackson shoved his hand into his pants' pocket, slipped a Benjamin Franklin from his money clip, then held the bill beyond Vincent's reach. "Scrambled well, no butter on the muffin. Blackberry jam."

Vincent plucked the hundred from Jackson's fingers. "I will lay the eggs myself, if necessary, sir." He departed with a determined gleam in his eyes, soon to batter the chef into preparing breakfast for the lady.

"You know me well," Celia said softly.

"I've known you a long time. We're thrown together often." His mouth curved in a tight smile. "I know your favorite charity is the Humane Society, yet you're allergic to most animals. You call Dahl Glouster, your personal trainer, Ball Buster behind his back. You love to run the show and hate to be controlled. Even by me. People find you sweet and delicate, but beneath the sugar, you're one strong, savvy lady."

A compliment from the big man of few words? "You find me savvy?"

"You hard of hearing?"

Jax hated to repeat himself. "Want to know how I see you?" She leaned toward him until their shoulders bumped.

He pulled his arm away, shrugged.

"You act tough. Invite the unexpected. Promise excitement." She ran her nails along his forearm. "Beneath the surface, you're infinitely tender and totally sensual. Despite your resistance, you desperately need me."

His jaw worked. "I'm never desperate, Celia."

"You're a loner, Jax." She'd watched him come and go throughout her life, a man unto himself. "Don't you get tired of going home to an empty house?"

"I have a pet rock."

"Pets resemble their owners."

He slanted her a look but didn't reply.

"Your dinner, Mr. Kyle," Vincent said triumphantly as he returned with a tray of covered dishes. After laying out their meal, he stood off to the side, inconspicuous yet available at the snap of a finger.

Celia ate slowly, all the while listening to the island band. The music was uninhibited and wild. On the dance floor, couples moved in a mating rhythm. Tongues and limbs tangled as men and women brushed, pressed, and ground their bodies together. Red floodlights illuminated the tiles, casting the dancers in a fiery glow. As the overhead lights dimmed further, the shadows on the wall writhed and swayed with tangible intimacy.

Celia shifted as if sitting on a hot rock. Beside her, Jackson remained unaffected, eating his meal as if seated alone in a quiet café.

When the band took a break, she drew in a breath, then slowly released the tension that wound her as tight as a corkscrew.

"I've been thinking, Jax," she said between bites, "I owe Daisy Alton a great deal. I wish to repay her."

"Owe? Repay?" His fork remained suspended over his plate.

She spread blackberry jam on her English muffin.

"The flapper brought Sex and Bree together. We had last night and dinner this evening because I'm under your protection."

He looked at her now, his eyes slits of suspicion. "Where are you going with this, Celia?"

"I'm going to throw a party in Daisy's honor."

Jax downed the remainder of his Cougar Black, shot two fingers toward Vincent, requesting a double shot of the whiskey. "Not one of your better ideas."

"Party pooper."

"I enjoy a good time as much as the next guy." He took a long, burning sip of whiskey when Vincent returned with his drink. "Sex, however, would never approve such a bash. Your brother hates the ghost."

"He doesn't know Daisy."

"And *you* do?"

She scrunched up her nose. "A Roaring Twenties costume party would please Daisy as well as the psychics on board."

"Don't go playing with the paranormal," he warned. "It's dangerous."

"Bree Emery will assist me."

Jax shook his head. "Sex doesn't do costume parties."

"Sex will dress up if you dress up," she insisted. "Help me convince him—"

"No."

"Is that your final answer?"

"As final as it gets."

"Then dance with me."

The band had started the next set with a slow song, and Jax had promised her a dance. His expression tight, he slid out of the booth. When she followed, stood before him, he took her hand and pulled her into his arms.

To her surprise, he encircled her waist, locked his hands at the base of her spine. She wound her arms about his neck. Her stilettos gave her height. Her cheek grazed his chin as she snuggled close. Beyond the crush of the crowd, she swayed against him.

Jackson remained composed and detached as he fulfilled his duty-dance. Knowing the song was soon to end, she grafted herself to his body. Like two sticks rubbed together, they suddenly burned. Ignited, his sex now nudged her belly, thick, hard, and enormous.

He remained close when the music ended, his expression stark with untold emotions. "Satisfied?" he growled near her ear.

Satisfied beyond measure. She felt the wild beat of his heart, the rampant need that matched her own. Desire and indecision warred in the depths of his fierce brown gaze, soon changing to disgust at his momentary weakness.

A stirring at his groin sent shivers along every inch of her skin. A stirring that increased. *Vibrated.*

"My pager." Jackson released her.

Reaching into his pants' pocket, he read the text message. "Damn," he muttered. "A message from Captain Nash. Daisy Alton's strolling the promenade deck. She was last sighted on the bridge."

"Daisy's looking for Bree Emery." Celia knew it without question.

Jax punched in his own message. "I'd better notify Sex."

Half a minute, and a second message flashed. "Your brother's returning to the *Majestic*," he informed her. "I'm to meet him at reception."

So much for romance. She forced a smile. "We'd better head back. Thanks for dinner and the dance."

He shrugged, once again indifferent. "We needed to eat."

She stood aside as he paid the bill. Then walked next to him into the night, along a busy Bay Street, across the docks, and up the gangplank. The *Majestic* was alive with boisterous passengers, loaded with rum punch and souvenirs, and ready to sail for Puerto Rico.

Once aboard, rumors of Daisy Alton roaming the ship spread rapidly. Travelers locked themselves in their staterooms, and an uneasy silence settled on all decks. The silence of the dead.

Sex and Bree Emery arrived within five minutes of Jackson and Cecelia. Celia watched them approach. The sexual and the ethereal. To her practiced eye, Sex appeared dazed, as if he'd been punched in the gut and was still sucking air. Bree, on the other hand, looked relaxed. Incredibly so. Her hair was beautifully braided, her nose sunburned, her body loose as she greeted Celia, then turned to Jax.

"Where's my ghost?" Bree asked.

Jax studied his pager. "According to the captain, Daisy's headed belowdeck. Back to her cabin."

Bree turned to Sex. "I need to find her."

"I'll join you," Sex said, then instructed Jackson, "Stay with my sister. Keep her safe."

Celia saw Jax swallow, saw his hands fist. Reluctance darkened his brown eyes. "Will do," the big man agreed.

"Be careful," Celia called to Sex and Bree as they took off down the staircase. Then biting down on her bottom lip, she looked up at Jax, all innocence and sweetness. "Back on duty?"

His face was as stony as his pet rock. "Only until you fall asleep."

"I'm not the least bit tired."

He took her by the elbow and escorted her along the corridor. "You will be after a glass of warm milk."

She made a face. "I hate milk."

"Too bad. Tonight you'll drink a gallon, if necessary."

Eight

Bree Emery pushed her body to hurry. After the massage, she wasn't certain her legs would respond to any sense of urgency, yet finding Daisy Alton was utmost on her mind. The ghost had sent passengers scurrying for safety. Silent and deserted, the staircase and corridors stretched out before her. Not a living soul in sight.

"Where to?" Sex asked, his footsteps rapid behind her.

"I'm not sure." Bree stopped suddenly, turned, listened.

Sex nearly took her out. Avoiding a collision, he sidestepped, one broad shoulder hitting the wall with a resounding thud.

"Give me some space," she advised. "Don't ride my heels."

He held up his hands. "Beep. Beep. Backing up."

Drawn to her cabin, she hit deck seven, then slowed. Slowed to the point that she could barely lift her feet. Feet that now felt like cement blocks. Lightheaded, she braced her hands on either side of the wall for balance. Her shoulders sagged, as did her knees. She folded like an accordion.

Within seconds, she'd settled in a time when short-term decisions held lasting consequences.

May 28, 1925
Deck Seven

Randolph St. Croix strode with purpose, his steps delivering him to Cabin 7001. Daisy Alton's cabin. He knocked on the door, one rap, then two. Pressing his ear to the door, he listened for the slightest sound.

Where was Daisy? He'd scoured the ship in search of her, bending propriety to its breaking point by coming to her cabin. Tongues would wag if any of his acquaintances caught him at the flapper's door.

If truth be told, he was damn tired of the dictates of society that separated his life from someone as fresh and funny as Daisy. She made him feel alive. Two days had passed since he'd last seen her. Since they'd enjoyed breakfast at the Palm Court.

Beneath her boldness, he'd glimpsed her gentle spirit. Her shyness. Damn if he hadn't missed her smile, the giggle that escaped when happiness seized her soul. She haunted him. His own heart swelled when she looked at him with trust and, he was certain, admiration.

Her zest for life and curiosity as to how the other half lived made him long to dress her in the finest fashions, to satisfy her desire to dine in splendor, then to dance with her beneath the chandelier in the grand ballroom. Even for just one night.

The repercussions of such actions would change his life forever. His blood hummed with the anticipation of living outside the rules of his breeding. Above all else, he must confess his St. Croix heritage. He prayed Daisy would not hold the lie against him.

A creak, and to his surprise, the cabin door opened, just a crack. It was not enough space for Randolph to wedge a hand or a foot.

"Miss Alton?" he questioned, the slight catch in his voice surprising even him. "It's Randolph Ambrose. I wish to speak with you."

"Now, belowdeck, in my cabin?" Her question slid around the doorjamb.

"Open the door." He lowered his voice. "We can't talk this way."

She allowed him entrance. He found her cabin cramped, the scent of mothballs suffocating. Pipes and rivets protruded from the walls and ceiling. A porthole, the size of a fist and smudged by sea spray, cast the cabin in gun-metal gray. There were no frivolities, save for a small potted plant, yellow-leafed from lack of sun.

Embarrassment over his wealth, over the fact that her cubicle could fit in one corner of his stateroom, brought heat to his cheeks. He stood uncomfortably beneath Daisy Alton's stare.

"You've very little room," he stated the obvious.

"With the light out, and the sea hissing and booming within an inch of my ear, I feel like Jonah in the whale." She motioned with her hand. "Berth or fold-down seat?"

He chose to stand, as did she, her spine straight, her gaze unwavering. A spring green day dress hung on her, clean, but wrinkled. Her low beige pumps were in need of polish.

She tilted her head, and her hair swept her cheek,

blond and shiny, as if brushed a hundred strokes. Her face was painted, her lips a hedonistic red. "Slumming, Mr. Ambrose?"

Her question was followed by footsteps in the hall, and the sound of snickering. Randolph nudged the door closed, yet the voices were too sharp and too clear to ignore.

"Did you see that dirty brown dress on that woman," a female asked, her tone snobbish and superior. "And those shoes! Black, scuffed, and thick-soled."

"How about the ripped shirt on her husband?" a second voice pointed out.

"Rats in third class," a man joined in, his tone jeering, nasal, and high-pitched.

Randolph recognized the man's voice. Phillip Foster, heir to a newspaper fortune and a pompous ass.

Laughter filled the corridor, followed by Phillip's snort of disgust. "A game of tug-of-war out on the deck? Both men and women grunting and groaning and gritting their teeth like animals. How unsavory."

Daisy bit down on her bottom lip. "I played tug-of-war this morning." Her words were angry and low.

Randolph clenched his hands into fists. He knew the dictates of the sea. It was a gross breach of etiquette for upper-class passengers to visit the quarters of the lower class. Yet over the years, he had witnessed the violation of good taste as parties of arrogant aristocrats explored the lower decks, entertained by the tatters and boisterous pastimes of steerage.

As the threesome moved on, Randolph made a mental note to post a steward at both the bow and stern, near the companionways that led below, to prevent further humiliation of those in third class.

Meeting Daisy's gaze, he found her face flushed, her

shoulders set. "Most first-class passengers have more tact than those three. Their boredom leads them to belittle others."

" 'Sall right," she returned. "I'm no shrinking violet."

Randolph admired her starch. "I have a confession, Miss Alton," he began. "I've lied to protect my identity."

Her gaze swept him as if seeing him for the first time. She stiffened visibly. "Are you on the lam? An escaped convict? A notorious mob boss?"

Randolph shook his head. "Nothing illegal, I assure you."

"Then pray tell?"

"My name is Randolph Ambrose St. Croix," he confessed. "My family owns the *Majestic,* along with six other ocean liners."

Randolph St. Croix looked ill at ease, expecting her to cast a kitten. She liked him too much to make him squirm. "I'm still Daisy Alton," she replied simply. "I dance at gambling clubs often raided by the police."

He looked relieved. "It doesn't bother you—"

"That you've got serious scratch?" She scrunched up her nose, shrugged. "Everything's Jake. No icy mitt."

"I'm glad we cleared the air." His relief was tangible.

Silence reigned as he scratched his head, rubbed the back of his neck, slapped his palms against his thighs. Daisy had him so deep in thought.

After several minutes, he cleared his throat. "I have a proposal for you, Miss Alton. One I hope will bring you delight."

Proposal? Daisy's heart jerked, jammed against her ribs. The man was already engaged. That left only one offer. "I'm not looking for a sugar daddy."

"I never believed you a gold digger," he assured her. "My suggestion offers an evening abovedeck. Dinner

143

at the captain's table and dancing in the ballroom to the Scat Cats Band."

Daisy looked down at her faded shirtwaist, her worn-down pumps. She looked a fright. "Secondhand clothes aren't in fashion."

"I would dress you for the occasion," he went on to explain. "With an appropriate gown and jewels. Give you a new identity for the night."

She found it hard to swallow. "Are you ashamed of me?"

"Certainly not." He stood straighter. "I wish to offer a memorable night at sea." He laid out her new identity. "A whisper to the deck stewards, and word will spread that eccentric socialite Darlene Altman, heiress to lumber and paper mills, has grown bored in her stateroom and wishes diversion. On the arm of a selected escort, you will create a sensation."

He winked. "Wealthy socialites allow no boundaries to restrict their behavior. You can be restless, flirty, or giddy, as the mood strikes you. No one can trace your bloodlines from the ocean liner."

Such a grand proposal! Daisy's heart beat so rapidly she could barely breathe. For one night she could walk unchallenged as a popular girl. Could live her dreams. "You feeding me a line?"

His brown eyes twinkled. "I will send a trusted steward to escort you to my stepbrother's stateroom."

Uneasiness settled in her belly. "Stepbrother?"

"Ramsay chose not to make this voyage. He remained in New York. Once you settle in, a maid will help you dress. I'll then locate a proper escort."

As quickly as her excitement had popped, like a cork on a bottle of champagne, it now fizzled, flat and tasteless. "You'll attend with Eloise Hogue?"

He frowned ever so slightly. "It's expected of me, Miss Alton. The roll of the ocean has confined my fiancée to her stateroom. Bouillon and biscuits have finally settled her stomach. Tonight she ventures on deck."

Daisy took a deep breath. The chance to live her dreams lay ahead. She could be ritzy and refined. Yet the man she was stuck on was engaged. Bound to a woman who'd been born to the life Daisy would enjoy for only one night. One incredible night.

She licked her lips, asked. "Why are you doing this?"

"For purely selfish reasons," he explained. "You are bold, irrepressible, express yourself so freely. You intrigue me, Miss Alton."

He saw her as a novelty. A real live wire.

"Are you up to the challenge?" he pressed.

She forced a smile. "Pos-i-*lute*-ly! I'm obliged loads."

He saluted her with two fingers. "Until tonight."

Tonight Daisy would sit among the polished and pampered. The resplendent. White tie was de rigueur for gentlemen, designer gowns and jewels for their ladies. She would look down her nose at those who addressed her, dab her lips with a pristine linen napkin, and try not to slurp her soup.

"Damn it, Bree, open your eyes!"

The thump of a palm between her shoulder blades straightened her spine and her head snapped back. It took several seconds to open her eyes, focus, recognize her surroundings.

Bree realized that Sex was on his knees, his hair tousled, his blue eyes honed on her, his Nordic cheekbones slashed with color. He looked out of his mind with concern.

Cradled against his side, she relaxed, allowing her present to detach itself from Daisy Alton's past.

"I'm back," she said after several minutes had passed.

He curled his fingers over her upper arms, squeezed. "I waited like you asked me to, not wanting to disturb your vision. Yet when I called out your name, you didn't respond. You left me for twenty minutes."

"I didn't mean to worry you," she said softly.

"You made me crazy," he muttered.

"You're touching me." The strength of his hands flowed into her arms. The man had great hands. Wide palms and long fingers. Experienced hands that knew a woman's body. The oils from the spa continued to buffer her from his previous conquests. "I feel only you."

"How do I feel?"

"Nice." *Amazingly nice.* She shook off images of Sex as a lover and concentrated on Randolph St. Croix, a man who had gifted Daisy Alton with a night to remember.

Shifting slightly, Bree moved to sit cross-legged in the middle of the corridor. Sex followed suit. Bending his right leg, he rested his arm across his knee.

"I need to tell you about my vision," she said.

"Keep it straight, keep it honest."

He believed she'd alter the truth to put Daisy in a more positive light. "Randolph St. Croix went to Daisy Alton's cabin."

He looked at her as if she'd lost her mind. "Randolph went belowdeck?"

"He sought her out," Bree repeated. "After having breakfast together at the Palm Court, he found he missed her."

"Missed her like a death wish."

His sarcasm stabbed deeply. "Once inside her cabin, Randolph and Daisy overheard a group of first-class travelers belittle those in steerage. That bothered Randolph. Bothered him so much, he offered Daisy a night abovedeck."

His face went tight. "Such a night would break every rule of society. Randolph would never have jeopardized his standing with his peers."

"He broke those rules for Daisy."

His hard eyes swept her face. "I don't believe you."

"Believe what you will, but allow me to finish," she said. "You're paying for my psychic services."

"Give me my money's worth."

Bree sensed his hatred of the flapper. He saw Daisy as a murderer. No amount of persuasion would change this man's mind.

Nonetheless, she laid out the facts. "Randolph proposed to change Daisy's identity. She would play an eccentric socialite. He would move her to Ramsay's stateroom—"

"Never happened."

"—provide a maid, and dress her in a designer gown and jewels," she went on.

The coil of his tension tightened. "Eliza Doolittle of the Jazz Age?"

The similarities to *My Fair Lady* were strong. Yet Daisy had lived long before Rex Harrison and Audrey Hepburn graced the big screen. Daisy and Randolph would not have a happy ending.

"Randolph found Daisy intriguing," she added. "He'd never met anyone like her."

"His circle of friends didn't include murderers."

Needing to bring their conversation to an end, Bree scrambled to her feet. Looking down on Sex, she crossed her arms over her chest. "Daisy Alton did not kill Randolph St. Croix," she said with conviction. "She may have been rebellious and wild, but her heart was in the right place. She admired Randolph, was attracted to the man, not his money."

"So you say."

She was ready to call it a night. "Thank you for the tour of Nassau, the spa, and dinner," she said stiffly. "I had a nice day."

"So did I." He lifted one hand, let it drop back to his side. She sensed he wanted to kiss her, wanted to heal the breach Daisy had made between them. She would have responded. She hated going to bed mad.

Her heart ached when he turned away. " 'Night, Bree."

He left her standing in the corridor. Damn, what a day. He'd gone from stud to dud in one afternoon. Even the memory of the butterfly tattoo on the soft, pale skin of her belly caused him to stir but not stiffen. His soldier had no salute.

Frustration compressed in his chest. He hated arguing with Bree. He'd wanted to kiss the lies from her lips, force her to tell the truth. Her romantic notion that Randolph and Daisy were destined for each other made him crazy. Fresh air would clear his head.

Reaching the top stair of the companionway, he crossed paths with Mimi Rhaine. Her smile broke, her breath hot against his cheek.

"Sex!" Mimi's delight in seeing him nearly knocked him down the steps. Her wild red hair whipped in the late night breeze, her green eyes as bright as the full moon. He clutched the handrail as she leaned in toward him. "I was regressing, thinking about our past lives together, and—" she snapped her fingers "here you are."

"Lucky, lucky me," he managed before she grabbed his arm and pulled him toward her. Beneath a cream sweater, her nipples poked the front of his shirt, and the snap on her straight-legged jeans rubbed the button above his zipper.

"Do I have a story for you," she elaborated. "We once lived in Greece, during the time of Caesar and Cleopatra. Major toga party."

Sex preferred lying on sheets, not being wrapped in them.

Mimi grasped his arm, tugged him along, her jeans so tight she walked like Frankenstein's monster. "Stroll with me on deck. It's a night for lovers."

They were the only couple on the promenade. The majority of the passengers remained sheltered from the threat of Daisy Alton. The deck shifted beneath his feet as the *Majestic* left Nassau Harbour for the open sea. Mimi's fingers dug into his arm.

"How was lunch at the Purple Parrot?" he asked.

Mimi tossed her hair. "Ram ate two bowls of conch chowder and Harlan managed one, filled with oyster crackers. When we returned to the ship, Harlan requested a nap, and Ram joined me at the pool. I parked his wheelchair beneath a beach umbrella. He was well-protected from the sun. Although a tan would cover his liver spots."

She stopped short. "You need a sign by the pool. If nude sunbathing isn't allowed, rules should be posted."

Damn. A buck-naked Mimi, visible to God and every passenger aboard. Including his great-grandfather. Sex was certain she'd created quite a stir. His deck stewards would have scrambled to cover her with a towel. "A sign will be posted as quickly as the paint dries," he assured her.

"Do you think ghosts sunburn?" Mimi asked.

Strange question. "Doubtful. Why?"

"I felt Daisy on the sun deck, thought she might be catching some rays."

"*You* sensed the flapper?"

"As if we were joined at the hip."

Hard to believe. "Where's Daisy now?"

Mimi stared into space. "Daisy's in Bree Emery's cabin, asleep on the top bunk."

He shook his head. "No bunk beds in the cabin."

"Then Daisy's floating, like a ghost."

"Daisy *is* a ghost."

"Yes, yes, I see that now."

Sex shook his head. Mimi Rhaine was as psychic as a cuckoo clock.

Mimi glanced at her watch. "Time for bed. Care to join me as Zorro?"

Mimi and her role-playing. He didn't have the time or the energy to slap on a cape and mask and mark her stateroom with a *Z*. "I've business to attend to."

She released his arm and hummed. " 'Here comes Peter Cottontail.' "

A jack rabbit?

"Does the gift shop sell batteries?"

He nodded. "Back by the cameras."

"Hippity-hoppity." She winked, then minced steps toward the companionway.

Sex laughed out loud. Mimi would find her satisfaction without him. The woman had toys.

150

"What's so funny?" Jackson Kyle approached him near the bow.

"Mimi Rhaine," was all he had to say.

Jackson dragged a hand down his face. "Sex with that woman would lock you like a Chinese finger puzzle."

"She's into bunnies. The vibrating kind."

"Whatever gets you through the night."

The night would be lonely for Sex. Despite her deceit, Bree Emery remained foremost on his mind. He hated the fact that Daisy Alton stood between them. Leaning against the rail, he glanced over at his friend. "I assume my sister is tucked in for the night."

"Tucked in, but not sleeping," Jackson was slow to admit. "I made her drink three glasses of warm milk—"

Sex made a face. "She hates milk."

"And now hates me," Jackson said gruffly. "I'd hoped the milk would make her sleepy."

"It makes her nauseous," Sex told him. "I'm surprised Celia puts up with your strong-arm tactics."

The big man shrugged. "She listens to me. Sometimes."

"Listens to you more than most. Thanks for keeping an eye on her. No telling what Daisy will do next."

"Speaking of Daisy," Jackson said, "I'll warn you in advance: Your sister wants to throw a nineteen-twenties party in her honor."

"Honor Daisy?" Sex started. "No way in hell."

"Celia is going to enlist Bree Emery's assistance." Jackson had the nerve to smile after delivering that tidbit of news.

In that case, Sex was doomed. *"No party,"* he reiterated. "Daisy's out to ruin my life. I refuse to celebrate her existence."

Jackson crossed his arms over his chest. "Celia believes Daisy brought you and Bree together. She believes in—"

"Destiny." The same word Bree had used for Randolph and Daisy. Soul mates drawn together over time. No matter his fascination with Bree, partying with a ghost was out of the question. "You'll stand beside me, back me up—"

Jackson grimaced. "And have Celia make my life a living hell? You're on your own, man."

Sex drilled Jackson with a look. "Since when do you care how Celia reacts?"

"Since you've assigned me to guard her," Jackson replied. "She's not as even-tempered as you might think."

Sex couldn't help smiling. "Celia goes after what she wants. Always has. She accepts *no* as well as she does milk."

"The milk went down. *No* she won't swallow."

Sex felt the weight of the party settle on his shoulders. "So what should I do?"

"Simple, man. Dance with the ghost."

Nine

"Care to plan a party?"

Bree Emery glanced up from her crossword puzzle. Cecelia St. Croix stood in the doorway, her lips pursed, her eyes wide, a *Majestic* coffee mug held in each hand. She looked lovely in an ice blue ribbed tank and matching linen slacks. A jeweled Zodiac medallion hung from a gold chain around her neck. Bree patted the narrow bunk, welcomed the younger woman. "You're up early. Care to join me?"

Cecelia hesitated. "If Daisy Alton shouted *boo* and jumped out at me, I'd scream the ship down. I'm not good around ghosts."

"Yet you braved your way belowdeck."

"I knew I'd find you here."

"Daisy won't harm you," Bree assured Cecelia. "She's trapped in limbo. Until I solve the mystery behind the nineteen twenty-five murder-suicide, she's stuck on board."

Cecelia eased into the cabin, gracefully slid onto the bunk. "Chocolate caramel latte?" she offered.

Bree set her crossword puzzle aside and accepted the mug. "My morning favorite."

Cecelia took a sip of coffee, then lowered her voice. "Sex hates the flapper. He'd kill her if she wasn't already dead."

Bree understood. "Sex wanted Daisy off the ship yesterday. Unfortunately, he'll have to wait."

"He's not good at waiting," Cecelia continued on a whisper. "He's used to getting his own way."

"He can't charm the panties off a ghost."

Cecelia giggled. "You haven't fallen for him either. A first for Sex."

Bree slowly sipped her latte. "I'm not interested in a shipboard romance. Sex hired me to find Daisy Alton."

"You found her," Cecelia said, "and I want to throw a party in her honor."

Bree was taken back. "Sex would shoot down the idea in a heartbeat."

"Not if *you* approached him."

"I have no power over your brother."

Cecelia cut Bree a sideways glance. "I think you'd be surprised."

Bree wasn't as certain. After their argument last night, she and Sex weren't seeing eye to eye. "What kind of party?" she ventured.

Cecelia lit up, her excitement contagious. "The theme is a nineteen-twenty speakeasy, perfect for clandestine drinking, dangerous clothing, and scandalous dancing."

"My life before I met Randolph St. Croix." Daisy had joined them. Her voice was gentle, wistful, and clouded with memories.

"We would prefer a sophisticated nightclub. Perhaps Club St. Croix?" Bree suggested.

"Hotsy-totsy!" Daisy's spirits picked up.

Goose bumps skittered on Cecelia's arms. "*We?* Has Daisy put in an appearance?"

"Daisy's in the cabin."

Celia paled. "Then I'd better leave. Come with me to talk to my brother," she requested.

"Your brother is right here."

The scent of Armani reached Bree within a heartbeat of his words. She turned to find Sexton St. Croix leaning negligently against the doorjamb. His dark blond hair had been combed away from his face; the blades of his cheekbones and nose were sharp and aristocratic. A pale blue pullover complemented his eyes; his tailored navy slacks fit to perfection. The corners of his mouth twitched. "Think of me and I appear."

"Telepathy?" Cecelia asked.

"Reading thoughts puts me at an advantage." He stared directly at his sister. "I've tapped into a party. Care to elaborate?"

Celia's breath caught. "You—you couldn't know."

Bree smoothed her hand down her thighs, flattening the creases in her denim shorts. "Unless someone told him."

"Jackson!" Cecelia's face heated. "Wait until I get my hands on him."

"Word's out, no need to choke the man," Sex defended his friend. "While *no* is on the tip of my tongue, I'm into bribery and persuasion."

Daisy's party had been dumped in her lap. Bree wondered what it would take to draw a *yes* from Sexton St. Croix. By the hot look in his eyes, seduction would work well. She went with straight talk.

"We thought a nineteen-twenties' costume party might enhance the psychic cruise experience," Bree told him. "A party honoring Daisy Alton."

"No."

The man needed convincing. Bree cut to the chase. "What would it take for you to say *yes?*"

Sex motioned to Cecelia. "Privacy, please."

Cecelia rose from the bunk, looked down at Bree. *Good luck,* she silently mouthed before leaving Bree to twist her brother's arm. Or any other body part that might get his attention.

Once his sister was out of earshot, Sex pushed off the doorjamb, crossed to the bunk, eased down beside her. Their knees bumped, and he jerked back, breaking all contact. He appeared uneasy, hesitant, leaving as much space between them as was humanly possible. Strange behavior for a man who had kissed the soul from her body at the spa.

Looking at her now, he said, "I'm glad you kept your beaded braids. Very pretty."

"And my tattoo."

His gaze glanced at her belly, now covered by a poet's shirt. Knowing where to look, he caught the hint of blue wings visible beneath the sheer white cotton. "Very nice."

"You could be *nice* by allowing your sister this party," Bree hinted.

"How badly do *you* want this party?" he asked.

"How much do you hate the idea?"

"I despise Daisy Alton."

"I'm quite fond of her."

A muscle jerked in his jaw. "So you continuously say."

The quiet was intense, as tangible as the man seated beside her. "Would this party make you happy?"

"As happy as you'd be unhappy."

He scratched his jaw. "What's in it for me?"

"A chance to dance the Charleston."

"Not the entertainment I'm seeking." A further pause, followed by, "The *Majestic* will soon be docking at Calle Marina, south of Old San Juan. See the island with me."

"I'd wanted to remain in my cabin today."

"A total waste of time in port."

"Not a waste if I solve Randolph's murder."

"Daisy killed him. What more do you need to know?"

Bree rose from the bunk, dodged Sex's knees. She set her mug on the mirrored dresser, then faced him fully. "The truth will be told. Only then will Daisy be free of her past."

"Told through *your* visions?"

"As clearly as I can interpret them."

"Would you lie for her?"

She sucked in a breath. "I've lied twice in my life, each time to ease someone's pain and discomfort."

He looked angry. "So you would stretch the truth."

"The people were dying," she calmly defended. "My eighty-year-old neighbor asked if her estranged son still cared about her. They'd had a fight, and out of stubbornness neither had apologized. I told her he thought about her often. She died peacefully. The other was a family friend with terminal cancer. The man had five dogs, no wife, no children. He trusted me to have the animals euthanized. When the time came, I couldn't put them down. I kept them all. A pet sitter moved into my home while I'm on the cruise. The animals are well attended."

His jaw worked. "You have *five* dogs?"

"Two harlequin Great Danes, a black lab, a bulldog, and a beagle."

"Small to extra-large." Pause. "Date much?"

"Love me, love my dogs."

Sex shook his head. "No wine and roses for the lady. Bring a box of Milk Bones for her dogs."

"The way to my heart. Along with tug toys, tennis balls, and rawhide chewies."

He rubbed his hands together. "Can't promise canines, but spend the day with me and we'll see reptiles."

"Reptiles in exchange for the costume party."

"Damn," he muttered. "Win one, lose one." He pulled his cell phone from the pocket of his slacks, dialed. "Party's on." Pause. "Jackson will assist you." Longer pause during which he grimaced. "Purchase what you can locally, fly the rest of the items in." Ending the conversation, he said, "Cecelia thanks you, told me to give you a big hug."

Bree waited for the hug that never came. He'd grown antsy, looking everywhere but at her. The silence grew embarrassingly long. The man didn't want to touch her.

"Where do we find reptiles?" she finally asked.

"Hiking El Yunque," he informed her. "We're headed to the National Rainforest on the eastern side of the island."

Second to jogging, she loved to hike. High elevations, merged with the clouds, gave her a rush. She gnawed her bottom lip. "I didn't pack my hiking boots."

"We'll stop at a store and buy you a pair," he said. "We'll also need an umbrella and mosquito repellent. It rains every day. The temperature remains cool up there. Wear a long-sleeved shirt and jeans."

"*Soap the inside of your socks to avoid friction and blisters.*" Daisy whispered her two cents.

"I'll change clothes and meet you—"

"Come by my cabin," he instructed. "I have several

phone calls to make, a few loose ends to tie up, before we disembark."

Thirty minutes later, Bree arrived at the owner's suite. Once again, Sex stood before her in a state of undress. She couldn't help admiring his marvelous backside. Lean and sinewy in black boxers with a Jack-in-the-Box pictured on his buttocks. He turned slightly, and she caught *Pop Goes the Weasel* on his fly. She swallowed her smile.

Sex disengaged his cell phone. Glancing toward Bree, he caught her eyeing his fly. His body hummed. He wanted to crank and pop his weasel, yet his sex remained utterly lifeless. There would be no rise in his Levi's today.

Clasping his hands over his fly, he forced a smile. "I've called for a car. Twenty minutes max. I'll be ready shortly."

Entering his bedroom, he put on clothes similar to Bree's: long-sleeved cotton pullover and jeans. Thick socks and hiking boots. He kept his closet stocked for every island adventure. Grabbing a backpack, he stuffed it with an umbrella, bottled water, mosquito repellent, Band-Aids, and an instant camera.

Near the docks, driver Carlos Chavez stood beside a black Mercedes. "*Señor* St. Croix," he greeted in broken English. "You climb to *los nubes,* no?"

Climb to the clouds. Sex spoke enough Spanish to converse easily. He clasped the man's hand. "Mount Britton," he informed the driver.

Chavez had been a St. Croix employee for several years. He was enthusiastic, dedicated, and loyal, with the eyes of a hawk. "Carlos, meet Bree Emery," he said.

"*Muy bonita,*" Carlos murmured.

Bree smiled, then blushed as Chavez gave her the

hot Hispanic once-over. Sex understood the look. The psychic looked amazing in jeans. The worn fabric cupped her ass like a man's hands. The slim-cut style flattered her long legs.

Sex cleared his throat and Chavez dipped his head. "No disrespect, señor," he quickly apologized.

The driver was as appreciative as Sex of an attractive woman. Bree Emery hit Sex on all levels. He liked her mind, her spirit. Her body. If only his shaft would stand up and act like a man.

Once settled on the backseat, Sex hugged the passenger door. He was afraid any contact with Bree might transmit his growing interest in her, along with his inability to express that interest.

Slipping in behind the wheel, Chavez started the engine. The Mercedes responded with a deep purr. The driver kept the car in tip-top running order.

From the backseat, Sex instructed, "Stop at Almacen de Zapato. We need to purchase a pair of hiking boots."

An hour later, Bree had chosen a pair of Red Wings. She was safe to climb; there would be no slipping or sliding along the dirt path.

An additional stop at Delgado's Market, and Sex stuffed his backpack with empanadillas, turnovers stuffed with lobster, fried plantains, and banana cupcakes.

A thirty-minute drive brought them to El Portala, the entrance to the rainforest. Chavez held the car door open for Sex and Bree.

Once standing in the parking lot, Sex hooked the backpack over his shoulders, then instructed the driver, "Go back to the ship and pick up Harlan, Ram, and Mimi Rhaine. Take them for a leisurely drive through Old San Juan, then past El Morro Fortress. Harlan wants to take the ferry to the Bacardi Rum Distillery in Catano. No free samples," he stressed. "The men can't mix liquor with their medications."

"Cuando debo volver?" Carlos asked.

"Pick us up around three."

Chavez nodded. *"Esta bien."*

Sex turned to Bree. "Ready to take a hike?"

She smiled. "I'm game."

He selected a marked trail. "Three thousand seventy-five feet to the peak of Mount Britton."

Bree moved out ahead of him. "I'm ten feet closer to the top," she called over her shoulder.

He was more than happy to allow her the lead. Her backside would be his compass up the mountain. Several hiking trails soon split off the main trail, some paved, others dirt and gravel. The air grew cool, fresh and scented with inevitable rain.

Beneath an overcast sky, palm trees, giant ferns, orchids, and bromeliads flourished. The croak of the tiny tree frogs known as *coquis* serenaded their every step. High above in the branches, beady-eyed lizards and spiny iguanas tracked those who trespassed in their tropical forest.

Nearing La Mina Falls, Sex motioned Bree toward the surface boulders that bordered the pool beneath the cascading water. "There are petroglyphs on them," he noted. "They can be seen in shadow but appear invisible up close."

She ran her fingers over the rock carvings, felt the depressions. "A turtle," she said slowly.

He traced a second set of depressions. "Hourglass? Or a very curvy woman."

She followed suit. "Frosty the Snowman."

161

"According to Indian legend, the good spirit Yuquiyu reigned here on his mighty mountaintop throne, protecting Puerto Rico and its people," he informed her. "There's no mention of Yuquiyu packing snowballs."

Hefting the backpack off one shoulder, he dug for the camera. "Stand between the waterfall and the pool," he instructed. "I want to take your picture."

She made a face. "I'd rather take a picture of you."

A short, stocky man with carrot-red hair and kind eyes approached them. "I'll take a picture of you both," he offered.

Sex handed him the camera. "Much appreciated."

Together they moved toward the jutting rocks near the waterfall. Bree climbed onto the first boulder and Sex edged in beside her. Their bodies brushed, the contact tight.

To their left, water splashed off the rocks, sending a light, cooling spray into the air. "Say *sex*," the cameraman shouted, trying to be heard over the cascading falls.

Bree caught Sex's eye and laughed out loud. A chuckle broke from his throat at the exact moment the light from the camera flashed. "Nice-looking couple," the man said as he returned the camera. "Keep your camera handy. A hundred feet ahead, the Puerto Rican parrots are thick as thieves."

The parrots were a sight to behold. Dozens of them gathered in the palms, bright green with blue wing feathers. They eyed Bree and Sex with casual indifference, as if to say, you've seen one hiker, you've seen them all. Sex captured the haughty, superior tilt of their heads on film.

"Ready for an empanadilla?" he asked when they reached the picnic facility.

Bree nodded. "Sounds delicious."

Shaded by Jurassic-sized ferns, they'd finished their lobster turnovers, golden plantains, and started on their cupcakes before Sex noted, "There aren't many hikers today. It's unusually quiet."

"Quiet is good."

"You're a woman of silence." He admired her for not chatting just to hear herself talk. "You see beyond the human eye; you move among the dead."

"It's been that way all my life," she confessed. "Ghosts hold as much interest for me as most mortals."

He took a bite of his cupcake. "Skeptics?"

She reached for a bottle of water. "More than I can count. People fear what they don't understand, yet won't take the time to learn what exists—"

"Don't you mean *lurks?*"

"—beyond their sight," she finished.

He licked banana frosting from his fingers. "Ever been scared?"

She grew thoughtful. "Once, at age four, during my first sighting. My grandmother had passed away, and she came to me one night, hovered at the foot of my bed. We'd always been close. I got up, went to hug her, and caught only air. It knocked me for a loop. Yet though I couldn't touch her, I sensed her presence, felt her love, long after she'd died. That love is timeless."

Bree rested her elbows on the table, steepled her fingers. "It's the same love Randolph and Daisy still share."

Sex finished off his cupcake. "It's too nice a day to debate Daisy."

She lifted her gaze to the sky. "Actually, it's going to rain."

He looked also. The clouds had shifted, were now

163

dark gray and swollen with the promise of rain. "Even with an umbrella, we're going to get wet if we continue. Would you rather backtrack?"

"I'm still game for the climb if you are."

A woman who didn't scream and scurry for cover at the first drop of rain. He liked the fact that she didn't melt beneath a sun shower.

The sun shower soon proved a downpour. Mother Nature hit them with lightning and thunder and a strong wind. Another hundred feet, and the first drops hit. Big, fat drops that splattered and dampened both skin and clothing.

"There should be a shelter ahead," he informed her.

When he would have pressed on, Bree stopped on the trail and tilted her face to the sky. Her eyes closed, she parted her lips, catching raindrops on the tip of her tongue.

She looked beautiful. A rainforest nymph with her damp face and spiked eyelashes. The amethyst and crystal beads in her braided hair glistened from the moisture. He went for his camera instead of the umbrella. Took her picture. A picture to remember her by, should she, at the end of the cruise, depart the ship and his life.

The very thought left his chest tight.

Slowly opening her eyes, she smiled at him. "The mountain will soon be washed clean."

They would soon be washed off the mountain if the dirt trail got any more slippery. Jamming the camera in his backpack, he reached for her hand, urged her to follow. "Climb, Bree."

She kept up, jumping puddles, dodging tree branches, a woman of speed and stamina. The deluge had them both panting by the time they reached the shelter. His umbrella would have been no match for the whipping wind. As abruptly as the storm had started, it ceased. The dark clouds scooted out to sea, and the sun reappeared, filling the air with a humid haze.

"We weathered the storm." One look at Bree and he wished he'd included a change of clothes.

Rain plastered her shirt and jeans to her skin. She could have been naked. Yet it wasn't the outline of her body that enthralled him. It was the tilt of her head, the brightness in her eyes, the happiness in her smile.

The revelation hit him square between the eyes, so sharp and poignant and intense, it suddenly hurt to breathe. *Turning point* flashed in his mind. His days of chase, catch, and climax were over. Bree Emery was the first woman ever to engage his heart. He liked the way she made him feel. A whole hell of a lot.

His life would never be the same.

He was crazy for her.

Staring at her now, he stammered, "You're, uh, wet."

Bree shook out her braids, breathed in the clean-smelling air. "More like soaked."

Sensing his gaze on her, she looked up, took him in slowly, from his wind-blown hair and damp lashes to the jeans molded against his body. Prominent pecs and abs were chiseled beneath his cotton shirt; his male package was outlined beneath the soft, damp denim. Water ran from the hem of his jeans into his hiking boots. He had a squishy climb ahead.

"Warm rain. We'll dry in the sun," he assured her.

She tugged on her shirt, but the fabric stuck to her breasts; her bra was now visible, the pink hue of her pebbled nipples easily detected. Her butterfly tattoo was no more than a blue smudge near the bottom button of her shirt. "We should keep moving."

"I'm right behind you." He didn't, however, move. His gaze remained on her breasts, his desire as palpable as the fire in his eyes. A subtle, yet perceptible, longing swept her senses as he looked into her soul, touching her deeply, heating her from the inside out.

Lost in the moment, Bree found herself unable to take that first step. The step that would move her beyond a situation soon to get complicated.

The air around them now hummed, nearly vibrating with awareness. Color claimed his cheeks, embarrassment darkening the hue. He'd grown uneasy, visibly hesitant to touch her.

On a dirt path two thousand feet above sea level, Bree leaned in for one light kiss. He tasted of rain and banana cupcakes, and arousal. She wanted more.

Nuzzling his cheek, she nipped openmouthed kisses along his sturdy jaw. A kiss to the pulse point at the base of his throat drew a groan. His return kisses came slowly, each one given with great hesitation. As if he didn't want to start something he couldn't finish.

After endless long moments, he made his move. He made love to her mouth with a timeless sensuality that touched on forever.

When he slipped his tongue between her teeth, a spiraling sweet heat started deep inside her, thick and swelling, filling her completely. He was a man of heaven and heat.

Her need to touch him was strong. Skimming her palms over his chest, she clutched his shoulders, drawing him even closer. Her heart raced, her nipples hardened, her body craved his touch. Yet his hands remained at his sides. His sex was as soft as putty against her belly.

She pulled back, swallowed hard. "I'm sorry. I thought you wanted me."

He raked one hand through his hair. "It's, uh, not you, it's me."

Not you, it's me. Standard line for getting dumped. Her stomach sank.

He looked ill at ease. "I have a confession to make, Bree."

"So do I," she said. "But it can wait. I'm more interested in what you have to say."

He dug the toe of his boot into the dirt. "This isn't easy for me."

"Nothing worthwhile ever is."

"It's embarrassing as hell." He inhaled, exhaled. Appeared fortified. "In wanting to make sex perfect for you, I'm suffering performance anxiety. I couldn't get it up if my life depended on it."

She was stunned to silence.

Her silence made him wince. "It all started at the spa. I wanted magic. Multiple orgasms and stars in your eyes. Instead I fizzled like a burnt sparkler." He sighed heavily. "I've always believed one female was pretty much like the next. Not so anymore. Not after meeting you. I really like you, Bree."

The man wanted her beyond a quickie on the massage table. She took his hand. "The feeling is mutual."

Sex looked as relieved as she now felt. Glancing down at their joined hands, he said, "You're touching me and not going off like a blowtorch. Rain doesn't buffer the skin."

"That's what I wanted to tell you. I have feelings for

you. I find you exciting and charming and incredibly sexy. While I can still read others and connect with Daisy, I can no longer read you."

He looked as if he could kick himself for telling her about his problem.

"Don't regret your confession," Bree said. "I thought you were—"

"All chase and no capture."

"I had no idea you couldn't—"

"Pop my weasel." He shot her a self-deprecating smile. "Sex is who I am."

"It's time to reinvent yourself," she stated. "But keep the great boxers."

Cool mountain air blew down from the peak. Mosquitoes swarmed overhead. "We're going to need that repellent."

Sex snagged the bottle from his backpack and released a small amount onto Bree's palm. She rubbed it on her face, neck, and hands. He did the same.

"Time to climb." Her own socks squished in her boots as she moved out ahead of him. Thirty minutes later, her clothes no longer clung to her skin, they hung on her. Without a dryer, her shirt billowed, loose and wrinkled, her jeans were baggy, slipping off her hips. She was in need of a belt.

Sex looked much as he had before the rain. Whether wet or sun-dried, he pulled off rainforest casual with aplomb. The man had been soaked to the skin, yet his clothes showed not the tiniest crease.

He looked rugged, assured, spectacular.

While she appeared rung out on the clothesline.

Just ahead, through a clearing in the clouds, Bree glimpsed Mount Britton. A tower had been erected at the peak, resembling a giant misplaced rook out of a chess set.

Rounding the final bend, she found the stairs that led to the tower. On the wall outside the entrance, she noticed a small bronze plaque. She ran her fingers over the raised lettering. PRESERVATIONISTS OF EL YUNQUE.

The list of contributors was short. One name jumped out at her. "McIntyre Foundation," she murmured. Scholarships, a spa, and now saving the rainforest— Alex McIntyre's eclectic interests fascinated her.

"McIntyre has his fingers in a lot of pies," Sex said, but did not elaborate. He had his camera out, and as the clouds shifted, snapped pictures of the island below, all lush and green and edged by turquoise water.

She heard the click of the camera and found he'd turned toward her, getting several shots off before she covered her face with her hands. "No more pictures."

"They're for your photo album."

She'd never had a photo album. All her memories were stored in her heart. "Let me take one of you," she insisted.

He handed her the camera. "Just one."

Illuminated by sun and sky, his hands now shoved in his pockets, he stood casually, the hint of a smile on his lips. When she zoomed in on his face, his Nordic blue eyes held such a sensual heat, she almost forgot to snap the picture.

Her hand shaking, she returned the camera to him. Taking her hand in his, he squeezed it gently. Without conscious thought, her fingers laced with his. His smile was as understanding as it was knowing. Although a

169

1920's flapper stood between them, a bond had formed on the mountainside, invisible, yet tangible.

Together they climbed the tower stairs, caught the panoramic view from the parapet. Standing there, Sex finished shooting the roll of film.

"I like scenic views," he told her as they made their descent. "Lush, unspoiled beauty."

"You could have been a photographer."

He slowed his steps. "Thought about it once. Took several classes, worked in a camera store one summer out of high school." He shrugged his shoulders. "Life steered me on another path."

A path of wealth, women, and cruise ships. "Hobbies are good."

"That's why I took up sex."

She rolled her eyes. "And perfected it."

"You be the judge of that . . . someday."

Someday. Three days remained of the psychic cruise. She couldn't predict the future beyond that point. She did, however, plan to enjoy Sexton St. Croix in between her contacts with Daisy Alton. The murder must be solved, the flapper set free.

Silence became their companion during the descent. At the base of El Yunque, Carlos Chavez awaited their return, along with Harlan, Ram, and Mimi Rhaine.

Chavez met Sex with an apologetic grimace. "Aiy-yi-yi, Señorita Mimi, she delay us. Sample *mucho* Bacardi. We miss the ferry from Catano—" he held up two fingers—"*dos veces.*"

"Harlan and Ram?" Sex was quick to ask.

"*Los hombres viejos estan bien,*" he assured Sex. Then, eyes wide, he whispered, "Mimi, she wish me to be a Spanish Conquistador and she an island maiden sacrifice." He held up his hands. "*No comprendo.*"

Bree saw Sex's lips twitch before he assured their driver, "Nothing you have to worry about, Carlos. I'll deal with her."

"Deal with me, *how?*" Mimi had slipped from the car, taken two steps, tottered dangerously. Unable to maneuver a straight line, she called to Harlan, "I need your walker."

Sex crossed his arms over his chest, shook his head. "Mimi, Mimi, good day at the distillery?"

Giggles escaped. "I've a fondness for rum."

"So I now see."

Harlan rolled down his window, grunted. "She's buzzed."

"At least she's a happy drunk," Ram added. "Sat on my lap through the last half of the tour. Chavez pushed my chair."

"Sat on your lap?" Sex's jaw dropped. "In the wheelchair?"

Mimi rubbed her bottom. "Rammy-bammy has bony knees."

Ram nodded. "My thighs fell asleep."

"So did my left foot." Mimi rolled her ankle in a circle. "It's still tingly."

"Tingle yourself into the backseat," Sex said. "We need to return to the *Majestic.*"

Mimi reached out, stroked his cheek. "Care to fool around in the back?"

"Backseat's full," Harlan told her flatly.

"Frontseat works." Mimi moved for the passenger door.

"Dios mio." Chavez jumped between Mimi and the car.

"Well *hello*, my sexy conquistador," Mimi purred. "Care to conquer me now?"

"Ayudeme," Chavez pleaded.

171

Bree came to his rescue. Stepping forward, she smiled at Mimi. "Cecelia St. Croix has planned a nineteen-twenties' party for this evening. We should get back to the ship."

"Party? I'm there." Tilting sideways, Mimi fell onto the backseat next to Harlan. "Hi Harley."

Harlan wrinkled his nose. "I'm not a motorcycle, booze breath."

"Woman can't hold her liquor," Ram agreed.

"How much did you have to drink?" Sex asked Mimi.

"I lost count," she returned on a yawn. "I sampled for everyone."

"She went after Chavez like a cat in heat," Ram chuckled.

Heat suffused Carlos's face. "I try tell her *no.*"

"When I want to hear *'yes, yes, yes'!"* Mimi's voice pitched like a rising orgasm.

Ram nudged Harlan. "Roll up her window." Harlan obeyed.

Sex shucked off his backpack and handed it to Chavez to shove in the trunk. Then he motioned to Bree. "We'll ride in front."

Once seated in the car, Sex tucked her tightly against his side. She fit perfectly under his arm. Bree chuckled when Mimi broke into "Ninety-nine Bottles of Rum on the Wall." Shortly thereafter, she turned to past life regressions.

Carlos Chavez nearly drove off the road when Mimi claimed he'd once been a Sioux chief, all bare chest and loincloth, and she'd been his white captive, her clothes ripped and disheveled, her flesh hot and burning for his big, bad hands.

172

Ten

"I could use a hand over here," Cecelia St. Croix called from a ladder.

Jackson Kyle crossed to her. "I've got two."

"Grab the end of those lights and tack them in the corner," she instructed. Jackson did as he was told.

Celia glanced his way. Muscles flexed beneath his black T-shirt as he stretched and tacked a strand of white and silver lights high overhead. Completing his task, he plugged them in, and the room flickered with the evanescence of fireflies.

She clapped her hands. "Lovely."

Jackson reached for her. "Let me help you off the ladder."

She turned slightly, shook her head. "I can make it down—"

"I don't want you falling." His long-fingered hands spanned her waist and lifted her against his chest. Held closely, she felt his heat, the kick of his heartbeat, before he released her.

Turning away from him, she surveyed the grand ballroom. "Club St. Croix is taking shape."

"You have an eye for decorating." Jax stood stiffly beside her.

She cut him a sideways glance. "A compliment from the *squealer?*"

He looked down his nose at her. "It's my job to keep your brother apprised of your antics. You're lucky he agreed to the party."

"Bree Emery persuaded him."

A hint of a smile touched the corners of his mouth before his expression hardened. "It's costing him a damn fortune."

"I want everything authentic."

He grunted. "Down to the telephones."

She loved the squat black telephones with the whirling dials, heavy receivers, and sprocketed cradles. Phones that were once marched about by white-jacketed captains and delivered to club guests for important conversations. "Centerpieces only. No one can accept calls." She tapped one finger against her chin. "If I'd had more time, I would have had them rewired for use." She bit down on her bottom lip. "Wish the champagne would arrive."

He blew out a breath. "Another trip to the airport?"

"Local delivery."

"What else needs to be done?"

Cecelia pointed to the tables. "I want them set up for two, four, and six people."

Jackson turned to the deck stewards already scurrying about. "I don't think they can work much faster." He glanced at his watch. "Five hours and counting."

Taking a breather, Celia stood off to the side. From her vantage point, she watched as Jax hauled tables from one end of the room to the other, stacked chairs, and directed the stewards. She loved the way his muscles filled out his black T-shirt and stretched the short sleeves rolled a notch over the bulge in his upper arm. The way his thighs flexed against the faded fabric of his jeans. The room hummed and buzzed as the stewards hustled to keep pace with him.

Jax was hers for the day, and possibly the night, if she played her cards right. Sex had ordered him to help set up for the party. But she knew from his curt replies and stony expression that her project grated on Jax's nerves.

As if sensing her gaze on him, Jackson stopped shoving tables together and looked over his shoulder. He straightened slowly. Their gazes locked, and neither could look away.

A muscle jerked in his jaw as he motioned toward the cloakroom. "A private moment?" She crossed to him.

Stepping inside, they stood jammed between hatboxes and metal hangers. Jax hit the light switch, then closed the door and slid the lock. A dim bulb shone overhead. He gazed down on her, his cheekbones cast in shadow.

"Find something to do," he ground out.

"Besides looking at you?"

"You have lists a mile long. Get to them."

"I'd rather get to you."

He raked his hand through his hair. "Are you insane?"

"I'm crazy for you, Jax."

His jaw worked. "Don't mess with me, Celia."

"Or you'll what? *Squeal* to Sex?"

His hands flexed, clenched, as if ready to choke her. She pushed him harder. "*Tattletale.*"

"Name calling?" His lip curled in disgust. "What are you, five?"

175

"*Blabbermouth.*"

"Don't take a tone."

"*Chatterbox.*"

He glared daggers. "You could piss off the dead."

"*Ratfink,*" she dared.

"Damn it, Celia, knock it off."

She stuck out her tongue.

Jax was on her before she could retract her tongue. His mouth came down on hers with the force of a very angry man.

Angry at her for acting like a child.

Angry at himself for allowing her to provoke him.

She could taste his temper. Ignited and hot. First on her lips, then on the tip of his tongue as he thrust into her mouth.

Magic and fever. The air came alive with arousal.

Pure male dominance pinned her against the wall. She welcomed his strength, his need. His wildness.

Jackson Kyle had lost control. His own frustration goaded him as much as Celia St. Croix. Fragmented thoughts filtered through his mind. Rational thoughts of loyalty and honor. Of trust. Thoughts soon lost to all-consuming desire. He had no judgment where Celia was concerned. For ten years he'd had the mindset of a Tibetan monk. Two days on the *Majestic* and his dick spoke for him.

She'd broken his resistance. Once again.

He was going to hell.

Skimming his hand beneath her tank top, he traced the arc of her ribs, stroked the warm underside of her breasts through her pale pink bra, no more concealing than a blush. His callused fingers worked the front clasp. Her breasts spilled onto his palms. They were shaped to be held. Creamy, soft, and aroused. Her nipples peaked, rosy and tight.

Impatient as he, Celia jerked his T-shirt from the waistband of his jeans. She slid her hands swiftly up his back, her touch so light, he almost didn't feel her. The raking of her nails straight down his spine caught his full attention. His body arched, his sex twitched, the muscles in his back now rigid. He growled low in his throat.

Their hands brushed, battled, as he went for the button on her slacks, and she reached for the snap on his jeans. He shoved her hand aside, had her zipper and slacks pulled down in a single heartbeat.

He pressed his open palm to her flat stomach, spread his fingers wide. She shivered against the stretch and contraction of his hand as he felt his way lower. Edging the elastic above her pubic bone, he traced the tiny pink satin triangle. She leaned into his hand. Moaned against his mouth. He caressed the satin until she grew wet. Then he pulled down her thong.

Her scent had him sucking in air. The sight of her Brazilian wax brought him to his knees. He rocked back on his haunches, openly admired the expanse of smooth flesh on either side of the narrow strip of tight, blond curls. Sexy, yet virginal. A man's wet dream.

"You like?"

His insides twisted. "Very much. When?"

"This morning at Nemo's. Massage and a wax."

His appreciation came in a nip to her inner thigh. His masculine stubble scraped her sensitive skin. His nostrils flared, breathing her in. *His woman.* All sweet and slick. The beast tightly coiled within him began to unwind. He gentled his touch.

Cecelia sensed the change in him. The wildness turned calm. Almost reverent. Her own breathing quickened as his big hands cupped her bottom and tilted up her hips. Her eyelids half lowered on a soft moan.

He nudged her legs apart with his thumbs.

She grasped his impossibly wide shoulders.

"Shatter for me, sweetheart." Flicking, licking, he penetrated her with his tongue.

Lost to his mouth, she tangled her fingers in his shirt. Desire pulsed, pleasure streaking along every nerve. She felt both flushed and chilled. Quivering against his rhythmic assault, she grew impatient for her release.

Jax, however, withheld her orgasm, his skill profound in exerting the right pressure, deepening her passion. Until she ached for him. To the point where she wanted to scream.

Within seconds, her muscles tensed and her spine stiffened. She'd hit her breaking point. She shattered. For him. A blinding sunburst flashed behind her lids, followed by spirals of heat and erotic spasms. She dug her nails into his shoulders to keep from melting onto the cloakroom floor.

He'd pleased her greatly.

Lightness played through her body. Peace settled in her soul. She would have folded had he not held her up. Eyes now wide open, her heartbeat still rapid, Celia urged him to his feet. Once standing, she gripped his hip, fingered his zipper. Felt his enormous erection.

His intake of breath was raw and sharp. Anticipatory.

She squeezed him through the faded denim. "Take me against the wall."

While she made fast work of his snap and zipper, he extracted a condom from the pocket of his jeans. The denim dropped, exposing his gray jockeys, then his sex.

He was primed, jutting and engorged. His jaw and neck muscles worked as she stroked him, cupped his testicles. Questing, squeezing, drawing him out, she made him sweat. She drew his body so tight, his muscles knotted. The kinks in his shoulders were visible.

"Good Lord!" He nuzzled her hair, the softness of her neck, the silken sweep of her shoulder.

Unrelentingly solid, he pressed her to the wall with his chest and hips as he fitted the condom. While one hand cushioned her back, the other soon cradled her bottom. He lifted her. Wet and aroused, she clutched his flanks with her thighs, then slid onto his shaft. She took him in deeply.

Need darkened his pupils.

She nearly went blind from sensation.

Her hands rested on his shoulders.

His were now splayed at the small of her back.

She moved on him, slow rolls of her hips, then rising, sinking, controlling their climax. Her face was flushed, her body captured by the pleasure.

She rode him to an all-consuming madness. Exquisite and ongoing. Intense and shared. Mindless, yet memorable.

Her orgasm was so intense, it rocked through his body.

He jolted so wildly, she felt his spasms clear to her toes.

Once their breathing slowed, he settled her back on her feet. Even sated, his sex was impressively large. She felt his gaze on her and looked up. He didn't look the least bit happy.

She lifted her chin. "You look like you've committed a sin."

He glared at her. "I'm not proud of what just happened."

"Don't detach when we're so close to connecting." She bent, stepped into her thong, eased it up her legs. "Chances are good it will happen again."

"Not if I can help it."

"You've said that before," she reminded him. "The fact is, we're good together."

Silence stretched as he snatched up his jockeys and pulled them on. Then he went for his jeans. Zipping, then snapping, he stood fully clothed. His gaze finally returned to hers. "What feels good at the moment is never long lasting." His voice was as hard as his expression. "In three days we return to Miami. What we've shared on the cruise remains on the *Majestic*. It's not reality."

It was real to her. So real, in fact, that she didn't want to live without this man in her life. "I've never wanted anyone but you."

"I don't give in to wants."

Harsh, even for Jackson. The man's head was as thick as a concrete block. Trembling, she scooped up her linen slacks and managed to finish dressing. She bit down on the inside of her cheek to keep her voice steady. "Tell me we're more than sex."

He shrugged, cool and indifferent. "Believe what you will."

Frustration stabbed deep. Surely she was more than a wild romp in a cloakroom to this man. Yet his gaze remained steely, his expression intractable.

Her throat thickened. Pride emerged. "You're a jackass, Jackson Kyle. Stubborn to a fault," she forced out. "Take the afternoon and spend it as you wish. I'm no longer afraid of Daisy Alton, so I don't need a body-guard. Any one of the ship's stewards can head the decorating committee." A moment's pause. "Have a good life."

She left the cloakroom without a backward glance.

With her departure, Jackson slouched against the wall, released his breath. *Have a good life* echoed through his mind. His life would suck without her.

After taking her against the wall, he'd come close to bending down on one knee and asking her to marry him. Confessing his love would have been the greatest mistake of his life.

He tucked in his T-shirt, adjusted his belt, then kicked a hatbox. Was the woman blind to their differences? Every time he touched her, his calloused hands abraded her soft skin. She deserved patience and gentleness. One kiss, and he turned into a wild man. While he would defy gravity for her, he'd left her with the impression he'd used her for hot, shipboard sex.

He'd been cruel, yet a clean break was necessary. In the long run they would be better off. While his financial portfolio grew with his investments, he remained middle class compared to the St. Croix fortune. He would never marry Celia for richer or poorer, when he came in on the short end of the stick.

He ground his palms into his eye sockets. What to do next? Celia had fired him. He almost smiled. She was mad, but she'd get over it. She would eventually move on. Without him.

His loss ate him alive.

Bree Emery needed a shower. Her day-long hike had left her calves tight, her skin sticky from the humidity. Although Sexton St. Croix had opened the door to his suite, she hadn't wanted to impose. Needing downtime, she'd chosen Nemo's Spa. The whirlpool would both soothe and recharge her batteries.

Returning to her cabin, she grabbed her black maillot, along with a change of clothes, and stuffed them in a tote bag. She ascended to the promenade deck. Nemo's was nearly deserted. A half-dozen men worked out with free weights, while two women exchanged gossip on stationary bikes. In the far corner, Cecelia St. Croix jogged the treadmill in hot pink sweats. Her ponytail swung wildly, her expression grim. She was burning off steam.

Bree approached her. "Mad at the world?"

Celia nodded, then broke into a run. "Mad at one man: Jackson Kyle."

"Because he told Sex about the 1920's party?"

"Because—" She caught herself, hesitated. "Let's just say we don't see eye-to-eye on most matters."

"Perspectives often differ."

Celia pumped her arms, pushed herself harder. "He's a jackass."

"Men can be stubborn," Bree agreed.

Celia was panting now. "Jax has selective memory."

Exhaling sharply, she slowed to a walk. Reaching for the towel that hung over the heart monitor, she dabbed perspiration from her brow. "I'm headed to the whirlpool. Care to join me?"

Bree patted her tote bag. "I brought my swimsuit."

Celia stepped from the treadmill. She preceded Bree down the hallway to Mermaids.

Nearing the locker room, Celia stepped aside to allow a woman and her daughter access to the sauna. Coming up behind her, Bree bumped Celia's arm.

Passion, pleasure, orgasmic heat. So hot, Bree felt burned. Her jaw dropped, and she slapped at her shoulder as if it were on fire.

"What can I do?" Celia gasped.

"Back up a step," Bree requested. Celia complied. Bree rubbed her shoulder until the sweeping fire faded to a sparkler's sizzle.

Celia covered her heart with her hand. She looked stricken. "You're clairsentient. We brushed arms. What did you feel?"

"One hot sex life."

The blood drained from her face. "My lover?"

"I didn't draw a name." Bree tried to put her at ease. "It was an accident. I had no intention of reading you."

Her voice shook. "No one can ever know."

"I can keep a secret."

"I'll hold you to your word."

Twenty minutes later, Celia and Bree sank beneath the bubbling, churning water of the therapeutic whirlpool. Celia's red thong bikini showed off a lot of skin. So much skin, Bree couldn't help noticing the beginning bruises on her left buttock. *Fingerprints?* Her lover had a strong, wide-palmed hand.

"Mmm, tension be gone," Celia moaned as the jets pummeled her shoulders. Leaning her head against the blue ceramic rim of the whirlpool, she inquired, "How was El Yunque?"

"Wet, lush, beautiful," Bree said. *A time of confession.*

"I'm not one for hiking," Celia confessed. "My brother, however, loves the outdoors. My idea of roughing it is the Ritz without room service. Sex enjoys camping, fishing, bathing in an icy stream."

Bree blinked. "He doesn't appear the type to leave civilization behind."

Celia smiled. "No other St. Croix has the heart of a hunter. One summer Sex participated in the Everglades Challenge. Twenty high school seniors were taught survival techniques, then dropped off by air-boat in the middle of nowhere with only a compass. Four days passed, and there was no sign of them. On the fifth day, the group located the ranger's station. One boy had a broken wrist, two others sprained ankles. Sex had taken control and led the group through the swampland. He won an award. My brother has the survival instincts of a Navy SEAL."

A playboy and an adventurer. Interesting combination.

"Sex also scuba- and skydives," Celia continued. "He collects classic cars."

"Collects both cars and women," Bree murmured.

Celia scrunched up her nose. "He's dated heiresses, swimsuit models, and beauty queens. But never a psychic."

Bree skimmed one hand over the bubbling water. "We're not exactly dating."

"He took you to Caribe Bleu and the Pink Conch. You hiked El Yunque. Places he's never taken another woman."

Bree shrugged. "There's a first time for everything."

Celia looked at Bree. "My brother keeps coming back."

Bree trickled water over her face, commented, "Jackson Kyle appears the strong, silent type. Trusting and honorable."

Celia sighed. "Some men take honor to an extreme."

"Have you known him long?"

"Since I was eighteen." Celia's expression softened as she drifted into a memory. "Jax showed up at my birthday party looking for Sex. I came across him first."

"You've been friends a long time."

A flicker of sadness, then frustration, darkened Celia's light blue eyes. "Yeah, just friends."

Just friends? Did Celia St. Croix want more than friendship from Sex's right-hand man? Judging from the bruises on her bottom, perhaps they'd already been intimate.

"Some men are worth waiting for," Bree said softly.

Celia grew uneasy. Checking the wall clock, she rose from the whirlpool. A willowy, classical beauty who would always turn heads. Twisting the damp ends of her hair, she said, "Zara Sage predicted I'd meet my husband on this cruise."

"Perhaps you already have."

"Perhaps I need to keep looking." She snagged a fluffy blue towel from the cabinet by the door. "Better run. I need to finalize my list for tonight's party." She stopped, snapped her fingers. "Forgot to mention, you're invited to dine at the captain's table this evening. Captain Nash requested your presence. Crystal Dining Room, seven o'clock."

Bree smiled. "I'll be there."

A quick shower, a change of clothes, and Bree returned to her cabin. She stopped dead in the doorway. Directly in front of her sat Daisy Alton's dome-topped traveling trunk, the lid now cracked enough for her to peek inside.

Hesitantly, as if afraid to wake the dead, Bree dropped to her knees and lifted the lid all the way. The hint of age and memories rose from the trunk. Memories so sad and devastating they broke her heart.

A plain white cotton nightgown lay on top, yellowed by time. Beneath the gown, she found several drop-waist spring dresses, the Peter Pan collars threadbare.

She uncovered a blue mesh cloche followed by a pair of two-tone pumps worn down at the heels. She clutched a cream teddy with side hooks and eyes and rosettes in the center. Then she ran her fingers over a pair of turned-down stockings with a run at the toe.

An empty tin of My Sin dusting powder by Lanvin lay at the bottom of the trunk. The scent had long since dissipated.

"Dig deeper." Daisy had arrived. Her secretive tone gave Bree the goose bumps.

Following the flapper's direction, she ran her fingers around the corners of the trunk, then pressed down hard. She watched with surprise as the bottom dipped slightly. Catching one corner with her nail, she pulled upward. The fake bottom gave way. Bree gasped, stared.

"Putting on the Ritz," Daisy said softly. *"For one night, feel as beautiful as I once felt. The dress was a gift from Randolph St. Croix."*

With the greatest care, Bree unfolded the 1920's gown. It belonged in a museum. Floor-length and fashionable, the rich rose silk was trimmed with Venetian glass beads. The designer gown combined refinement and elegance. A glass-beaded clutch purse matched the dress. A pair of shoes with rose-floral designs completed the outfit.

The look was totally Daisy.

Emotion welled in Bree's chest. "Thank you."

Daisy's blessing came in a burst of warm air against Bree's cheek. A cosmic kiss. *"Knock 'em dead, kiddo."*

Bree pressed the rose silk to her cheek. The Venetian beads brushed her chin, tickled her neck. She sat quietly, imagined Daisy splendidly attired and confident as she stepped into Randolph St. Croix's world.

Embraced by the flapper's optimistic warmth, Bree felt pleasure beckoning, first to dress, then to dine. Then to dance. The night fanned out in a spectrum of hope and promise. Soothingly slow, like a massage to her temple, reality shifted and time receded. She was soon captured by anticipation and excitement and love.

Daisy's world became Bree's own.

Deck Seven
May 28, 1925

Daisy Alton's heart beat so rapidly, she could barely breathe. Tonight she would dine and dance with the cream of society. Tonight she would live out a dream.

All because of Randolph St. Croix. The man had a generous heart and a conspirator's mind. Daisy delighted in her venture abovedeck. As Darlene Altman, Daisy planned to kick up her heels and shock first-class speechless.

A knock on her cabin door revealed a deck steward in the corridor: a trusted man chosen to deliver her safely to Ramsay St. Croix's stateroom.

"Tal at your service, ma'am."

Daisy took him in, from his long, narrow face to his hair combed back and stiffened with slickum. He bore a permanent squint from mid-ocean glare, his face, neck, and hands burnished mahogany.

She could barely find her voice. "You're here to escort me abovedeck?"

"With all discretion."

No further words were exchanged as he took her by the elbow and steered her along passageways and up stairwells. His palm felt rough against her skin. When he released her at Ramsay St. Croix's stateroom, he flexed his hand. Daisy caught countless white scars and a fresh scab on his palm.

Was the man recruited for donkey work? Perhaps he was assigned manual duties beyond setting up deck chairs for passengers wishing to take in the sea air.

A click, and the steward's pass key gained her admittance. As she took a hesitant step into the suite, Tal quickly closed the door behind her.

The wealthy traveled in style, she noted. Hepplewhite furniture gleamed with polish and cream silk brocade. Matching curtains covered the square portal. A stir-about fan buzzed in one corner. Beneath the fan sat a table large enough to seat four. A silver ice bucket, a tray, and long-stemmed glasses awaited a champagne toast.

Walking deeper into the suite, she ran her fingertips over the rosewood of a wing-back chair. She wondered what it would be like to curl up on the brocade and read *Vogue* in silk lounging pajamas and fluffy marabou mules.

An electric brass lamp with a frosted white ball shade cast light on a cane-back chair pushed up to an oval writing table. She slid open the top drawer, discovered a Mont Blanc fountain pen and letter paper. She fingered the stiff, cream-colored sheets, each bearing an engraved, AT SEA ABOARD SS MAJESTIC. She had no one to send a letter.

Separated from the main room, the bedroom and private bath were the ultimate in luxury. The bed's headboard and footboard were made of walnut inlay. Incorporated along one side from pillow to thigh, a polished side rail promised safety in the event of rough water. Her own small bunk lacked such a rail. Twice now, the pitch of the Atlantic had landed her face-down on the floor.

Directly across from the bed stood an antique high-boy with curving Queen Anne legs. A gold-backed hand mirror, a boar-bristle brush, and a deck of cards lay atop the linen runner. She fanned the deck. Shivered. Six aces stacked the deck. Ramsay St. Croix cheated at cards.

The doors to an old French armoire stood open. Hung on a padded hanger, a beaded rose gown shimmered with the vibrancy of the night. The stylish shoes beneath looked ready to dance. A tin of bubble bath along with My Sin dusting powder invited her to bathe.

Her jaw dropped when she entered the bath; it boasted porcelain fixtures and a massive tub lodged beneath a quartet of taps, two salt- and two freshwater. The desire to submerge herself in a mound of bubbles drew a giggle. Tonight she would pamper herself to death.

To death . . .

Eleven

Bree Emery jerked out of the vision. A tightness gripped her chest. She fought against the fear that sifted into her soul. Time grew short. If her visions continued, remained clear, a day, perhaps two, and she would witness Daisy Alton's death. She did not look forward to that final scene.

"Get a wiggle on." Daisy broke into her thoughts. *"Time to doll up."* She hummed "Yes Sir, That's My Baby." *"My toes are tapping. My dogs are itching to dance."*

Clutching the beaded rose silk to her chest, Bree slowly stood. She had an hour to ready herself for the evening ahead.

Once on, the gown clung with shimmering intimacy. She removed the crystal and amethyst beads from her braids and combed out her hair. The tightness of the braids left a gentle wave no amount of brushing could tame.

Daisy insisted Bree should "paint her face," but Bree

191

downplayed the cosmetics, using a mere touch of mascara and a pink lip gloss.

"*Very vamp,*" Daisy approved. "*And waterproof.*"

Sexton St. Croix arrived promptly at seven to escort her to the Crystal Dining Room. He wore his black tux with ease, as if it were everyday attire. No man had the right to look so handsome. Nor smell so good. The scent of Armani would always remind her of him.

Close by, Daisy openly admired the man. "*Hotsy-totsy.*"

Sex took Bree in with a laser-hot look.

Daisy caught his stare, giggled. "*Don't sprain an eyelid.*"

"Drop-dead gorgeous," he finally managed. "Great dress."

He might as well know the truth. "A gift from Daisy."

"What are you wearing underneath?"

"Dusting powder."

He leaned in, sniffed. "My Sin?"

"How did you know?"

"My grandmother wore it until the day she died."

So had Daisy Alton. Bree forced a smile. "The Galleria Gift Shop had a small box of powder in stock. I thought the scent appropriate for tonight."

He rubbed the back of his neck. "Where did Daisy get such an expensive gown?"

"From Randolph St. Croix," Bree said. "I had a vision earlier this evening. Daisy wore the gown on the night he welcomed her into his world."

Sex's eyes narrowed and a muscle jerked in his jaw. "Sorry, Bree, but I can't accept the flapper as first-class."

Randolph had viewed Daisy as more than a flapper. He'd recognized her as genuine. Had found her zest for life irresistible.

Bree refused to allow Sex's disbelief to dampen her

spirits. "Take me to dinner, Sexton St. Croix," she requested. "I want to enjoy this evening with you."

"As I want to enjoy you." Tucking his hand in the inner pocket of his tux, he plucked out a black satin box. He laid it on her palm. "I want to give you pleasure," he said softly. "Since we're not sleeping together, allow me to give you this gift."

He helped her open the satin box.

Arrayed against black velvet, a vintage filigree locket hung from a platinum chain. It was delicate and exquisite, and crafted for a loved one.

"Detectives found this locket in Randolph St. Croix's coat pocket the day he was shot," Sex told her. "Family assumed it was meant for Eloise Hogue. Inside you'll find a miniature of him. The opposite side awaits a picture of his wife."

Using the tip of her nail, she slipped the tiny clasp, and the locket sprang open. The black-and-white photograph revealed a dark-haired man with a strong yet kind face. Solemn. Aristocratic. The faintest hint of a smile made him human.

A smile reserved for Daisy Alton.

Sadness pierced Bree's heart. His was a life cut short. So much left unshared. The locket had been meant for Daisy Alton, the love of Randolph's life. A love so powerful, it transcended time and stole her very breath.

"I carried a torch for Randolph." Daisy's words ached with loss.

Bree's own eyes teared at the corners.

Sex wiped the moisture away with his thumb. "The locket wasn't meant to make you cry."

Her tears were for all the memories that had died with Randolph and Daisy. She gave him a small smile. "It's the nicest gift I've ever received."

He lifted the necklace and placed it around her neck. Gently brushing her hair aside, he kissed the soft spot behind her ear, then fastened the clasp.

Bree caught her reflection in the mirror above the dresser. She looked herself, yet felt beyond herself. A woman adorned in a gown and a locket lost to an enchanted time of unattainable love.

Moving to stand behind her, Sex rested his hands on the curve of her shoulders. "Time to dine." His gaze shifted, taking in the tight space. "Will Daisy remain in the cabin, or will she join us in the Crystal Dining Room?"

Bree felt the flapper's warmth surround her.

"Pull an extra chair up to the table. I promise not to eat much." Daisy giggled.

"The party is in her honor," Bree reminded him.

He looked resigned. "I'm sure she'll liven things up."

The night had a Gatsby-esque quality, Bree noted as Sex swept her through the reception room, then past double-wide doors into the Crystal Dining Room. A collection of old photographs hung on the starboard wall. She felt as if she'd stepped back in history, dining in the presence of ghosts.

Amid the modern mauve, olive, and peach hues, the past prevailed in the wide, etched-glass windows and coffered wood ceilings. The room exemplified the grandeur of another age.

The quietly dignified maître d' showed them to the captain's table. Captain Nash greeted them as old friends. Within minutes, Cecelia St. Croix joined them, exquisitely attired in fringed red satin and a matching boa.

Bree grinned at the younger woman. "You look fabulous."

Celia couldn't take her eyes off Bree's gown. "Your dress is exquisite."

"A Daisy Alton original," Sex told his sister.

"A gift from a man of means," Bree said simply.

Celia sighed. "Daisy had an admirer? How romantic."

Sex snorted. "Not romantic, lethal. She pulled the wool over Randolph St. Croix's eyes."

"Randolph saw beyond Daisy's brash behavior," Bree said softly. "He became fond of the flapper."

Cecelia frowned. "I thought Randolph loved Eloise Hogue."

"Randolph damn sure did love the Hogue woman," Ramsay St. Croix announced as Mimi Rhaine pushed his wheelchair to the table. "They were close to marrying before that Alton floozy took his life."

Harlan took a chair next to Cecelia. "Daisy's dead and gone—"

"She's still on the damn ship," Ram reminded him.

"Let's not talk about Daisy Alton." Mimi took a seat between the elderly men. "She gives Ram indigestion." After straightening her low-cut black tuxedo blouse, she patted his arm. "Watch your swearing, sugar lips."

From across the table, Ramsay narrowed his gaze on Bree's vintage locket. "I see you're wearing the locket found on Randolph's corpse."

Sex rolled his eyes. "Takes the romance out of the gift."

Bree fingered the delicate filigree. "I find it lovely."

"The locket was intended for Eloise Hogue," Ram said.

"Or for Daisy Alton," Bree countered softly.

Ramsay's nostrils flared. "Never," he said with such finality his dentures clicked.

Mimi reached across him, grabbing his waterglass. "Take a sippy-sip and cool down. There's no need to get all worked up over crazy Daisy."

"I agree." Sex leaned close to Bree and lowered his voice. "No more Daisy talk. Ram has a pacemaker. He doesn't need the stress."

"I hadn't realized he'd get so upset," Bree returned. "Should I take off the locket?"

Sex's breath fanned her cheek. "Since my hand can't rest between your breasts, I want the locket there instead."

Heat spread across her chest and climbed higher, into her cheeks. She reached for her own glass of ice water.

Captain Nash cleared his throat. "We have one chair vacant. Who are we missing?"

"Jackson Kyle won't be joining us until Club St. Croix," Sex stated. "I spoke to him earlier." He cut Celia a look. "He mentioned you'd fired him."

Celia bit down on her bottom lip. "We had a disagreement."

"Agree to disagree, but don't keep my right-hand man from dinner," Sex told her.

Celia's reply was lost as Zara Sage approached. "Good evening, everyone," the Ouija master said as she passed their table.

Captain Nash rose, inquired, "Would you care to join us?"

Zara glanced at Harlan, who gave her a quick nod. "I'd love to."

The moment she'd settled at the table, two waiters appeared. They handed each person a menu card. "Cocktails or champagne?" the taller of the two asked Sex.

He contemplated the menu longer than Ram wanted to wait. "Heidsick Monopole nineteen-o-seven," the elderly man ordered.

"Heidsick Monopole. Champagne for the Czars of Russia," Daisy said as she swept by their table. Flighty as a hummingbird, the flapper had yet to settle anywhere.

This rare champagne had been drunk during a time of gaiety and giddiness, Bree sensed. A time when Randolph St. Croix raised his glass to Daisy Alton.

"Bree?" Sex was looking at her now, his concern evident. "You look a little pale."

"My mind wandered," she confessed. "I'm fine, really."

Taking her hand in his, he clasped it to his thigh. "Concentrate on me."

She could manage that, after she consulted her menu card. The five-course meal offered the finest cuisine. Ramsay, however, was not impressed.

"Saltimbocca alla Romana? What the hell is that?"

"Veal, Ram," Sex informed him.

"Everything's so damn fancy," Ram scoffed. "Whatever happened to plain old meat and potatoes?"

"The chef will prepare a meal of your choice." The waiter had returned with a bottle of Heidsick Monopole. Popping the cork, he poured a small amount for Sex to sample.

"Superb," Sex declared after tasting the champagne. "Ram and Harlan will have no more than a sip. Bring them club soda and lime."

"Just a sip for me also," Mimi piped up, now sober and repentant following her afternoon at the distillery.

The champagne glowed like liquid gold in the long-stemmed crystal goblets, as if proud of its age. Sex toasted the table, then squeezed her hand against his thigh. "To the beauty of the night."

In that instant, Bree felt spoiled and pampered. Protected. Her heart was lost to this man.

Shortly thereafter, the waiter delivered silver trays of caviar and fresh oysters, along with a basket of bread-sticks and crescent rolls for Harlan and Ram. Then he nodded to Bree. "Your first course, ma'am?"

She studied the selections on the menu card: lobster Veloute, French onion or chilled fruit soup. "Chilled fruit soup," she requested.

"No cream of potato?" Ram sounded cranky.

From behind Bree's chair, Daisy coughed with disgust. *"Cream of potato tastes like paste."*

Bree hid her smile behind the menu card.

"Can't sink my teeth into sole with lemon butter sauce," Ram complained once again as he buttered a crescent roll.

Harlan grunted his agreement. "Sole, the ocean's answer to pork chops."

"You've got taste on your face, puddin'." Mimi applied the corner of her napkin to a smudge of butter on Ram's chin.

Without conscious thought, Bree picked up her soup spoon. She traced the rounded edges, the shallow dip, then turned it over.

Real silver. Her stomach took a sudden dive. She blinked against the images that skirted just beyond her vision. "How old is this spoon?" she asked.

"As old as the *Majestic*," Celia said. "Some pieces sprout legs and disappear after every meal, but we try to use the real silver for special occasions."

Special occasions. Struggling to stay focused, Bree

curled her fingers around the spoon and clutched it tightly. The handle dug into her palm. Time crooked a finger and beckoned to her.

As the past flicked into full focus, the spoon slipped from her hand and fell to the floor.

Crystal Dining Room
May 28, 1925

Daisy Alton ran her fingertips across the three spoons arranged to the right of her plate, chose the furthest one for her cream of potato soup, then glanced up expectantly. Randolph St. Croix gave her a discreet nod. Not having been born into society, she'd survived the first course by the skin of her teeth.

Tonight she dined among men who considered selecting the right bottle of wine strenuous work. And their women exerted themselves no further than to lift a finger to flash their diamond rings.

Seated at a table for six, she shared company with Randolph, Thomas Hogue, his wife, Frances, and their daughter, Eloise. Her escort, Phillip Foster, hovered at her elbow, overly attentive. She'd never taken to men with patent-leather, center-parted hair. Hair as slick as the man himself. A regular dewdropper.

Daisy couldn't have been more surprised when Phillip arrived at Ramsay's stateroom. Here was the man who, hours earlier, had passed belowdeck with two women, belittling the passengers in third class. She'd recognized his voice immediately. Nasal, and rather high-pitched. Phillip hadn't perceived her as Daisy of the tug-of-war; otherwise he'd be scrunching his nose as if she were garbage. He only saw her as Darlene Altman, prized and prominent passenger.

She'd sat quietly, wearing a small smile, nodding appropriately as the men at the table discussed economics and politics. Thomas "Tommygun" Hogue openly condoned the rise of police investigations into banking and money laundering, a topic on which he seemed well versed.

Peering across the pristinely draped table, between candelabras adorned with lemon-scented candles and freshly cut jonquils, she caught Thomas's eye. The older man winked at her.

How bold! Daisy dipped her head. The mob boss made her skin crawl. Particularly because she'd seen beyond his charm and good manners. She'd witnessed firsthand his sinister soul.

Thomas cleared his throat and addressed her. "Randolph mentioned your family is in lumber and paper mills and that you reside in the Northeast. Maine, I believe."

Daisy feigned a yawn. "I'm not as reclusive as my parents. I'm known to bore easily and escape to the bright lights of New York City."

Frances Hogue of the sharp eyes, tight lips, and large bosom, straightened the silver fox stole about her neck before she looked down her nose and sniffed. "Surely you're not one of the cynical, disenchanted youth, Miss Altman?"

"A smarty?" Phillip asked.

Smarty. High hats never said flapper outright. It was as if the word would soil their tongues.

Everyone at the table eyed her keenly, awaiting her response. Despite her dazzling dress and fairy-tale lineage, she remained Daisy of the gin joints and backdoor speakeasies. Far more outrageous than refined.

She cut loose, just a little. "I'm enchanted with jazz, the Charleston, and late-night parties," she confessed.

Frances and her daughter, Eloise, reached for their fans. Daisy's words had tainted the air, and they needed to clear it.

Phillip, however, leaned closer. His elbow now rested on the arm of her chair. "Utterly fascinating, Miss Altman. Tell me more about yourself."

Daisy smiled sweetly. "I recently sat for a barber and had my hair bobbed. Cloche hats and short skirts are all the rage."

"Bobbed hair is immoral." Eloise Hogue stuck her square jaw in the air. Her high forehead and widely set brown eyes gave her a horsey look. For one so young she dressed like a fuddy-duddy in heavy black velvet with a peach-and-ivory cameo pinned at the high neck. Worn on the fourth finger of her left hand, her engagement diamond was the size of a dime. "I much prefer osprey plumes, hobble skirts, and long hair."

Killjoy, Daisy thought, still unable to comprehend Randolph St. Croix's interest in Thomas Hogue's daughter. A Bluenose, Eloise held everyone to her own high standards. Since only the most daring and popular girls ever got kissed, Eloise would stand at the altar with virgin lips.

She cast a quick glance at Randolph. He looked spiffy in his white grosgrain shirt and impeccable tux. His hair was neatly parted but not slicked down. His gaze, when he looked up and caught her staring, warmed ever so slightly.

Not wanting to draw any undue attention, Daisy sipped her champagne. Heidsick Monopole, rare and extravagant. The bubbles teased her nose. Randolph had shared with her the significance and history behind his purchase of the wine. A Swedish merchant ship carrying cases of champagne destined for the Czar of Russia sank in 1916, and only a dozen bottles had been salvaged. One such bottle had been opened in celebration of Darlene Altman's introduction to society.

"What else do you enjoy?" Phillip pressed her, openly intrigued and more than a little smitten.

Daisy pursed her lips. "I like to gamble and nip bootleg gin under the table."

"Heavy petting?" Phillip's whisper carried across the table.

"Splush!" She playfully swatted his forearm. "You've let the cat out of the bag."

"Fast morals!" Frances made a noise that sounded like she'd swallowed her tongue.

Eloise gaped like a fish.

"My deepest apologies," Phillip made quick amends, yet continued in the same vein. "Do you smoke?"

"Camels or Chesterfields," Daisy admitted. "Or a very thin cigar."

A speculative gleam brightened Phillip's gray eyes. "Perhaps you'd join me in the smoking club after dinner?"

A male-only preserve. "Perhaps I might."

Thomas Hogue raised one brow, his wife paled, and their daughter nearly bit off her lips.

"Forgive me—" Daisy put her hand over her heart, looking contrite "—I've shocked you."

"Not shocked but delighted." Phillip smiled at her. "You're quite daring, Miss Altman."

Randolph St. Croix silently toasted Daisy Alton with his glass of champagne. Leaning back in his chair, he watched how she handled herself amid his peers.

Smart and witty and fun, she was more than a beautiful bundle of clothes.

She'd beguiled Phillip Foster to the point that the man would, no doubt, propose marriage before midnight. While Thomas Hogue appeared mildly amused, the Hogue women looked appalled. Daisy was outrageous and bold. She would never conform to the upper-crust. She wasn't a snob.

Why was he marrying Eloise Hogue? The question had haunted him the live-long day. Her father had suggested the match. At the ripe age of thirty-two, Randolph had accepted the fact that he might never marry for love. His introduction to Eloise proved her shy but amicable, a young woman reared with propriety and virtue.

Although they held similar interests, there was nothing stimulating about their future together. Their lives would move forward at a slow, predictable pace. He would be sitting on the porch in a rocking chair by the time he hit forty.

The thought depressed him greatly.

Across the table, her blue eyes flashing, Daisy Alton offered him smiles and sassiness, and a future that would never be boring. She brought him joy.

During a lull in the conversation, his gaze shifted to Eloise Hogue. Like mother, like daughter. He caught Eloise plucking at an uneven pleat in her black velvet bodice at the exact moment his future mother-in-law tried to smooth a crease on the sleeve of her gown.

"I should have brought my own maid," Frances complained. "I can't depend on the stewardesses to get out all the wrinkles."

Randolph squinted. Such tiny wrinkles, nearly obscure to the naked eye. Yet such trivial matters caused the women great distress.

"Perhaps the stewardesses aren't trained to iron," Daisy said simply. "I have two maids. Might I send you one in the morning?"

Randolph bit his inner cheek, held back his smile. Daisy's boasting would cost him a servant.

Daisy's generous offer put her in a new light. Frances could no longer tag Daisy undesirable if Frances accepted Daisy's maid. A deep sigh, and the older woman came to her decision. "How thoughtful of you, Miss Altman. The trip will be less a fright with a maid in attendance."

"We certainly wouldn't want to lift a finger for ourselves," Daisy agreed.

Randolph nearly choked on his sip of champagne.

Daisy met his gaze across the table. His look was not one of reprimand, but of amused disbelief. Smiling to herself, she dipped her head and sampled the cream of potato soup.

It appeared creamy and thick with potatoes, celery, and pearl onions. Unfortunately, it tasted like paste. The consistency stuck her tongue to the roof of her mouth and glued her lips together. She made an indelicate smacking sound that drew everyone's attention.

"My apologies." She dabbed her mouth with her linen napkin. "My pleasure in the soup escaped me."

Beside her, Phillip smacked his own lips. "I agree. The soup's delicious."

The meal continued with Phillip imitating her smallest blunder, as if it would elevate him in her eyes. It was both charming and irritating. While she was slicing her lamb, a bit of mint jelly cleared her plate and landed on the pristine tablecloth. She blushed, only to burst out laughing when Phillip *accidentally* dropped a bite of duckling and applesauce onto the linen.

Silly man! Her laughter caught on the air, carried across the solemn, dignified diners. Gazes shifted, drawn to her table. People looked down their noses at her. Distaste crossed in their features.

Randolph St. Croix saved her life. He smiled. A full-blown smile that reached his eyes and relaxed his features.

A smile Daisy Alton would take to her grave.

He lifted his glass of champagne. "You've made our meal enjoyable, Miss Altman. A memory to savor."

"Savor like an éclair," Phillip added.

Frances and Eloise Hogue were slow to join the toast. They sat stiffly, shocked by Daisy's indelicate behavior. They looked at Thomas, who had, without hesitation, raised his glass in good cheer. Their expressions tight, the women acknowledged the fact that Darlene Altman was an equal.

After several bites, Daisy decided lamb was an acquired taste. She finished her green peas with too big a bite, and several scattered back onto the plate.

"Shot like marbles," Phillip commented from the corner of his mouth while eating his creamed carrots.

While known for his high style, Phillip Foster had infused their meal with humor in hopes of capturing her heart. Daisy's heart, however, beat for only one man: Randolph St. Croix.

Shortly thereafter, an array of cheeses appeared, from mellow Bries and Camemberts to a seriously smelly blue cheese surrounded by grapes, sliced apples and pears.

"What might I serve you?" The waiter hovered by Daisy's chair.

Daisy wrinkled her nose. Not the blue cheese. The

scent alone could fell a rhino. Taking her time, she finally said, "The Brie and a slice of apple."

It was no surprise that both Frances and Eloise went for the blue cheese without any fruit to mellow its pungency. Their picky palates salivated over what Daisy found offensive.

Randolph, Thomas, and Phillip selected the Camembert with slices of pear. When the dessert tray was passed, Daisy's eyes widened with delight. Unable to contain her excitement, she claimed a chocolate eclair, French ice cream, Waldorf pudding, and a sampling of petit fours.

Having made her selection, she looked up and caught the horrified gazes of Frances and Eloise upon her.

She'd made a faux pas.

"Have you never eaten dessert, Miss Altman?" Frances questioned, her tone superior and unkind. "You've stacked your plate like someone starved in steerage."

Daisy felt the color drain from her face.

Randolph St. Croix cleared his throat. His look was thoughtful. "I rather admire a lady with a healthy appetite." He glanced from Frances's to Eloise's plate. Each had selected a wide slice of cheese, yet had eaten very little of it. "Such a waste when women pick at their food like birds."

Frances Hogue looked duly chastised.

Eloise sat silently, her lips pinched in a line so thin they were nonexistent.

"I'm tempted to sample a little of everything myself." Philip smoothed the waters by choosing both a chocolate and a vanilla éclair and peaches in Chartreuse jelly.

To Frances's obvious disgust, her husband also filled

his dessert plate, as did Randolph St. Croix. The women sat with the aftertaste of blue cheese in their mouths.

Engaging Randolph's eye, Daisy Alton held his gaze for three heartbeats. In those heartbeats, she crossed the lines of wealth and breeding and took him fully into her heart.

She would love this man forever.

"Did she bump her head on the table?"

"Did the plate break?"

"Do we need a doctor?"

Question after question sifted through to Bree Emery. She heard the concern but couldn't reply. A part of her was held fast in 1925, while the other part was pulled toward the present.

"I need you, Bree. Find me." She recognized Sex's voice. Her consciousness honed in on the man who called her to him.

Forcing her eyes open, she found herself still seated at the table. She focused on Sex amid the sea of faces hovering over her, all staring, their distress tangible. Sex's color was high, his eyes wild. His hair was spiked from shoving his hands through it.

Her throat was dry, her words drawn slowly as she spoke to him. "No shaking, no slapping, you're getting good at waiting for me to return to you."

He exhaled sharply. "You scare the hell out me, woman. One minute you're playing with a spoon, the next you're facedown."

"Sex caught you just before your head hit the table," Cecelia told her. "You could have knocked yourself out."

Sex stroked Bree's cheek. "You were almost out for the count."

"What happened?" Zara Sage asked.

"I had a vision." Bree reached for the silver spoon that had fallen to the floor. She held it on her palm. "The spoon triggered it. I witnessed Daisy dining with Randolph St. Croix."

"Impossible," Ramsay sputtered. "My brother would never have allowed a flapper in the Crystal Dining Room."

"I side with Ram," Zara agreed. "Daisy Alton spoke to me this very afternoon through Ouija. She was in a jealous rage. Angry with Randolph for spending time with Eloise Hogue and not showing her attention. I'll soon take her confession."

The air around Bree vibrated with indignation. *"Take my confession?"* Daisy blew her top. *"Woman's blowing hot air."*

Beyond the hot air, Zara Sage had attacked Bree's credibility. Why would the Ouija master knowingly lie? And to what purpose?

"Zara is right on target," Ram stated with finality. "Zara's older, more experienced than Bree. Zara calls it straight."

"Zara knows all," Harlan parroted.

"Perhaps there's more here than meets the eye." Sex remained impartial. "We'll talk later."

"Talk all you want," Zara sniffed. "The truth lies in Ouija."

Captain Nash cleared his throat and spread his hands wide. "Might I coax everyone back to dinner? The cuisine is excellent."

Conversation slowed, slipped into silence, as the waiters delivered, then removed each entrée with polished discretion.

Though the food smelled wonderful, Bree found it

tasteless. From the chilled fruit soup and oriental salad to the chicken sauté and chocolate soufflé, each bite went down with difficulty.

"There's nothing like meatloaf and mashed." Ramsay patted his stomach. "I'm so full I'm about to pop."

"Unbutton your pants," Mimi Rhaine suggested.

"I'd rather take them off."

"Not here, butterball," Mimi returned with a smile.

Ram grunted as he loosened his belt and button.

Folding her linen napkin, Celia asked, "Shall we adjourn to Club St. Croix?"

Sex nodded, turned to Bree. "I'd love to hear some jazz. How about you?"

The Jazz Age. The Charleston. Bathtub gin and goldfish-swallowing contests. Cuddling. A time of rebellious youth and unguarded virtue.

The time of Daisy Alton.

"I'm in the mix." The flapper slid in beside Bree, snapping her fingers. *"Let's hear some Cat with balloon lungs and a Finger Zinger get down."*

Twelve

Cecelia St. Croix had transformed the grand ballroom into a testament to the Jazz Age. Passing beneath a green canopy over the entrance, Bree, Cecelia, and Sex were immediately greeted by a blue-uniformed doorman.

The doorman bowed as he unhooked the solid-gold chain linked between two metal posts and allowed them to enter. Bree looked around, completely captivated. Illuminated by a chandelier, mirrors reflected the sleek black décor set off with silver adornments.

Starboard, the bar ran the full length of the wall. On a shelf above the bar, colossal globed brandy snifters blended with slender champagne flutes and triangular martini glasses. Set at each bartender's station, silver chafing dishes with shimmering flakes of ice cradled cocktail onions, slices of lemon and lime, and stalks of celery.

A six-foot square wine list hung next to black-and-white autographed photographs of Clara Bow, Mary

Pickford, and John Barrymore. Movie stars who once frequented the *Majestic*.

A roving photographer fired blinding barrages from a flash camera. The rattling of ice in cocktail shakers, the pop of champagne corks, and spirited laughter mixed with the sudden blare of a trumpet. The band was warming up.

"This way, please." The host swept his hand for them to follow.

Sex pressed his hand to Bree's back, directed her around chairs and between tables until they reached a prime yet private corner table for four. Ram and Harlan had begged off the club, preferring to play cards in their suite. Mimi had claimed a date.

Once seated, Sex draped his arm across the back of Bree's chair. He grazed her shoulder with his fingertips.

A flapper in a short, black fringed dress and sequined headband danced over to their table. After crossing and uncrossing her knees with her hands, she looked up and smiled. "Vintage cocktail?"

"Party like it's nineteen-twenty-nine," Sex said. "Two silver fizzes and a sidecar."

The flapper shimmied to the bar and quickly returned with their drinks. Sex signed for the cocktails and tipped her heavily.

"Bee's knees!" the flapper exclaimed, then danced off.

Settling comfortably on his chair, Sex crossed one ankle over his knee and asked, "Have you recovered from your vision?"

"Somewhat," she admitted. "Each one gets stronger, clearer, as if I'm living the moment along with Daisy Alton."

"Zara Sage believes you're out in left field."

She held his gaze. "What do you believe, Sex?"

"I want to accept what you see," he said slowly. "Your visions, however, go against every bit of evidence gathered during the investigation of the murder-suicide."

"Perhaps Scotland Yard wasn't thorough."

One corner of his eye twitched. "You're claiming a love match that defied society. Randolph would never have chosen a cheap flapper over Eloise Hogue."

The evening was disintegrating rapidly. "Love brings men to their knees," she said.

"Not rational, intelligent men. Randolph was upstanding and committed to marrying Eloise Hogue," Sex insisted. "According to Ramsay, family meant everything to both him and his stepbrother."

Bree bit her tongue. Discussing Daisy and Randolph drove Sex crazy. Voicing the fact that she questioned Ramsay's loyalty to Randolph would drive Sex over the edge.

Turning slightly, Bree focused on the chatter and gaiety of the club. All around them, the tables were filled with psychics and their predictions. People grew boisterous as each claimed to know Daisy's thoughts, along with her whereabouts. One psychic went so far as to claim Daisy would soon leave the ship and live with her.

Bree scanned the room. Daisy had yet to appear at Club St. Croix. She'd drifted from Bree's side on their way to the grand ballroom. What was the flapper up to?

Bree glanced at Cecelia St. Croix, who hadn't taken her eyes off the entrance. Whom was she anxiously awaiting? By the softening of her face, then the stiffening of her spine, it could only be Jackson Kyle, who now swung through the door with a dark cloud over his head. He approached their table with hard eyes and a barely restrained temper.

Sex nodded to his friend. "Glad you could make it."

"I came at your request." Jackson looked about the room, then at Celia. "Place looks decent."

"We managed without you."

Tension filled the air, sharp and tangible. Jackson dropped onto the only available chair, between Bree and Celia. His hand brushed Bree's and she jumped. Jackson wore his emotions on his sleeve.

Love. Anger. Desire on the explosive edge. He burned for his woman. His passion was held in check only by a sense of honor and decency.

Bree slowly massaged the heat from her hand. She smiled at the big man. "Looks like a fun night."

"Depends on your definition of fun."

Clearly, he wasn't having the time of his life. Bree would bet his good time hinged on Cecelia. The younger woman sat stiff as a mannequin. Bree raised her voice over the music. "Celia, the jazz is hot. Where did you find such a great band on such short notice?"

"Cell phone, telephone directory, and a gold American Express," Jackson answered for her.

Celia shot Jackson a poisoned look. "Actually, I heard them play at a club in Miami. It was their night off, and I persuaded them aboard."

Jackson cut Sex a look. "Company Cessna to and from."

"You'd have preferred they swim?" Celia asked.

"A strong free-style would have saved your brother money."

Celia flipped her hair. "As if money matters."

"As if . . ." Jackson set his back teeth.

Sex chuckled. "Children, behave. Enough bickering. Kiss and make up."

Celia blanched, and Jackson's scowl darkened.

Sex ignored them.

Even though Bree tried her best to keep things light, Celia closed up like a clam. Jackson turned to stone. Long stretches of silence pushed the couple farther apart.

The jazz band took a break, and the regular ballroom band stepped on stage, so there would be no break in the music. The popular modern songs drew couples to the dance floor. "I Swear" seeped into Bree's soul.

"Dance with my sister," Sex said to Jackson as he rose and took Bree's hand, "while I dance with my favorite psychic."

Held tightly against his chest, Bree embraced Sexton St. Croix. Sighing, she tilted her head up and asked, "Are Jackson and Cecelia dancing?"

He rubbed his cheek against her temple. "He's standing, she's still sitting."

"Expressions?"

"Hers is tight, his even tighter."

"Why are they so angry?"

He shrugged. "Might have something to do with her firing him."

"Perhaps she had a good reason."

"Reason being: He didn't pay enough attention to her."

Bree faltered, stepped on his toe.

"Spiky heels. Thought you'd be more graceful."

"Your answer surprised me."

He shrugged. "My sister's crazy for Jackson. She has been for most of her life."

"How does Jackson feel?"

"At the moment, about to kill her." Sex craned his neck, chuckled. "He's grabbed her by her boa and is tugging her onto the dance floor. She's spitting feathers."

"He wouldn't hurt her, would he?"

"Celia deserves a good spanking," he said. "She's spoiled and used to getting her own way. Jackson seldom allows her her own way."

"Does Jackson care for Celia?" Bree asked.

He hesitated. "I believe so but can't say for certain. I always thought Jackson treated my sister as if he were a second big brother. Not so anymore. There's enough charge between them to power an electric plant."

"Pretty steamy," Bree agreed. "Does that bother you?"

"Only that they've never acted on it. At least not in front of me. Behind closed doors, who knows?" he mused.

"Jackson would make a good husband for Celia."

"I've thrown them together at every opportunity possible, without being obvious. Neither has taken the bait."

"They might think you wouldn't approve of the match."

Sex blinked. "Jackson's my best friend. He always has my back. No one has ever looked out for Celia the way he does."

"Jackson once pulled a woman off your back." She recalled Jackson's comment in her cabin the night of the psychic cocktail party. It was a story as yet untold.

Sex grinned. "Cherry Rome, a body builder. We'd spent August together on Long Island, and when it was time for me to return to college, she didn't want the summer to end. I'd tossed the last of my suitcases in my Beemer, turned to say good-bye, when she jumped me."

A chuckle broke from his chest. "I danced around, trying to shake her off. It took Jackson to finally break her hold. I swore after that I'd never date another woman who could beat me at arm wrestling."

"Some women refuse to let go."

His voice lowered, soft and serious. "I have no intention of letting you go, Bree Emery."

She liked being in his arms. Yet Daisy Alton stood between them. A woman condemned of a crime she never committed. Bree would do everything in her power to prove Daisy's innocence.

A second slow song followed the first. Bree nudged Sex to check on the angry couple. "Jackson and Celia?"

"They're dancing now, stiff as brooms."

"Bend a little, Celia," Jackson growled. "You have a pole up your ass?"

She stared at him. He'd never spoken to her so crudely. She was a marvelous dancer, or so she'd been told. She wasn't a tight ass without rhythm.

Her anger seethed. When she'd resisted dancing, he'd snagged her boa and dragged her onto the dance floor like a Neanderthal. The feathers still tickled her nose. She sneezed. "Release my boa; you're choking me."

He did so, reluctantly.

In return, she bent for him. Just a little.

On the edge of the dance floor, his back to the crowd, Jax's big body blocked her completely. With his left hand secured at the small of her back, he placed his right on her nape and began a slow massage. She fought him for all of six seconds before succumbing to his magic. Her temper was soon lost to his strong yet gentle strokes. The knots eased, as did the strain between them.

On a sigh, she sank against him. A brick wall of a man with incredible hands. "I've bent to your will."

"I don't want us to fight." His tone a husky whisper.

"Then don't tick me off."

"Always my fault."

"Only when you don't agree with me."

He tilted up her chin. "What I said earlier today in the cloakroom stands. We can no longer be lovers."

The man was honorable and decent, and a dedicated pain in the ass. The urge to rant was strong. It took every ounce of her will to remain calm. "Don't sweat any bullets." She forced a smile. "I gazed in the crystal ball you left in my bedroom and saw my future. It didn't include you."

Jackson Kyle's heart stopped right along with the music. As the band continued with "Here and Now," he tucked Celia closer and picked through her words. He'd expected her to fight him, as she always had.

Not tonight, however. Tonight she'd used the sorry excuse of a crystal ball to let him down easy. He'd shoved her away so many times, she was now distancing herself from him. He should be pleased with the break. Celia was now free to seek the husband she deserved. His elation proved bittersweet.

Soft and feminine and flush against him, Celia drifted with the music. Her cheek rested at the curve of his neck, her breath warm against the pulse point at his throat. His leg slipped between her thighs. The sharp crease in his formal black dress pants brushed the silk of nylons. Rough against smooth. Man against woman.

Provocatively intimate.

Sexually challenging.

Inevitable combustion.

His desire for this woman drew him outside of himself with a need to be inside of her.

He was so hard he hurt.

His desire to mate challenged his good sense.

With a resolve as stiff as his sex, he set her roughly from him. "I'm calling it a night."

Surprise flickered in her blue eyes, yet she didn't protest as he'd expected. As he'd hoped. "Enjoy yourself."

Turning on his heel, Jackson Kyle left Club St. Croix for his stateroom. The cold voice of reason was a sad replacement for Celia's cries of pleasure in his bed.

Sex took a close look at his sister when she returned to their table. She was putting on a front. Her eyes were too bright, her smile forced. He'd noticed Jackson Kyle leaving the ballroom, and Celia's retreat to her seat.

"Where's Jackson?" he asked casually.

Her throat worked, her gaze riveted on the entrance. "The club didn't appeal."

"Still arguing?" Sex pressed.

Celia straightened on her chair. "Don't concern yourself."

"I think there's reason for concern when my sister looks ready to cry and my best friend storms from the room."

Celia waved her hand. "His loss."

"Did he hurt your feelings?"

"He tests our . . . friendship." She met his gaze. "Let it go, Sex. Don't play big brother."

He rubbed the back of his neck. "I want you happy."

"Happy to dance." Celia pointed to the returning jazz band. A man now stood on stage, snapping his fingers. "That's Milford Waite, a dance instructor from Miami Shores. He flew over with the band and will teach the Charleston."

With the first beats of "Sweet Georgia Brown," the band once again hit a 1920s' rhythm. Short, wiry Mil-

219

ford in an outdated leisure suit and scuffed brown shoes, hopped off the stage and motioned to the crowd to join him on the dance floor. Sex hoped the man danced better than he dressed. The song was for beginners, starting out slow and sultry, then picking up to a Charleston tempo.

The man had crazy legs. Sex had never seen anyone dance so exuberantly.

"Are you game?" Cecelia nudged Bree.

Bree looked at Sex. He shook his head. "Count me out."

"Singles or couples," Milford Waite called above the music.

Bree debated until Daisy entered the picture.

"I'm no wallflower." Daisy vibrated with energy and enthusiasm. *"I dig that jazz."*

Bree pushed back her chair. "Let's do it."

She'd taken one step when Sex snagged her hand, drew it to his lips and kissed her palm. "Have fun."

His mouth was warm and moist and made her shiver.

Once on the dance floor, Bree fell into step beside Celia, who was laughing at herself for tripping over her own feet. Milford Waite danced over and gave them personal instruction.

"Swing those hands forward and back in the opposite direction of the corresponding foot," he directed. "Rock left, step right, kick left, step left, kick right, knee right."

His instructions were as fast and snappy as "The Charleston," which the band now played. Bree could barely keep up. She giggled right along with Celia. She glanced at Sex, who smiled and gave her an encouraging thumbs-up.

Out of the corner of her eye, Bree caught flashes of Daisy Alton as the flapper swung her arms, kicked her feet, danced with liquid grace. Her image was faint but recognizable, from her bobbed blond hair and fringed lilac dress to the strand of knotted pearls around her neck.

Daisy's exuberance had made her visible.

"Y-you see what I see?" Celia had stopped dancing and now stared at the spot where Daisy danced the Charleston.

"Whoopee! Get hot! Get hot!" Daisy called wildly.

"Don't panic," Bree told Celia. "Keep dancing, don't draw attention to the flapper. We don't want a stampede for the door."

Celia covered her heart with her hand. "I can't breathe."

Bree didn't want Celia hyperventilating on the dance floor. "Go sit with Sex."

"My feet won't move."

Bree prayed the music would end.

With a flourish and a bang, the music stopped. Daisy crossed and uncrossed her hands on her knees and sang out, *"La-de-dad-da dum-dum,"* then clapped her hands. *"Didn't that just chill ya?"* Her question faded with her appearance.

"Is she gone?" Celia asked, her gaze scanning the room.

"I'm here to hoof." Daisy remained near, yet not visible.

"Daisy will close down the club," Bree said. "I'm in need of the powder room."

Cecelia was on her heels. "I'm coming too."

The two women crossed the dance floor and found the ladies' room at the far side of the bar. Pastel wallpaper, pale lighting, and vases of freshly cut tea roses added a feminine touch. Bree sat on one of six cream satin stools before a pink marble vanity. She stared into the mirror with a gilt frame.

The stool shifted beneath her, its legs wobbly, throwing her off-balance. Suddenly dizzy and disoriented, she clutched the edge of the marble vanity. Her palms grew damp, her fingers slippery.

Oxygen seemed scarce. She took a jerky breath. When she again focused on the mirror, it was not her face that stared back at her.

Bree now looked through the eyes of Daisy Alton.

Ladies' Lounge
May 28, 1925

Daisy Alton perched on a stool in the ladies' lounge. She drew her powder puff from her evening bag and lightly dusted her nose. Then she applied a bright shade of pink lipstick to match her beaded satin gown. She blew a kiss at the long mirror, smiled, deliciously happy.

Setting her bag on the vanity, she ran one hand over the cold, pink marble. It felt rich. Perhaps as rich and cold as the women she'd met that evening. Frances and Eloise Hogue didn't give two snaps of their fingers for her. Their looks had been haughty, at times sneering. Had Randolph St. Croix not provided a congenial buffer, Daisy would never have survived the evening.

She'd enjoyed the smoking club. Escorted by Phillip, Thomas Hogue, and Randolph St. Croix, she had braved the brass-studded leather doors and invaded the hallowed sanctum where access was traditionally denied to all women. She'd craved a ciggy, and smoked one of Randolph's Camels.

The initial shock and fidgeting of the male members soon led to pleasurable smiles and gentle teasing. The club had provided good fellowship, fine cigar smoke, and relief from female chatter. But only because she stood next to the owner of the cruise line did high society find her tolerable. Alone, she would have been tossed from the all-male preserve.

Randolph St. Croix had been a perfect gentleman, but Phillip Foster had turned fresh. He'd fed her line after line, then claimed her a cuddler. Shortly thereafter, he'd tried to steal a kiss in the companionway outside the smoking club. Diving beneath his arm, Daisy had pinched his elbow. Phillip had taken the pinch as her playing hard to get.

Then, in the grand ballroom, she'd danced until her dogs barked. Upon Daisy's request, the Scat Cats Band had moved from waltzes and fox-trots to tangos and Charlestons. Dreamy "Swanee River Moon" had lost out to jazzier numbers. She'd escaped to the ladies' lounge to collect herself.

The door to the lounge opened and the music danced in, followed by a stodgy Frances Hogue and her horse-faced daughter, Eloise. They walked as if their thighs were stuck together.

"Darlene Altman is walking the path to hell," Frances stated with the inflection of a priest.

"The Charleston is unorthodox and primitive," Eloise agreed.

Daisy's eyes crossed. She had no desire to face these women. She stood and hid behind a white lacquered screen that provided privacy for making adjustments to a lady's undergarments. She stumbled over several discarded girdles. Liberated from the ironsides, whomever the garments belonged to could now move easier to the Black Bottom, the Shimmy, and the Charleston.

Their mothers would be horrified.

Across the lounge, Frances sniffed distatefully. "How could Randolph put us through such an evening? Miss Altman may be rich, but money can't buy morals."

"Do you believe she *smoked?*" her daughter asked. "And at an all-male club!"

"Scandalous!"

Fuddy-duddies, Daisy thought.

"Randolph joined her." Eloise pouted.

"Are you feeling neglected, dear?" Frances inquired.

Daisy heard Eloise's agitated sigh. "Randolph glances at me, yet stares at Miss Altman."

"Men may stare, but they never marry outrageous women. Your fiancé doesn't give a fig for her," Frances assured her daughter. "Heavens! His closest friends would shun him should he involve himself with her."

"Perhaps she's trying to trap Phillip," Eloise suggested.

Daisy rolled her eyes. She wasn't looking for a sugar daddy. Phillip was as stuck on himself as he was on her.

The click of a clasp, and the women grew silent. No doubt powdering their noses. Daisy stood still, barely breathing. She'd die if she were discovered.

Eloise sniffed. "I'm not certain how I will endure the remainder of the evening."

"Do you wish to claim a migraine?" her mother asked.

"I feel one coming on."

"Excuse yourself, and I will attend you."

The rustle of skirts, the opening and closing of the door, and Daisy inched from behind the screen. She stood alone, a dull ache about her heart. Such a sap. She didn't give a flip what Phillip thought of her. But she couldn't live with herself if she'd embarrassed Randolph St. Croix.

It was time to blow. Clutching her purse to her chest, Daisy Alton slipped from society.

"Do something!" Celia hit Sex on the shoulder for the third time in thirty seconds. His sister had signaled him the second Bree delved into her vision. He'd found her crumpled on the floor.

"I'm doing all I can," he told Celia, his tone sharp with concern. "Stop hitting me."

Celia looked as panicked as he now felt. "She's so pale."

And clammy. Kneeling beside her, he'd felt her forehead for cuts or bumps, then taken her hand in his. It was cold and lifeless. He squeezed her hand. Hard. "Bree, I'm here, beside you."

Her eyelids fluttered. "Ladies' room," she said faintly.

"You fell off the vanity stool. What can I do?"

"Hold me."

He rolled onto his hip, then eased her onto his lap. She slipped her arms about his middle, sank against him. Her cheek was now pressed to his heart. His own arms wrapped her shoulders, his chin resting on her pale blond head.

"The visions are coming faster and stronger. I can't control them." Her voice was no more than a whisper. "I'm drained."

Sex sensed her weakness. Her body was so limp, she could barely lift her head. He stroked her nape, her shoulders, down her spine. Infused his energy into her.

Celia bent down beside them. "What did you see?"

Slowly, but precisely, Bree told them about Daisy's

evening in high society. Ending with Daisy's decision to leave Randolph's life.

"Such grandstanding, Bree Emery." Zara Sage had entered the ladies' room with several psychics on her heels. She clapped her hands, her tone sarcastic, "I applaud your efforts."

Bree's body stiffened in his arms. Over the top of her head, Sex met Zara's gaze. "Her efforts?"

"Bree has no connection to Daisy whatsoever," Zara stated. "The flapper is within *my* realm, and has chosen to speak *only* to me."

Sex lifted a brow. "What has Daisy told you?"

"The flapper had bold intentions and loose morals," Zara said simply. "She seduced Randolph St. Croix, and when he wouldn't marry her, she plotted his murder."

Bree shook her head. "That's not true."

Zara huffed. "Only truth flows through Ouija. Ramsay and Harlan believe me, why shouldn't you?" she asked Sex.

"I'm taking it all in before I pass judgment," he replied.

"You'll soon realize I'm right," Zara returned. "I will expect a check at the end of the cruise." She turned on her heel and pushed through the gathering crowd.

Bree blew out a breath. "The room's closing in on me. I need fresh air."

Sex scooped her up and held her high against his chest. He carried her from the ladies' room, out of the grand ballroom, and up to the boat deck. She was as light as the air she needed to breathe.

Outside beneath moonlight brighter than the electric lights, she began to shiver. An uncontrollable trembling he couldn't absorb. Settling her on a sun lounger, he snagged a lightweight blanket left behind by an earlier passenger and wrapped it about her shoulders. Then, motioning to a deck steward, he ordered a snifter of Courvoisier. When the cognac arrived, he eased down on the lounger next to her and held the snifter to her lips.

"Very smooth," she sighed after her first sip.

Within minutes, her shaking eased and her body relaxed. Relief shot to his bones.

"You scared the living hell out of me," he confessed.

"Sometimes I scare myself," she admitted softly. "I went so deep into the last vision, I couldn't find my way out."

He stroked her cheek, ran his thumb over her lips. Soft, pink lips, full and tempting. He leaned in, flicked his tongue against the crease of her mouth, then kissed her lightly. She tasted of brandy. He placed a second lingering kiss to her lips, savoring her.

Warmth filled him, as if he had drunk the cognac. A hint of a breeze and the scent of My Sin rose off her skin. A taunting memory of a time best left alone. Uneasiness struck him. Bree mattered more to him than her visions. He didn't want her returning to Daisy.

"Stay out of the past. The crime scene's closed."

Closed? Bree struggled to sit up. "Are you taking Zara's side?"

"I want you safe in my present," he said. "You're wasting time, witnessing what's already been investigated."

"It's my time to waste." She tucked the blanket tighter around her shoulders, tried to explain. "Daisy's love and pain bind me to her. She won't leave the ship until the mystery is solved."

If Daisy remained on board, he would have to scrap the *Majestic.* He loved this old ocean liner. He also loved Bree Emery. "Be careful. I don't want to lose you."

"I have no plans to leave until after the cruise."

After the cruise. He'd been so wrapped up in Daisy and Bree's visions he hadn't thought that far ahead. Earlier that evening, he'd had a fleeting thought that appealed greatly: he and Bree getting married on the ship, perhaps in St. Thomas at sunset on the boat deck.

A radical thought, to say the least, since they had never even made love. Yet for the first time in his life, he desired a woman for something other than her body. He loved Bree for her intuition and her sweet disposition.

Despite his feelings for Bree, having Daisy Alton as a bridesmaid had killed his proposal. He refused to have a murderess at their wedding.

Thirteen

"I'm ready for bed." Bree shrugged off the blanket. "Walk me to my cabin?"

Sex laced his fingers through hers, drew her from the sun lounger. She absorbed the warmth of his palm, the strength in his fingers. "We dock in St. Thomas tomorrow and I have a special day planned for us," he told her.

Their steps matched as they crossed the deck. "Tell me," she said.

"I'd rather surprise you."

"You are a man who enjoys surprises."

"I enjoy the pleasure on your face."

"I'll plan to be pleasured."

He paused on deck and pulled her into his arms. He kissed her brow, the arc of each cheekbone, the tip of her nose before loving her mouth. Slow, deep, moist kisses that curled her toes.

The man could French kiss.

Just as her heartbeat returned to its regular rhythm,

a lusty shout rose from the dock area, surprising her. She and Sex moved to the side rail. Standing near the gangplank, they caught Carlos Chavez waving to Mimi Rhaine, one deck above him.

Bree squinted. "Is Carlos naked except for a leather vest and chaps?"

"And a well-placed silver star." Sex chuckled. "Looks like Mimi had a play date."

Any passenger within ten miles could have heard Carlos and Mimi's boisterous farewell.

"*Adiós,* Señorita Kitty," Carlos called.

Mimi blew him a kiss. "*Adiós,* Marshall Dillon."

Carlos snatched her kiss, made a smacking sound. Then, bowlegged as a horseshoe, he worked his way to the black Mercedes.

Sex gave a low whistle. "Hot time in old Dodge tonight."

Bree agreed. "Carlos and Mimi give a whole new spin to *Gunsmoke.*"

Sex hooked his arm over her shoulders as they descended to deck seven. At the bottom of the staircase, she hesitated, suddenly seized with apprehension. She walked the corridor cautiously, listening, her sixth sense heightened.

Darkness and negativity blended with aging memories. Someone awaited her . . . or perhaps he was meeting Daisy Alton. Bree could no longer distinguish between herself and the flapper. She felt vulnerable and at the mercy of others.

"Bree?" Sex tugged her hand against his chest. She clutched him so tightly, her nails scored his flesh.

"Someone's in my cabin," she whispered.

Sex reached for his pager. "I'm calling Security."

"They may not make it in time."

He held her back when she would have moved closer. "You can't enter your cabin."

"I . . . must."

As they reached the door, the vibration of the ship grew excessively loud. The thrumming of the engines held an urgent note, as if warning her to stand back. She staggered, bumped into Sex, then hit the wall. Time pressed her backward. She was suddenly trapped in the suffocating haze of 1925.

Deck Seven
May 28, 1925

Daisy Alton jerked the chain pull on a tarnished electric lamp, and a sliver of light pierced her cabin. "Stop skulking in the corner like a tailor's dummy," she said to the man awaiting her return.

Ramsay St. Croix pushed off the wall, moved toward her. "I'm not hiding."

"You're standing in the dark."

He looked her up and down. "You're mighty dolled up." He ran his finger down the sleeve of her beaded satin gown. "Glad rags on a ragamuffin. A gift from my stepbrother?"

She found his touch offensive. Hated his reminder that she belonged in steerage. Not owing him an explanation, she returned his stare. His appearance had altered drastically since their confrontation in the storage closet. Rings of purple circled his right eye, and his nose had been broken. Nervous fingers raked his dark brown hair, and his clothing could use a hot iron. He smelled of scotch, as if he'd been on a toot.

Tossing her beaded handbag on the dresser, she said, "Spill, then scram."

"I'm in no hurry. You were in my stateroom earlier, now I'm in your cabin."

Ramsay knew she'd been escorted abovedeck. That she'd changed clothes in his stateroom. "What's your beef?"

He dipped his head. "I've doubled my debt to Tommygun."

Daisy gaped. "For crying out loud! He'll bump you off."

Sweat broke out on his forehead. "The collector's tracking me."

Ramsay would soon be fish food.

"I need you to go to Randolph and beg the scratch."

"Dry up! I won't approach him on your behalf."

"Not on *my* behalf," Ramsay grunted. "I want *you* to request the dough."

Daisy shook her head. "I'm no gold digger." After tonight, she never planned to see Randolph again.

"Yet you wear a gown designed by the House of Worth. Randolph bought you for the evening."

Daisy's stomach took a dive. "I never asked him for the gown."

"But you didn't turn it down, did you?"

The beauty of the night turned as dark as Ramsay's scowl. Clasping her shoulders, he shook her. Hard. "It's time to spread that rumor I promised."

Daisy's teeth rattled. "Eloise Hogue has already seen us together. She knows Randolph doesn't give two snaps of his fingers for me."

Ramsay's brows shot to his hairline. "When did you meet Eloise?"

"At supper with her parents, Randolph, and Phillip Foster."

He released her so suddenly, she fell back a step. His

bravado fell to blathering. "Tommygun caught me cheating. If I don't repay my debt by dawn, I'll be buried at sea."

Daisy had no sympathy for Ramsay St. Croix. Earlier in his stateroom, she'd counted six aces in his deck of cards. In her experience, cheaters always got caught.

Taking a fortifying breath, she pointed toward the door. "Pull your socks up, man! I've had an earful. Go chase yourself."

Ramsay wiped the spittle from his lips. His sneer was vile. "You'll be sorry you wouldn't help me."

"I'd be more sorry if I did."

"How is Bree? Will she come around?" Jackson Kyle handed Sex a tumbler with two shots of whiskey, which Sex downed in one long sip. It burned his belly. Fortified him for a long night ahead.

Setting the tumbler on the dresser, Sex ground his palms into his eye sockets. It was two in the morning. Security had come and gone, along with the ship's doctor. Only Jackson remained. The big man leaned against the door frame in khaki slacks and a forest green Ralph Lauren Polo shirt Cecelia had given him on his last birthday. To Sex's recollection, Jackson wore the pullover at least once a week.

"Bree's vitals are strong, but her mind is exhausted," he said. "Dr. Walsh indicated a good night's sleep should return her to herself."

"Should we move her to your stateroom?"

Sex shook his head. "I'll stay with her here. Thanks for helping me get her on the bunk."

Jackson scratched his jaw. "The woman weighs all of a hundred and ten pounds with sandbags in her pockets, yet lifting her, she felt like dead weight."

That had bothered Sex the most. He'd carried her easily from the grand ballroom to the boat deck. Yet when she'd entered her vision and collapsed on deck seven, her body had grown lifeless, heavy, as if all her energy had been depleted.

"I'm taking Bree off the ship tomorrow," Sex said. "We'll take *Spank the Wave* to St. Serene."

"I'll alert the marina to your arrival," Jackson said, making a mental note of it. "She should enjoy the old banana plantation."

"A day away from Daisy should revive her spirits."

"Anything I can do while you're away?"

"Cecelia's my second biggest worry," Sex confessed. "She catches credit card fever on St. Thomas. I don't want the ship leaving port lower in the water than when we arrived. No cement garden statues this trip. However fanciful."

"No statues," Jackson repeated.

Sex crossed his arms over his chest. "You've gone above and beyond the call of duty where my sister's concerned. Once we return to Miami, ask me for anything and it's yours."

Jackson's gaze narrowed. "Anything, huh?"

"A long, paid vacation, a new Navigator, my little black book."

"Your black book?"

Sex looked down on Bree. Fully dressed, she lay on her side, still pale, her breathing shallow. She slept like the dead. "After this cruise, I plan to marry Bree Emery."

"You've set a date?"

Sex smiled ruefully. "I haven't even asked her."

"I like her."

"Thanks. That means a lot."

"Anything further?"

"No. You'd better get some sleep," Sex said. "At first light, Celia will hit the dock running."

Jackson nodded and turned. "Later, boss."

Sex wanted to change that boss to brother-in-law. Jackson wore honor and decency like Boy Scout badges. Sex wished the big man would come clean and claim Celia for his wife.

Shucking his tux, he fitted his body against Bree in the narrow bunk. The Venetian beads on her gown would leave imprints on his chest and thighs. Tucking her close, he suffered the cramped quarters, the musty odor, and the drum of the ship's engines.

Tonight was a first. He'd never spent the night with a woman and not had marathon sex. Yet at this moment, utter peace claimed his soul.

There was no place he'd rather be.

Bree stirred at first light. Heat suffused her skin, along with the hint of Armani. As she shifted, so did the male body that was spooned against her. She felt every inch of man and muscle, from the sinewed arm dusted with tawny hair secured beneath her breasts to the muscled leg entwined with hers. To the erection pressed to her spine.

Warm breath fanned her cheek, followed by a light kiss. "You awake?" Sex asked on a yawn.

Awake and cramped. "Awake and a little stiff."

She felt his smile against the soft spot beneath her ear. Heard the relief in his voice. "Yeah, so am I . . . stiff."

His stiffness sent shivers down her spine. She eased up on one elbow and straightened slowly. She rolled off the bunk, then looked down on him. He'd adjusted his boxers, gray satin imprinted with hammers, wrenches, and screwdrivers. A bright yellow tape measure ran the length of his fly, marking off eight inches. Eight fully aroused inches.

She couldn't help smiling. "You measure up nicely."

He scratched his stomach. "I wasn't sure the tape would stretch again."

"And now that it has?"

He swung his legs over the bunk, sat, and stretched. "I hate to waste a morning erection, but Daisy Alton's cabin kills the mood."

"I understand."

Sex glanced at his watch. "It's early yet. A shower, a change of clothes, and we'll face the day."

"Ah, yes, my surprise."

"Dress casually," he said as he rose from the bunk and stepped into his tux pants. "Pack Chapstick and sunscreen."

He held her gaze as he slipped into his dress shirt. "I won't press you to share my shower or my bed," he said. "When you're ready, I'm ready." Squeezing past her, he added, "Meet you in reception in an hour."

Having showered at Nemo's and readied herself for their outing, Bree located Sex in the lobby area. He stood amid the milling crowd, yet stood out from the other men. He was tall, lean, overtly sexual. His smile when he saw her was slow and charged with sin. It turned her on.

She admired him fully. The turned-up collar of his coral polo shirt framed his strong jaw and tanned throat. Dark olive cargo shorts and a pair of Air Jordans gave him a sporty look as he idly spun his black Bulgari sunglasses by the earpiece.

She walked up to him and returned his smile. "Ready whenever you are."

"Hold on. I want to look at you." Cupping her cheek, he took in her heart-shaped earrings and matching pendant. "Great crystals." He traced the curve of her shoulder, the V-neck of her crop top. Skimming his hand down her side, he felt bare skin above her hip-hugging shorts. "Slender waist, shapely hips."

She dipped her head, blushed. Purchased on a whim, the tangerine short set showed a lot of skin. Skin Sex found fascinating, judging by the sexual glint in his blue eyes.

"You look hot," he said, right before he kissed her. A light, I-like-you kiss that meant as much as any tongue-to-tongue.

"Where to?" she asked.

He slipped on his sunglasses, then twined his fingers with hers. "We're going to *Spank the Wave.*"

It sounded kinky. Not allowing her further questions, he nudged her toward debarkation, then tugged her down the gangplank.

Reaching Havenright Dock, they walked and Sex talked. He knew the island well. Unhurried, he allowed Bree to take in all the sights.

She stood like a tourist and watched the Paradise Point Tramway descend from the hills, the cable cars providing a skyview of the capital, Charlotte Amalie. Houses and hotels were banked on the lush green hillside. The marina was jammed with sporty powerboats and masted sailboats. Amid such beauty, she scrunched up her nose against the exhaust from the taxi-clogged roads that led into the capital.

The yacht harbor curved west from Havenright Dock. Bree's heart slowed along with Sex's stride as they turned toward an octagonal building assigned to the dock master. Air conditioned against the heat, the coolness inside fogged the windows. In the chill, goose bumps rose on her arms and her nipples puckered beneath her crop top.

Two seconds and Sex's gaze settled on her breasts. The man had nipple radar.

She watched with interest as an office door opened and a man with salt-and-pepper hair, Atlantic gray eyes, and a weathered face greeted Sex like family. Introduced to Bree as James Sharkie, the dock master reminded her of an old-time sea captain.

"Jackson Kyle called ahead," Sharkie said as they proceeded out through sliding glass doors and onto the docks. "You're fueled. Picnic basket's onboard."

Bree trailed the men as they walked among the boat slips. Boys and their very expensive toys. The slips abounded with high-performance fiberglass boats built for speed and sport. *Spank the Wave* was no exception. The sleek lines of the cigar boat would pound the surf at breakneck speed.

"Any plans to race this year?" she heard Sharkie ask Sex. "After you won the Miami and New York Super Boat International Grand Prix last summer, I'd thought to see you on the water early this year. *Spank*'s been serviced and ready to race."

"Racing's on hold," Sex told the dock master. "Several teams have approached me. If I don't race, I'll sponsor someone."

Sharkie pursed his lips. "I'm mighty fond of Trent Knight and his brothers. Both daredevil and decency run in their blood. They're due on the island tomorrow."

"Have Trent give me a call."

Sharkie slapped Sex on the back. "Appreciate your taking the advice of an old man."

Bree approached them then. "Nice toy, St. Croix."

"*Spank* winds up well."

Sharkie assisted in the cast off. Within minutes the powerboat cleared the harbor. Out in open water, the boat flew east across the water toward a burning morning sun. Sex handled *Spank the Wave* with skill. The vibration shook Bree's fillings, bounced her breasts, then shimmered down her body to the soles of her feet. Mussed and wild, her hair stuck to the corners of her eyes and mouth, and stood on end.

When Sex jerked his head toward a low fiberglass bench that banked the engine casing, she shook her head, preferring to ride it out flat-footed.

There was freedom in the wind and waves and wild ride. She'd never felt such a rush.

St. Thomas soon faded to a speck on the horizon. Less than an hour later, Bree caught sight of a small island sprouting out of the Caribbean, lushly green and overgrown with vegetation. Sex cut the engine to a slow drift, limiting the wake, as they docked on the calm leeward side of the island.

"St. Serene." Sex swept his hand wide.

Bree squinted along the shore. "No sign of life."

"It's a private island."

Sex was bold, but she didn't think he'd break any laws. "How private? Are we trespassing?"

He shook his head. "As an escape from the twenty-first century, the McIntyre Foundation recently purchased several small Caribbean islands. I was with Alex when he made the investment. Since St. Serene is close to St. Thomas, I thought you'd like to see the old banana plantation."

"A working plantation?" she asked.

"No, the island's gone back to nature," he explained. "McIntyre plans to turn the old plantation house into a small getaway hotel for yachties seeking five-star service and solitude."

The unspoiled beauty of St. Serene beckoned to Bree. She stood patiently while Sex secured *Spank the Wave*. Then he snagged the picnic basket and helped her off the boat.

Leaving the crystal-clear water behind, they stepped onto the shore. White and soft as talc, the sand held no marks but their footprints.

Sex pointed toward a break between the palms that fringed the coast. "We'll follow that path for about half a mile."

She pushed aside man-size philodendron leaves that overran the trail. "Snakes? Spiders?"

"Only butterflies and hummingbirds." He slid his sunglasses down his nose and winked. "And the occasional dinosaur."

The path ended at a three-story plantation house. A grand dame in need of refreshing her makeup, Bree mused, taking in the sun-faded rose paint and peeling brown shutters bolted closed. A wide veranda encircled the house.

Stepping around her, Sex unlocked the front door. She crossed the threshold, paused, listened for its heartbeat. The pulse was as faint as a last breath.

Time had taken its toll. The people who had once inhabited the house had long since passed on, leaving the place as cold as a morgue. And as silent.

Reconstruction had begun. The inside was fully gutted. Bare beams, pipes, and electrical wires showed everywhere like a skeleton, the house needed to be fleshed out. She moved to the newly constructed staircase that rose to the second floor. The steps were deep and wide and recently sanded smooth. She rested her hand on the newel post. "How many rooms?" she asked Sex.

"I've seen the architectural specs." He set down the picnic basket, crossed his arms over his chest. "There will be twelve deluxe suites on the second floor and ten on the third. All with private baths." He pointed beyond a pile of lumber. "At present, there's one functional bathroom off the pantry."

"Color schemes?"

"Tropical. Banana yellow, mango green, red ginger lily."

She could picture the transformation. The plantation house would welcome its new visitors. "It's going to be beautiful."

"You'll have to return once the house is refurbished."

She met his gaze. "If it's in the stars."

Sex prayed the cosmos continued to smile on him. He wanted Bree in his life. "What would you like to do first?" he asked. "See the island or have a snack?"

"See St. Serene."

They walked the six-mile circumference of the mango-shaped island, then cut through the middle. Dominated by twin peaks, a trail split the hillside, descending to the heart of St. Serene. All along the path, Kalabash, elephant ears, and green African tulips grew wild. A natural rock bridge connected two shallow waterfalls. At the base of the falls, banana trees flourished, heavy with fruit.

Sex picked two finger bananas. He peeled the first and handed it to Bree. "The smaller ones are quite sweet," he said, peeling his own. "McIntyre won't let all this fruit go to waste. Once the hotel is up and running, he'll begin working the plantation once again, and export the fruit, as well as providing banana muffins, pancakes, and mousse on the menus."

"McIntyre has diverse interests."

Sex agreed. "The man's got a good business head on his shoulders."

"How long have you been friends?" she asked, finishing off the banana in three bites.

"As long as I can remember."

A sudden wind snapped around them, ruffling the banana leaves. Sex glanced toward the horizon. Dark clouds drifted over the Atlantic, releasing sheets of rain. The storm would be upon them in no time. The plantation house was two miles from the banana crop.

He remembered El Yunque. He and Bree hadn't been able to outrun the storm then, and he doubted they would be able to now. They would soon be wet. Once again.

"How fast can you run?" he asked.

Bree's gaze tracked the storm. "Like a deer."

She took off through the underbrush, crashing through leaves and bushes, leaping over an uprooted palm. Branches slapped her bare skin. Sex dodged a huge puddle only to scrape his shins against a boulder.

By the time they reached the plantation house, the sky was black as pitch. The heavens broke when they were fifty feet from the veranda. The rain soaked them immediately. Panting and laughing and bumping into each other, they made it onto the wide porch.

Sex stared at Bree as she shook out her hair, laughter in her eyes and on her lips. "I like you wet."

She wrang out her crop top. "Wet is close to being naked."

"I'd love to see you in only your crystals."

"I'd love to see you setting out lunch."

He followed her into the plantation house. A narrow board between two sawhorses provided a table for their picnic. They sat on large spools wrapped with electrical wire. Puddles of water formed at their feet.

Amid the hot, heavy, humid air, Sex unpacked the wicker basket, laying out good china and crystal goblets. He lit a tapered freesia-scented candle in a sterling silver holder.

Unwrapping the sandwiches, he placed a double-decker peanut butter and jelly on her plate, along with a handful of potato chips. He filled the goblets with orange soda.

"Back to my childhood," Bree said enthusiastically, taking her first bite of PB&J. "Mmmm, grape jelly. I've died and gone to heaven."

He'd like to show her heaven, Sex mused, by taking her to the stars in a celestial climax.

"Tell me about your life away from the *Majestic*," she said between bites of her sandwich.

He bit into a chip, chewed thoughtfully. "My life before you was as exposed as a flasher. Every date hit every tabloid across the country."

"That's because you dated *naked*."

"I've let it all hang out," he admitted. "Skinny-dipping, nude surfing and parasailing. But not anymore. Since you, I'm zipped up. Only you can lower the tab."

She wiggled the fingers of her right hand. "Such power."

He leaned his elbows on the narrow board between them, his face now close to her own. "Feel free to abuse it."

She did, initiating a kiss. He flicked the tip of his

243

tongue against the crease of her lips. "More," he requested.

Her mouth softened, opened to him. The kiss deepened, now savoring and indulgent. Threading his fingers through her damp hair, he controlled, dominated, devoured her with openmouthed hunger.

He had the hard-on of his life.

Thunder so loud it shook the plantation house broke them apart. The storm had worsened. Sex eased off the electrical spool, moved toward one of the front windows. He peered through the shutters. The sky was midnight dark, the wind so wild it bent palm trees. Summer storms often hit the Windward Islands without warning. He and Bree weren't going anywhere for a good long while.

"It looks nasty outside," Bree said as she came up beside him.

His mouth curved up slightly. "Want to get nasty inside?"

His gaze was lit with heat, his blue eyes locked with hers, waiting, Bree knew, for her to make the first move.

"Protection?" she asked.

"Never leave home without it."

Their desire was tangible. Inevitable. Her heart beat like crazy. Needing to touch him, she traced the ridge of his Nordic cheekbones, strong jaw, and confident chin. Flashes of lightning made his golden good looks shimmer and shine.

Sexton St. Croix was an incredibly handsome man.

She stepped into his arms as if she belonged. Had always belonged.

His mouth tender, he kissed her forehead, her eyelids, the tip of her nose. Taking her mouth, his tongue glanced hers, teasingly. Unhurried, almost leisurely, he nurtured and gave and drew out her pleasure. All hungry lips and experienced tongue. Her surrender was pure, raw, and passionate.

She was a woman waiting and wanting to be taken.

Sex's hands were on a mission. Finding the hem of her damp crop top, he drew it up and over her head. She stood in a white sports bra, her nipples diamond points against the wet cotton. A snap of the clasp, and her breasts spilled forth, full and ripe and so heavy they hurt. He grazed her nipples with his thumbs. Arousal pulsed from her breasts to her belly. She grew wet.

Following his lead, she worked his shirt up his torso, spiking his blond hair when it caught at his forehead. She took in every inch of his amazing chest. Sinewy and sculpted for pleasure. She couldn't stop touching him.

Sexton St. Croix had moves. His hand stole down her side, his fingers lightning quick. Within seconds, her shorts and panties were around her ankles and she stood stark-naked before him.

His experience should have intimidated her. Instead she reveled in the intimacy and intensity of making love to a man who knew his way around a woman's body.

Her hands trembled as she unfastened his buckle, drew his leather belt through the loops of his cargo shorts. Sex assisted, unsnapping, unzipping, and dropping them in short order. He stood in emerald boxers decorated like a golf course, with clubs and tees, and HOLE IN ONE imprinted on the fly.

"Golf much?" she breathed against his mouth.

"I once dated a golf pro."

She tugged down his boxers. Their clothes now coupled on the floor. They kicked off their tennis shoes.

They stood so close, her nipples grazed his chest. His shaft rose against his flat, ridged belly, fully erect. A slight shifting of weight, and they were flush against each other. He caressed her bottom, the crease between her buttocks, before delving between her thighs from the front. Deftly he sought her damp, throbbing sex.

Flames flicked and flirted, drawing pleasure as strong as the white brilliance that built behind her eyes.

"We're going to christen the staircase," he told her between deep tongue kisses.

Snagging a condom from his wallet, he led Bree to the wide steps. Six stairs up, he seated her gently. "Not a bed, but the surface is smooth. Too many nails and splinters on the floor."

Bree met his gaze, her smile sweet. "Stairs are good."

Fragile and beautiful, yet adventurous, she connected to his soul. He felt her with every beat of his heart. Her love was pure and open, her scent one of clean rain and earthy woman. They would be good together.

Parting her thighs, he knelt before her. He stroked her cheek, her throat, her breast. Passion-flushed, her skin was as soft as the underside of an orchid. Closer still, he swirled his tongue around each nipple, circling in toward the center. Then gently nipping, he blew cool air to send a sexy chill down her spine. Her goose bumps rose.

Bree's hands were on their own quest. Tracing her fingernails from the middle of his inner thigh to the fold where his leg met his pelvis, she caressed the sensitive line with her nails. A hot spear of lust lanced upward from his sex, and his testicles tightened against his body. The pleasure was so sharp, so acute, it was almost painful.

Even though he'd rather take her with nothing between them, he tore the foil packet with his teeth and fitted the condom. Sliding her toward him, he brought her buttocks to the edge of the stair. He flattened his palms on the step on either side of her shoulders. She locked her legs about his hips. The muscles in his back contracted as he entered her, became part of her, was soon lost within her.

His consciousness settled into a primal haze. Pleasure flashed and surged as he found a rhythm that pleased them both.

Ecstasy burned. Sharp. Rising.

Sweet, sweet madness. He couldn't catch his breath. Could no longer command his sanity. Overcome, they found their release. He stiffened and she clasped him until every last quiver of pleasure subsided.

The climax left him slack-muscled and out of breath. Bree's short, shallow pants blew against his neck. He'd never had such phenomenal sex. The woman was amazing.

The shrill wind and violent rain held them indoors. Candlelight cast their silhouettes on the wall as his packet of condoms dwindled toward dusk.

More certain than ever, Sexton St. Croix wanted Bree Emery on top, beneath, or standing beside him for the rest of his life.

He'd lost himself in her.

Fourteen

"Everyone's leaving the ship," Cecelia St. Croix pointed out as she and Jackson descended the gangplank. A westerly breeze tossed her blond bangs, then kicked up the blue gauze skirt of her sundress, flashing her thighs. Even though his eyes were hidden behind mirrored sunglasses, she was certain Jax had caught the flash. The sight made one corner of his eye twitch. "Who's going to stay with Daisy?" she asked.

Jackson Kyle grunted. "The ghost will manage on her own. She has for eighty years."

"I, for one, am in need of a little retail therapy."

"Clothes and jewelry are fine, perhaps a painting, but no statues this trip."

Celia clipped Jax's arm, stopped him dead at the bottom of the gangplank, forcing the people behind her to step around them. "*Who* says no statues?"

He slipped his shades down his nose, his gaze as sharp as his tone. "You're looking at him."

She snapped her fingers. "Just like that I'm supposed

to curb my spending. Think again, Jackson *Layton* Kyle."

"There's no need to middle name me."

"Then stop being bossy."

"I'll stop being bossy when you stop demanding your own way."

Her voice lowered to a whisper as she pinched his arm. "I demand little from you."

He didn't even flinch. "It's your *little* demands I can't meet."

She knew very well what he meant. He liked her, but he didn't love her. He'd told her to move on with her life. Stepping out briskly, she said, "My crystal ball revealed a whole new wardrobe, several island paintings, and a dozen teak statues."

He caught her in two strides. "Don't push me, Celia."

She planned to do just that. When Jackson insisted they avoid the traffic and walk the short distance into town, Celia hailed a taxi. When he asked her to roll up the cab window to avoid the exhaust, she claimed it was stuck. Even though she hated breathing in the fumes.

Paralleling the waterfront, Main Street was the primary shopping area, with a seemingly endless supply of boutiques. That was where the taxi dropped them off.

Strolling the storefronts, they found out-of-work actors and comedians doing magic tricks, telling old jokes or sweet-talking customers into the countless shops. Competition for sales was high.

Cecelia had her favorite stores. She dragged Jax to each and every one of them. She tried on clothes she didn't need, and spent time looking at jewelry she had no intention of buying. She took one full hour in the art gallery.

When he finally suggested lunch at an outdoor French café, she claimed it was too warm to sit on wrought-iron chairs beneath an umbrella. Even though it was a comfortable seventy-five degrees. She shook her head when he pointed toward the Yellow Mango, with its island fare.

Her chance to decide where they would eat soon came to an end. Clasping her by the elbow, he hustled her into Khaki's, an American bar that served beer, hot wings, and fried cheese sticks. He planted her on a bar stool. Pulled one up beside her.

"My type of place, my kind of food," he stated, removing his sunglasses and slipping them in the front pocket of his gray knit shirt.

Adjusting from sunlight to darkness, Celia looked around. Very U.S.A. From the American flag and red, white, and blue leather booths to the Charlie Daniels music. One other couple conversed at the far end of the bar; otherwise they had the place to themselves. Although it was a far cry from Miami's Nobu, Rumi, or Emeril's, she liked Khaki's. Jackson appeared quite at home.

The bartender slapped a menu on the bar. He was a short, stocky man with BRUCE tattooed at the opening of his button-down shirt. He had muscles like Popeye. "What can I get you folks?" he asked.

Celia scanned the menu. "Everything's fried."

Bruce narrowed his gaze on her. "Don't be so persnickety. Little grease won't kill you."

Grease clogged arteries. It also put on pounds. She didn't want her liver looking like goose pâté.

Beside her, Jackson pulled several bills from his wallet. He laid them on the bar. "Coors, a basket of hot wings, and a side of fried zucchini," he ordered. "For the lady, iced tea and a salad."

Bruce puffed out his chest, huffed, "I don't make prissy salads. For anyone."

Jackson added another bill to the pile. "You've got garnish for your hamburgers. Toss a wedge of lettuce in a bowl with whatever vegetables you have in the kitchen. If you don't have dressing, she'll do without."

Bruce and Jackson had a glaring Mexican standoff before Bruce snatched up the bills and headed toward the kitchen.

"Thank you," Cecelia said.

"Yeah, no problem."

She ran one finger around the edge of the menu. "I don't make your job easy," she admitted. "I'm tough to baby-sit."

He folded his arms on the bar, looked straight ahead. "I'll live."

"Miami is only two days away. Then you're done with me."

Jackson Kyle's stomach took a dive. He didn't want to be rid of Cecelia St. Croix. He loved the woman. He was still pretty certain she loved him, despite her crystal-ball prediction that she'd move on with her life.

Sex had offered him compensation at the end of the cruise. How freaked would Sex be if Jackson requested Celia's hand in marriage? Jax was finally ready to test his best friend's reaction.

Bruce returned shortly with their meal. Jax was surprised by the care he'd put into Celia's salad. Wedges of tomato and hard-boiled egg, sliced onions, and a few black olives nestled among the finely chopped lettuce. Thousand Island dressing was served on the side.

Nodding to Jax, Bruce turned, grabbed a rag and began wiping down the bar. Jax heard him mutter, "Man must be pussy-whipped to pay fifty bucks for rabbit food."

Celia's breath caught. "I haven't a clue as to the price of lettuce, but you paid a great deal. Bruce has mistaken your kindness for being whipped. I, however, know the difference."

So, she'd overheard Bruce as well. He couldn't very well tell her that he'd have bought the seeds and grown the lettuce for her salad if that was what it took to please her.

He shrugged his shoulders. "No big deal."

She ate an olive. "I have the rest of our afternoon planned."

He groaned.

"Don't think you're getting off early today, because you're not," she stated. "I want to buy a pair of jeans—"

One brow shot to his hairline in surprise.

"—and a T-shirt."

The woman who matched jewelry, cosmetics, purse, and shoes to every outfit she owned wanted to break in jeans? "Why?" he asked.

"I don't own a pair," she said simply. "You once said you'd like to see me in jeans. This may be one of our last times together."

His throat constricted. "Yeah, fine, we'll get your jeans."

Once they finished eating, they again hit the crowded sidewalk. They were jostled, bumping into each other with every step. Their arms and hands brushed, and giving into impulse, Jax twined his fingers with Celia's to keep her close.

"Don't want to lose you," he said gruffly.

"I don't want to be lost."

Jackson took her to Arabella's, a boutique with designer jeans and sequined T-shirts. For her first time out, she'd feel more comfortable in a Rodeo Drive label.

Arabella met Jax at the door. A transplant from California, she was only five feet tall, with a geometric haircut and a sharp chin. She greeted him warmly. "Mr. Kyle, your timing is impeccable. I've just returned from the West Coast with the latest fashions."

She glanced around him, eyeing the street. "Is Mr. St. Croix with you today?"

Jackson couldn't help smiling. Sex had a running account with Arabella. The women he entertained aboard ship ran up monumental charges whenever the *Majestic* was in port. Charges that financed Arabella's exotic vacations.

"Not Sex, but his sister," he informed her. "Arabella, this is Cecelia St. Croix."

Arabella took Celia's hands. "Such a beautiful lady. Such divine coloring," she admired. "What might I show you, my dear?"

Jackson caught Celia scanning the rack of cocktail dresses. "We're here for jeans and a T-shirt," he said, drawing Celia back to the purpose of their visit.

"And maybe a cocktail dress or two or three." Celia moved swiftly, already picking through the one-of-a kind gowns.

Dropping onto a dainty brocade chair, Jackson sat uncomfortably for ninety minutes straight while Arabella fawned over Cecelia. "The jeans?" he pressed at the two-hour mark. He stood, stretched, pulling his arms back to relieve the strain on his spine.

Cecelia made a face but complied.

Ten minutes later, she stepped from behind the dressing room door in a black-and-white sequined

T-shirt portraying a vampy woman with pouty red lips. *Pretty Is As Pretty Does* was scripted in the same red as the cartoon's mouth. Low-rider jeans hugged on her hips. She'd wiped her face clean of makeup and cast off all her jewelry; her hair was gathered in a ponytail. She looked all of eighteen. The memory of Celia and their first meeting at her birthday party hit him hard. His sex strained at his zipper.

She strolled toward him, her gaze warm, her smile easy. "The jeans are so stiff, they could walk on their own."

Usually a quick thinker, he could barely put two words together. "Washing will ease the fit."

Her smile faded. "I've never washed my own clothes."

"Never made your own bed, grocery shopped, or fixed your own meal." He ticked off the list on his fingers. "Always charged on plastic but never paid a bill. Never—"

She waved him to silence. "I'm pretty pathetic."

"Not pathetic, Celia," he corrected. "Merely in need of less pampering and more self-sufficiency."

"I wish I were more like you," she confessed. "Nothing was ever easy or given to you. Look at the incredible man you've become."

Incredible? File that under *C* for curveball. "I work hard and do what's expected of me, same as the majority of the people on the planet."

"You're more than most." Her expression suddenly softened along with her voice. "You ground me, Jax. You make me a better person."

He was stunned speechless. Arabella saved him from replying. "I've located the hand-painted St. Thomas T-shirt you requested," the owner called to

Celia from the back of the boutique. "One left. Size small, still in the original package."

"Add the T-shirt to the cocktail dresses and second pair of jeans," Cecelia said. "Put them on my brother's account."

Arabella quickly tallied the total. She handed Jackson three shopping bags bursting with tissue paper and clothing and escorted them to the door. "May the island sunshine warm your day," she said as she waved them off.

Once on the sidewalk, Cecelia took a final look in the window of the boutique. She pressed her fingers to the glass. "I could own and operate a boutique."

Cecelia in the work force? "You might break a nail."

She pursed her sweet mouth. "I'd keep a manicurist on the premises."

Jackson rolled his eyes.

Wiggling her hand through the handle on one of the shopping bags, she curved her fingers over his wrist. "So I don't get lost."

They walked in companionable silence until they hit Island Imports. Jackson ground his teeth. He should have been paying more attention. Instead of enjoying Cecelia's soft hand over his, the light brush and bump of her hip against his thigh, he should have been watching for the import shop. He'd have walked around the block to avoid the store of a zillion statues.

The bounce in Celia's step indicated she'd spotted the place. *No statues.* He'd have to carry her bodily across the street to keep his word to Sex.

She was one step ahead of him. Releasing her hold on his wrist, she darted through the door before he could shift the shopping bags and snag her hand. Damn! Flinging the door wide, he caught her shaking hands with the manager, Wilton Moss. *Cha-ching*. Dollar signs appeared in Moss's eyes.

"Celia, it's getting late. We need to return to the ship," Jackson said sternly.

"After I browse."

Browsing would lead to buying. She glanced in the jewelry case, then passed row after row of small, manageable, mantel-sized statues before heading toward the back room, where the larger-than-life statues were displayed.

Statues that weighed a ton and would fill the *Majestic*'s hull to capacity. Sex would have a fit.

He nearly collided with Celia when she stopped before an enormous pink coral statue of a naked man. Smooth, his torso broad and ripped, the figure stood on a crystal pedestal with a challenge in his eyes, his sex prominent.

Cecelia was entranced. "He's beautiful," she sighed, her eyes glazed, her lips slightly parted. Stepping closer, she ran her fingers over the statue's chest, the firmness of his buttocks, the thickness of his thighs. She touched him as if he were mortal.

Jealousy stabbed Jackson. If Celia was going to touch someone, it was going to be him. Not some twelve-foot piece of coral.

"I want this statue," she said to Wilton Moss.

Moss was at her side in a heartbeat. "Then it is yours."

"*No*, it's not hers," Jackson said, his tone hard. He cocked his head toward a corner of the room. "A moment of your time?" he requested of Celia.

He followed her blue-jeaned backside across the room, becoming mildly distracted by her denim butt. Several washings and the fabric would hug her bottom. Nicely.

"Don't make a scene." Celia spun on her heel.

He set down the shopping bags and crossed his arms over his chest. "Then don't buy the statue."

"I happen to *like* the statue."

He'd *hated* the fact that her fingers had lingered on the statue's coral ass. "Find pleasure in a smaller one. There are hundreds of teak and bronze statues at the front of the store."

She bit down on her bottom lip. "No other statue will suffice. The coral one reminds me of . . . you."

Of him? His gaze narrowed. "Come again?"

"The statue is strong, challenging, imposing," she said. "And he's amazingly endowed, just like you."

He glanced back at the statue, shook his head. "I'm not *that* big."

"Inside me, you're enormous."

Inside her. How vividly he could recall her sleek wetness. Her readiness to take him deeply. A pronounced bulge pressed his zipper. He shifted his stance. "However flattering, I'm standing firm. No large statues."

Cecelia's chin shot up, her gaze mutinous. "Only one person will ever tell me *no,* and that's my husband."

Every muscle in his body tightened. Jax took a deep breath, exhaled. With or without Sex's blessing, the time was upon him. He no longer wanted to fight with this woman. He only wanted to love her. For the rest of his life. "How about your fiancé?"

She started, her expression wary. "I'd listen to my fiancé."

"*He's* telling you 'No statue.'"

Celia began to tremble. "He who? *You?*"

Jackson took her by the shoulders and sheltered her in his arms. He kissed the top of her head. "For richer or for poorer, for a limit on your credit cards, for a smaller house, for learning to cook, I'm asking you to marry me, Cecelia St. Croix."

She started to cry, not just little whimpers but full-blown tears and a runny nose. Jax accepted the handkerchief Wilton Moss discreetly slipped his way.

Jackson recognized her happy tears. They usually fell the longest. In this case, a solid five minutes. When she looked up at him, her eyes bloodshot, her nose red as Rudolph's, his heart embraced her, and he took her to his soul.

"A big or small wedding?" Celia asked, dabbing at her eyes with the handkerchief.

"Don't suppose you'd settle for a justice of the peace?"

She sniffed. "Nor Las Vegas Elvis."

He sighed. Getting her to the altar would involve Vera Wang, a wedding planner, a catering service, a florist, and a dance band. The works. "I love you enough to wait six weeks."

She wiggled in his arms. "Six months."

She was pushing his love. "Any negotiating room?"

Celia kissed him full on the mouth. "Persuade me."

"Once we get back on the ship."

Her lips lingered near his. "I love you, Jackson Kyle."

"Even though your crystal ball told you to move on?"

"Not every fortune teller's on target."

He drew her hand up between them. Kissed the fourth finger on her left hand. "You'll need an engagement ring."

"I have one in mind." Easing from his embrace, she waited while he retrieved the shopping bags. Then she led him to the front of Island Imports.

Bronze, gold, and coral rings, pendants, and hair

clips lined a glass case near the register. Cecelia quickly spotted the ring of her choice. A narrow band of pink and white coral with two gold hearts.

"What, no diamond?" he asked.

"I'd wear a cigar band for you."

Jackson took out his wallet and handed Wilton Moss his credit card. "The ring and the coral statue." Catching Celia's shocked expression, he explained. "My wedding gift to you. Shipped to Miami, but not on the *Majestic*."

Her eyes teared once again. "The statue would look great in an entrance hall."

Jackson envisioned the sculpted coral decorated for the Christmas holidays. A garland would wrap the statue's neck, a *large* wreath positioned over his privates.

Cecelia squeezed his hand. "What about Sex?"

Jax didn't bat an eye. "I'll tell him—"

"*We'll* tell him."

"—when we get back to the ship."

He signed his Visa slip, provided a shipping address, then snagged the shopping bags. "Where to now?" he asked as they left the shop.

"The *Majestic*," she said easily. "The sky's getting dark. A good afternoon to slip into bed and read. I've nearly finished *The Japanese Art of Sex: How to Tease, Seduce, and Pleasure the Samurai in Your Bedroom*."

"I've got warrior in my blood."

"Then by all means, let me please you."

Bree Emery and Sexton St. Croix had made love until they were both exhausted. The stairs would leave a permanent ridge on her bottom, and Sex's knees would be bruised after their long afternoon together. Sex had scored like a superhero. The man had stamina. The moment one orgasm subsided, he'd kiss her until her body craved him again. And again.

Now, as the sun tinted the horizon, she sat on the low bench of the cigar boat while Sex fired up *Spank the Wave*. The storm had passed, but the sky remained dark. Recalling the afternoon, a smile curved her lips all the way back to St. Thomas.

Once at the marina, he called for a cab to return them to the ship. Weak in the knees, she was glad she didn't have to walk the short distance. He also phoned Jackson Kyle, announcing their arrival.

Jackson and Cecelia met them at reception. The area was empty except for one officer manning the desk. Bree immediately sensed the challenge and determination coming from Jax, along with Celia's own commitment to the big man.

"Have a minute?" Jackson was the first to speak.

Sex glanced at his watch. "Have fifteen before I need to check on Ram and Harlan. What's up?"

Jackson's muscles flexed. "A wedding."

Sex raised a brow. "Anyone I know?"

"Both bride and groom," Jax said. "The groom's looking for a best man."

"I'm listening, if someone's asking."

Jax's jaw worked. "*I'm* asking. I plan to marry your sister."

Silence filled reception as Sex studied Jackson, then Cecelia. "You wouldn't rather have my little black book?" he asked Jax.

Jackson smiled but shook his head. "I've been crazy for your sister since her eighteenth birthday. I never wanted to mix business with pleasure. I wasn't sure you'd accept me beyond as an employee."

"You've been like a brother." Sex shook his hand, slapped him on the shoulder. "Welcome to the family."

Jackson relaxed. "Thanks, man."

"No, thank you, for marrying my sister," Sex said. "She's held every man she's ever dated at arm's length. Now I know why. She was waiting for you."

"Jax took his sweet time." Cecelia smiled up at her fiancé. "More than one time I thought he'd walk out of my life for good."

"Never happen," Jackson assured Celia. "I'd have found my way back."

Sex rubbed his hands together. "So, when's the wedding?"

Celia blushed. "In six weeks."

"What's your rush?" Sex wanted to know.

Jax's smile broadened. "It took a little persuasion. I'm not one for long engagements."

Bree took in the scene. The strength of family and friendship between Sex, Jackson, and Cecelia. She was thrilled for Celia.

Bree hugged the younger woman. "Happy life, happy love."

Then she embraced Jackson. Whispering near his ear, she reminded him, "Wealth does not define the man."

"So I've learned."

"Dinner tonight?" Sex addressed the newly engaged couple. "I'd like to toast and celebrate your upcoming marriage."

"Make the dinner for tomorrow," Celia said. "I want Jax all to myself tonight."

"Tomorrow night, then," Sex agreed. He turned to Bree. "I need to check on Ram and Harlan and speak with Captain Nash. Where can I find you?"

She bit down on her bottom lip. Despite the joyous announcement, something dark and disturbing still lurked on the ship. "I wonder if there are vintage books in the ship's library? I think I'll do some research there."

Tucking his hand in his short's pocket, he scooped out a handful of coins and passed them to Bree. "If you have time before dinner, Ram and Harlan would love to beat you in poker," Sex said.

Bree pocketed the change. She had avoided spending time with the elderly men. Especially after Ram and Harlan had sided with Zara Sage and challenged her psychic ability. "Perhaps one hand."

"No strip poker," Sex cautioned as he turned to leave. "The old guys cheat. Mimi Rhaine was naked after six hands."

Bree had every intention of keeping her clothes on.

Jackson and Cecelia departed shortly after Sex, leaving Bree to her own devices. She took the staircase to the library on the lido deck. The room was small and windowless, yet cozy. The latest best-sellers, along with well-used mysteries and romance novels lined the shelves. In a glass case, turn-of-the-century baggage tags, concert programs, publicity brochures, and farewell dinner menus were memorialized.

Bree found Marilyn, as her name badge indicated, kneeling on the floor straightening a shelf of books. Clutching a higher shelf, Marilyn pulled herself to her feet. "What can I help you find?" she asked, smiling.

Bree wasn't certain. "Do you have anything pertaining to the St. Croix Cruise Line?"

Marilyn tapped two fingers to her chin. "The St. Croix Line was reviewed in *Luxury Liners of the Atlantic,*" she said as she went behind the counter and located a leather-bound volume. She brushed dust off the yellowed pages. Next came a scrapbook, jammed with black-and-white photographs, some loose but all labeled. She nodded toward a grouping of chairs. "These two items don't leave the library."

Bree gathered two books, then selected a comfortable chair for reading. She scanned *Luxury Liners of the Atlantic,* a tribute to an era of travel when galas, games, and exquisite dining was "half the fun in getting there."

Setting the book aside, she turned to a scrapbook. The earliest photos were of Robert St. Croix, Randolph and Ramsay's father. Next came Randolph. Bree traced his picture. His hair was dark and wavy. His face somber, yet expressive, speaking of his ambition, innovation, and pride.

The family resemblance was strong between Sex and Randolph. Sex had inherited his great-grandfather's jaw and aristocratic nose.

Fingering through the scrapbook, she came upon several pictures of the Hogues. Thomas, Francis, and Eloise looked exactly as she'd seen them in her visions. Big as a baby Grand, Tommygun stood unsmiling behind his tight-lipped wife and plain-looking daughter, both women seated on deck chairs.

There were ten photographs of the Hogues, all on deck, all rigid. A lone man had been captured in the background, someone setting up deck chairs. The man's gaze was on Tommygun, sharp and attentive.

Goose bumps chilled her. She felt she should know this man yet could not place his face.

"Marilyn," she called to the librarian. "Do you have a magnifying glass?"

"No, I don't," Marilyn replied. "But I do have a pair of prescription reading glasses. Would they help?"

Bree gave them a try. The man appeared larger now, and she studied him for several minutes. No matter how hard she tried, she failed to see further images related to the photograph.

A dark force seemed to block her reading.

Further photos depicted celebrity travelers. And as the years passed, there were pictures of Sex's grandparents and parents, followed by Sex and Cecelia as children. More recent ones showed Sex, posed with countless beautiful women. All sexy and smiling and clinging to him.

There was no commitment in Sexton St. Croix's expression. He'd been out for fun in the sun and nothing more.

The man he had once been was not the man he was now. Bree believed he cared for her. They would continue to explore their relationship once Daisy Alton was cleared of murdering Randolph St. Croix.

"I have something that might interest you." Marilyn waved several yellowed pages at her. "They're original manifests. I don't share them with many people. The paper is fragile and easily torn. I've protected them in Ziploc bags."

Holding the bags by her fingertips, Bree ran through the lists from 1920 to 1925. In many cases, the ink had either faded or smudged on the handwritten lists. The names of movie stars and men of fortune flashed before her eyes. One name listed under crew members held her interest. A name repeated on every cruise: *Deck Steward H. Talmont.*

Her heart quickened. Talmont, as in Harlan Talmont? Ramsay St. Croix's oldest and closest friend?

Had the man once worked on the *Majestic*? Had he known Tommygun Hogue?

Definitely a long shot. But one worth investigating.

After returning the book, scrapbook, and manifests to Marilyn's care, Bree put on her poker face. She was about to challenge Ram and Harlan to a game of cards.

Mimi Rhaine opened the door to Ramsay's stateroom. A scarlet tube dress stretched from above her breasts to just below her buttocks. Strappy stiletto sandals wrapped her feet. "Come in, Bree," she welcomed. "Have you come to see my boys?"

Bree nodded. "I'm looking for poker partners."

Mimi motioned her inside. "They're in the living room."

She followed Mimi and her mincing steps along a short entrance hall and into a room decorated with burgundy leather and bright lighting. A small table separated Harlan, who perched on the couch, and Ram, seated in his wheelchair.

Harlan noticed her first. "Here to penny ante?" he asked, shuffling the cards.

Bree pulled up a chair and settled between the two men. Reaching into her pocket, she scooped up a handful of change. "I'll play until I'm broke."

"Our mark," Ram said, exchanging a look with Harlan.

Harlan's rheumy eyes brightened. "Need my cheaters," he called to Mimi, who quickly brought his eyeglasses.

"*Cardsharps.*" The air around Bree cooled with Daisy's sudden appearance. "*Leave now. Danger!*"

Daisy's fear touched Bree, yet her need to stay was stronger. The flapper hovered, then retreated, unwilling to remain by the table. Bree sensed the wild fluttering of Daisy's heart.

"Blind Man's Hand," Ram stated, then rattled off the rules.

Rules that changed with every hand. Changed so the men continually won. Never allowed to deal, Bree was soon down to her last dime.

Mimi served club sodas with lime and bowls of unsalted nuts and wheat pretzels. Bree paused between hands to study the men. "How often do you sail on the *Majestic*?" she asked Ram.

Ram cupped a handful of peanuts, popped several in his mouth. "It's been ten years since my last cruise. My past caregivers never wanted to travel. Mimi, however, wants to see the world."

"We've planned a trip to Cancun next month," Harlan added.

Bree smiled at Harlan. "Do you travel with Ram?"

The two men exchanged a look. "I have for many years," Harlan replied.

She squeezed the lime into her club soda. "Do you prefer ship or plane?"

"I've never flown. I spent years—"

Ram broke into a coughing fit that cut off whatever Harlan might have said. Bree jumped up to thump him on the back.

"Oopsy-poopsy." Mimi minced across the room. "No tossing back nuts. One peanut at a time." Ram's coughs slowly subsided.

Returning to her chair, Bree nudged Harlan. "You were saying?"

"I spent time on the docks in New York—" his gaze once again locked on Ram—"loading steamer trunks, hatboxes, and baggage on the transatlantic liners."

Bree sipped her club soda. "You've a fondness for big ships?"

267

Harlan slanted Bree a sharp look. In that instant, she recognized his profile. He was definitely the man pictured behind the Hogues in the black-and-white photograph. "Lots of questions, little missy," Harlan said.

Bree tried to remain calm. "My apologies." She reached across Harlan for the pretzels. "You have age and wisdom, and I love old stories."

"We have no stories to tell," Ram said dismissively. "We're crotchety men with failing memories."

"Who hold a fondness for poker," Harlan finished.

Having snagged several pretzels, Bree purposely brushed Harlan's hand. She wanted to read this man.

"Don't let her touch you." Ram's warning came too late.

Bree cringed as sensations struck, fast and furious. The pretzels spilled from her hand as she struggled to free herself from Harlan's past.

"What's happening?" she heard Mimi Rhaine gasp. "Bree's white as a ghost. Is she having a seizure? I'm calling the doctor." The retreating click of her high heels sounded overly loud.

From the corner of her eye, Bree caught Ramsay St. Croix dip his head, his expression defeated. "Hell's bells. Time's caught up with us."

Harlan stacked the deck of cards at the center of the table. "Secrets never die."

Evil hovered in the room, as dark and sinister as a murderer. Daisy whimpered, took Bree's hand in a protective gesture. There was no escape. Time soon gave way to the past and all its painful memories.

Bree Emery found herself cast into the final moments of Daisy Alton's life.

June 3, 1925

Randolph St. Croix approached Daisy Alton's cabin. He'd had a difficult day. He'd broken his engagement to Eloise Hogue over morning bouillon and biscuits. Always quiet, always poised, Eloise had snapped, becoming a vicious shrew. She'd threatened a breach-of-promise suit, which, if necessary, he would pay. Money meant nothing to him. Daisy Alton meant everything. He needed to see her now.

After tugging down the sleeves of his herringbone suit, he brushed an unruly strand of hair off his forehead. A light tap on her door brought Daisy to him. His sweet, vivacious Daisy. She stared openly, as if she'd conjured his image and feared he might disappear if she should blink.

"Randolph?" Her voice caught breathlessly.

He nodded. "I wish to speak with you."

"I look a fright." She nervously plucked at her threadbare skirt. "What more is there to say?"

"Much more, if you'll allow me a private word."

She stepped back slowly, allowed him to enter. They stood so close, he caught the reluctance in her eyes, the panicked parting of her lips. She expected bad news, when he only wished her happiness.

He quickly alleviated her fears. "I'm crazy for you, Daisy." He spoke from his heart. "I want to marry you."

She swayed, as much from the motion of the *Majestic* as from Randolph's declaration of love. Her knees gave out and she dropped onto the narrow berth. The porridge she'd eaten for breakfast sat heavily on her stomach. She fanned herself with her hand. Surely he was feeding her a line.

Moistening her lips, she said, "You're engaged."

The roll and pitch of the luxury liner forced him to settle beside her on the bunk. He collected her hands in his, absorbed her trembling with a squeeze to her fingers and a gentle smile.

"I've broken my engagement to Eloise," he informed her.

The enormity of his actions stunned Daisy. He had damned propriety for her. "How did her parents take the news?"

"Frances claimed me ill-mannered and Thomas threatened my life or that of a loved one," Randolph said.

Daisy chewed her lip. "I have a secret I must confide." She spoke of her first meeting with his stepbrother, what she'd learned about Tommygun Hogue's real identity, ending with Ramsay's gambling debt to the man.

Randolph had the class to keep his composure. "Ramsay is weak and easily led. He falls in with bad company. I will settle my brother's debt to Tommygun Hogue. Thank God I've ended my alliance with that man."

Tears of happiness filled her eyes. The finest man she'd ever known wanted her as his wife. Daisy, of the backdoor gin joints and speakeasies, embraced her good fortune. "I am yours, forever."

Releasing her hands, he reached into the inner pocket of his herringbone jacket and removed a small square satin box. He flipped open the top with his thumb. "A fire opal to reflect your spirit," he said as he slipped it on her finger.

Her heart swelled as she admired its brilliance. "Cash or check?" she asked shyly.

Randolph leaned closer. "I'd like to kiss you now rather than later."

His mouth brushed hers, lightly, tenderly, with the promise of forever. "I love you, Daisy Alton."

Daisy loved him to the depths of her soul. She stroked his smoothly shaven cheek. "'Til death do us part, my darling."

They sat for some time in silence, holding hands and smiling, sharing a second gentle kiss. Until noise outside the cabin drew them apart. The sounds of heavy footfalls and heavier breathing came from the corridor. It sounded like someone running for his life.

"Ramsay!" A man with a stealthy tread called out. "This ship's too small. Sharks are circling."

The collector! Daisy recognized the voice immediately.

Randolph leaped from the bunk and threw open the door before she could warn him not to. "Who's there?" he demanded.

"Harlan Talmont," came a voice sharp with sarcasm. "As if you didn't know."

Randolph straightened his shoulders. "I don't know, sir—"

Without warning, two shots silenced Randolph St. Croix. Daisy sat in absolute horror as blood spattered on the door and wall. Movement slowed, as if meant to be captured for eternity.

Daisy heard his anguished moan as he clutched his head, then his heart. Staggering sideways, he banged into her dresser. The sharp corner caught and tore the leg of his pants.

"Daisy—" he choked out before he keeled over, falling facedown on the floor.

She screamed from the depths of her soul. Could not stop screaming. She fell to her knees beside his body, praying for his life. Tears blinded her to the blood pooling around her skirt and on the floor. Her hand shook so violently, she couldn't find his pulse.

"God, don't let him die." Her voice was as raw as her pain.

"God had no say in this," said a voice from the doorway. "Ramsay's life was ended by my hand. You got to kill to be on top of the hill. Ram became a liability."

"Ramsay?" Sobbing, shaking, Daisy jerked toward the man in the doorway. "You shot Randolph."

Harlan Talmont stepped into the cabin. Tucking the toe of his shoe against Randolph's stomach, he kicked him onto his side. Randolph's back brushed Daisy's knees.

"Son of a bitch," Talmont hissed.

Blood, so much blood. Daisy pressed one hand over the wound at Randolph's temple, her other hand over his heart. Blood seeped between her fingers, ringed her wrist, flecked her forearms.

Clutching Randolph tightly, she threw back her head, cried from her soul, "Please don't leave me. I can't live without you."

"You won't have to live without him."

There was a third gunshot, followed by the sensation of fire in her chest. The impact of the bullet jerked the breath out of her throat. The point-blank force pitched her over Randolph's body. Her vision blurred. She was suddenly starved for air.

A faint sound of footsteps halted in the corridor. "W-what have you done?"

Ramsay? In the darkness that pulled her down, Daisy recognized his voice. Had he come to save his brother? Save her?

"I saw your brother in profile and thought him you," Talmont told Ramsay, his voice cold, without regret.

"W-why did you shoot Daisy?"

"A gangland shooting requires silence. No witnesses."

"W-what should I do?" Ramsay blathered.

"Follow my lead and stick to my story. Tommygun will back us up," Talmont said. "We've got a crime of passion on our hands. Randolph was to marry Eloise Hogue. Daisy shot him in a jealous rage."

"Dear God, you have no conscience." Ramsay fought for control. "I can't live with such a lie."

"I can add yours to the pile of bodies." Talmont leveled his gun at Ramsay's chest. "Or you can pick your brother's pockets, pull the ring off Daisy's finger, and pay your debt to Tommygun. You'll soon be a free man."

"I'll never be free." Ramsay's voice broke.

Daisy's struggle with life ended with the touch of Ramsay's hand on her own. Her last sensation of life was the slide of the fire opal off her finger.

Bare finger. Bare soul.

She'd been labeled a murderess. She would never rest until the truth was told.

Fifteen

"Bring her back. Find a way!"

Pressure on her chest, breath blown in her mouth.

"She's flat-lined."

A hard thump over her heart, breath as strong as wind pushed into her lungs.

"Sex, Bree's gone—"

"To hell she is!"

A palm pressed her chest, pumped, released, continuous and steady, willing her back to life. Bree's body jerked with the single beat of her heart that returned her to the living.

"I'm here, Bree. Feel me. Find me."

Sexton St. Croix's voice grew as strong as her heartbeat. Unable to open her eyes, she forced out a squeak. "Alive."

Seated on the floor, his back supported by the wall, Sex held her now, hard against his chest, protecting her from the vision that had nearly killed her. Her loyalty to Daisy Alton had held her in the past longer than she should have stayed. Time had stood still while she ab-

275

sorbed Daisy's pain. Bree's own breath had been stolen in the tragedy. She had died alongside the flapper.

Focusing on Sex, her eyes stung, the corners gritty. Her throat was raw and her chest burned unbearably. Her hand shook as she reached for his, which still covered her heart. "How long have you been with me?" she finally managed.

"Long enough to catch you when you fell off your chair. About twenty minutes," he relayed. "Mimi called me right after the doctor. I came running. Doc and I performed CPR."

Bree tried to sit up, but dizziness claimed her. Sex's hands rose on her back, supporting her shoulders, until her head cleared. "I became Daisy." Her gaze found Harlan and Ramsay, who hovered nearby, their expressions grim. "I witnessed—"

"You don't need to talk about this now," Sex quickly assured her. "Tomorrow, next week—"

"*Now*, Sexton." Seated in his wheelchair, Ramsay's throat worked, and he had difficulty getting the words out. His voice was reedy. "We need to come clean. Bree witnessed a time when mistakes were made and innocents suffered."

Ram closed his eyes, drifted, drawing those in the room into his past as he relived memories that had died with his stepbrother.

Held against his chest, Bree felt every muscle in Sex's body tighten as he sat in stunned silence, taking it all in. He shook his head throughout Ram's accounting of the tragedy that took two vibrant lives. "Unbelievable," was all he could manage.

Ram's confession drew silence. A long, contemplative silence during which everyone in the room looked anywhere but at each other. Too many years had passed to prosecute Harlan Talmont. But the truth had resurrected Daisy's good name.

Despite Ram's declaration of guilt, Daisy's grief still clung to Bree. Her heart remained heavy with the loss of a great love denied two innocent souls.

Looking at Ramsay, she added to his story. "Daisy told Randolph about your debt to Tommygun Hogue. Randolph intended to pay it off."

Tears spilled from the older man's eyes. Mimi got him a handkerchief. "Everything happened so fast," Ram choked out. "I was running for my life when Randolph's own came to an end."

Holding on to his walker, Harlan dipped his head, his brows drawn together. He looked frail and very vulnerable. "I committed vile crimes in my youth. I survived by other's deaths. I have blood on my hands and regret in my heart."

Ramsay nodded. "There isn't a day that goes by that memories don't haunt me. I have nightmares about Randolph's death. I can still hear Daisy's screams."

Sex pressed a kiss to Bree's cheek. "Your visions were incredibly accurate."

"Always on target." Ramsay slumped in his wheelchair, a broken man. "Zara Sage is Harlan's granddaughter. We hired her to contradict any psychic who got close to the truth."

Bree now understood the looks exchanged between Harlan and the Ouija master. They were family, working together, steering Sex away from the truth.

"Randolph loved Daisy Alton." Bree wanted closure for the flapper. "He gave her a ring, vowed to marry her."

Ramsay's head snapped up. "I never sold the fire opal; it's in my wall safe. I kept it as a constant reminder never to gamble." He motioned to Mimi Rhaine. "Push me to the safe."

A removal of a painting from the wall, followed by a whirling of numbers, and Ram withdrew a small satin box. Mimi rolled him back to the group.

His hand shook as he handed the box to Bree. "You freed Daisy Alton from a past concealed by lies and ill-intent. She was a beautiful young woman. Her love for Randolph shone in her eyes. My stepbrother must have loved her deeply to present her with this family heirloom. It's priceless." He flicked open the satin box, then looked straight at Bree. "I think Daisy would want you to have her ring."

Emotion built in Bree's throat and she couldn't speak. The ring was one-of-a-kind. A six-carat fire opal surrounded by diamonds. As brilliant and fiery as Daisy's own spirit.

Sex nudged her gently. "Take it, Bree. It represents your connection to Daisy. One that will never die."

Tears formed and spilled, dampening her cheeks. Accepting the ring, she slowly slipped it on her finger. The band grew warm, the diamonds casting prisms across the floor. Daisy's future had been captured within the fire opal.

Bree silently prayed she, too, would experience the kind of love once shared between Randolph and Daisy.

She touched Ramsay's hand. "Thank you."

"I'm so very sorry," Ram said. "If I had my life to live over—"

"Regrets come through hindsight," Bree gently reminded him. "Live another hundred years in good conscience."

Exhaustion hit her then, her mind turning to mush.

"Take me to your bed," she whispered to the man who held her.

Sex rose to the occasion. Pushing himself to his feet, he scooped her up. Her eyelids drooped before they crossed the threshold.

Bree slept for eighteen hours straight, in his bed, in his stateroom. Sex remained by her side the entire time. He hadn't taken his eyes off her. He didn't want her slipping into anyone else's past. She was his future.

Martinique came and went, Point Simon Cruise Dock bustling with shipboard passengers. He'd missed showing Bree the island of fairy-tale romance and horrific disaster, love and death in a one-two punch.

Known originally as the birthplace of Empress Josephine, sweetheart and wife of Napoleon, Martinique had flourished, a sea-faring island, lush with island flowers.

Yet in 1902, tragedy struck without warning. The bustling cosmopolitan capital, St. Pierre, became a volcanic graveyard for thirty thousand souls. Few had survived.

Rebuilt, Martinique was now an island of quaint seaside villages, colonial ruins, and captivating beaches. Someday soon he'd return with Bree and show her all she'd missed.

Easing off the bed, he began to pace. He contemplated his future. In the darkest hours of the night, he'd rehashed Ramsay's accounting of the tragedy at sea. The truth had struck him like a bullet. Randolph and Daisy had loved, would have married, had Harlan Talmont not fired his gun.

He owed the flapper an apology.

Across the room, his private business line rang. The

line no one answered but him. Snatching the portable receiver, he moved into the living area before answering so as not to wake Bree.

"Alex McIntyre," he said. The caller was his secretary, Bridget Myers. A lady hired by Jackson Kyle, someone Sex had never met. His identity had remained a secret for ten years.

Bridget would never have called him aboard ship had the matter not been of utmost importance. His foundation needed his attention, and the conversation grew lengthy. So lengthy, he felt the walls close in around him. He shoved open the sliding glass doors that led out to the balcony and breathed in the salt air. He loved the ocean, the way the sun played off each cresting wave.

He began to tick off his immediate concerns. "Approve the expansion on St. Michaels, along with the purchase of the organ. Tell Southern Miami Baptist the foundation will buy the requested church pews. Get specs on the new addition for the animal shelter. Pick up the monthly grocery bill at the homeless center. Arrange permits for the restoration of the six historical homes in South Beach."

He paused, then went on. "Jackson will deal with the East End Skaters once we return to Miami. In the meantime, tell Risk Filleni, directly from me, that he's a punk if he doesn't attend summer school. A *C* in Algebra will guarantee him a new skate ramp at Center City Rec." That ought to motivate the kid.

Rubbing his jaw, he focused on Bridget's final question. "Cut checks from the McIntyre Foundation. Jackson will pick them up for my signature."

His head was filled with upcoming projects and calculations by the time he ended the call. Running his hand through his hair, he glanced up and caught Bree Emery's reflection in the sliding glass door.

She stood in his black silk pajama top, her hair pulled into a ponytail, her eyes wide, as if seeing him for the first time. "Alex McIntyre?" she said slowly. "You and he are one and the same?"

Heat sliced his cheekbones. "We're like Superman and Clark Kent."

The flat of her palms slapped her bare thighs. "There's more to Sex than sex."

He tossed the portable phone on a table, then adjusted his slate-blue silk boxers imprinted with a picture of the Supremes and golden music notes. "Set me free, why don't you, babe" ran across the fly. He approached her, his need to share his affiliation with the McIntyre Foundation strong.

"My middle name is Alexander, my mother's maiden name was McIntyre." He chose his words carefully. "I couldn't shake my reputation as a ladies' man, it was well-earned. After college, a part of me sought more from life than the next big orgasm. I could never eat three meals a day knowing there were homeless people on the street fighting over garbage. With Jackson's assistance, we formed the McIntyre Foundation. Any club, church, business, school, charity, or child can request assistance. I've never turned down a call for help."

"Why all the secrecy?" she asked.

He shrugged. "My life has been splashed across the tabloids and the society section of the newspaper since I was sixteen. The foundation allows me anonymity." He gave her a crooked smile. "I rather like being the mystery man behind good deeds."

She closed in on him. "You wear mystery well."

When they were inches apart, the heat from her body reached him. Their mouths touched, exchanging breath, but not kisses. "I want you wearing nothing at all."

He took her mouth in a sensuous kiss. She tasted of mint toothpaste. His tongue thrust. Slow entries. Slower retreats. There was no need for seduction. They belonged to each other. The quickening of her pulse echoed his own excitement. His sense of urgency.

Her throaty moan drove his hands down the silky sleeves of her pajama top. He unbuttoned his way up her body, exposing the tight skin over her belly, the arch of her rib cage, the swell of her breasts. His hands fanned widely, needing to touch and trace until her breasts flushed pink and her nipples puckered against his palms.

She hooked her arms about his neck, tucked herself into his body. She trusted. Accepted. Their desire was uncomplicated yet intense.

Fully aroused, he rubbed himself against her belly. When his hand pressed her pubic bone, his fingers seeking, he found her slick and swollen. His erection became painful.

With his mouth on hers, his fingers still teasing, he walked her backward until her calves bumped his bed frame. They hit the mattress with a bounce before sinking into its softness. Hot and willing. Wild and experimental. Her pajama top came off as quickly as his boxers. Her breasts rose and fell with the quickening of her breath. Full, tight, and berry-tipped. Her skin blushed the faint pinkish hue found in the center of tea roses. Her hips arched from the play of his fingers.

His muscles strained; his heart slammed wildly. He throbbed from his teeth to his toes. Seeking protection, he snagged a condom from his nightstand. Sheathed, he parted her thighs, then cupped the soft weight of her bottom. He tilted her hips to receive him.

Pure, sweet surrender.

His control slipped.

He was out of his mind.

Bree couldn't think. Couldn't breathe. She was so into Sex, she took him deeply with his first thrust. Lost in him, she forgot herself completely.

Her sensitized skin flared with his possession. She welcomed the slick friction that stroked her body to orgasm.

Matching moans.

Quick, breath-snatching cries.

Their lovemaking was compelling, heart-stopping, yet tender.

Time went away as she hit her breaking point, then soared beyond.

Her body arched and shuddered.

She absorbed his spasms.

The pleasure left her languid. Boneless.

Rolling onto his back, he drew her to his side. She draped her arm over his chest. Rested her head on his shoulder. Sexton St. Croix was a sexual being. His scent hinted of Armani. His smile was pure sated male.

She grazed his flat, brown nipples with her fingertips, the dip between his hipbones, the erection that swelled at a stolen glance. She glanced at him often.

Taking her hand, he kissed her palm, then pressed it to his heart. His voice was deep, his expression serious. "Marry me, Bree."

Her heart skipped, then slowed. "I don't come alone," she reminded him. "I come with dogs and the occasional ghost."

He stroked her hair off her cheek, tucked it behind her ear. "I can throw a Frisbee and take long walks in the park. The ghosts are welcome as long as *we* still go bump in the night."

Bree's chest warmed. The hottest, sexiest man alive would make concessions for her. Raising herself up on one elbow, she nuzzled his neck, then his jaw, his morning whiskers scratchy. Licking along his bottom lip, she paid special attention to each corner. Then she gave him a long, deep kiss. "I can do bump. And grind."

Fitting him with a condom, she straddled his thighs, sank down on his sex, and showed him grind. Their bodies fit together as if by design. She rotated her hips. And he threw back his head and moaned. "Damn fine grind."

In little time, desire condensed and coiled. She lost all focus as white-hot pleasure shot through her body. The force of her orgasm shook her. Tremors, like after-shocks, left her spent. Once again.

Making love to Sexton St. Croix had marked her forever.

Leaning forward, she kissed him soundly, the last of his drawn-out sighs warm on her mouth. His arms wrapped her to his chest. Their legs tangled. His voice was low and husky and serious. "I need to speak with Daisy Alton."

Bree pushed up slightly on her forearms. "She may have left the *Majestic*."

"Call her back."

Bree brushed her thumb over his lips. "Back? This from the man who wanted to dump the flapper overboard?"

He kissed the pad of her thumb. "I owe her an apology."

"Quite an acknowledgment, Mr. St. Croix."

"Daisy was an innocent victim and I was an ass," he confessed. "I should have listened and believed you from the start. Instead I stuck to the story handed down over generations. I'm still getting my head around the fact that Ramsay and Harlan lied all these years."

Compassion crossed his face. "Unsuspecting and in love, Daisy and Randolph were caught in the wrong place at the wrong time."

"The men spent their lives imprisoned by their memories with regret their constant companion," she reminded him. "Daisy's name has finally been cleared."

"All because of you." His hand grazed her back, stilled over her buttocks. "You're amazing, Bree Emery. Intuitive. Gorgeous. With a body that turns me inside out."

"You're smart and giving and too sexy for any one man."

He cocked a brow. "My woman finds me sexy?"

She pinched his shoulder. "Don't let it go to your head."

"It went straight to my groin." He tumbled her over, then rose above her. His gaze was as hot as his body as he settled between her thighs. "Compliments always get my full attention."

Sex was first to leave the bed. He'd shaved and showered and slipped on his boxers by the time Bree sat up and stretched. Glancing his way, she smiled. "Nice wiener."

She referred to his coral silk boxers decorated with small, reddish dachshunds and *I Love My Wiener* imprinted on the fly.

"I once dated a veterinarian," he explained as he

tugged on a pair of jeans. "If you want me to toss any or all boxers, I will."

She stood, all bare and beautiful, and approached him. "The boxers are you." She pressed a light kiss to his lips. "I do, however, plan to design my own pair once we're married. Ones that say *Property of Bree Emery.*"

He laughed out loud. His breath hitched in his throat when she presented her back and headed for the shower. She was one exquisite female. Slender shoulders. Sleek spine. Superb length of leg. She enhanced his life. He welcomed old age with this woman at his side.

Once she'd toweled off and dressed, they took the elevator to the boat deck. The sun colored the sky amber as it set. The stern stood empty except for a lone jogger. Bree stood at the railing, Sex close beside her, his arm hooked about her waist.

"Daisy?" Bree softly called to the flapper.

Seconds drifted into minutes before a shimmer of silver flashed against the sky, followed by the faint outline of the flapper. No longer in brilliant color, her imagine now appeared in shades of gray. She looked older, her smile tired.

Bree elbowed Sex. "Can you see her?"

He shifted his stance, a whole lot curious yet a little uncertain. "Sure can. Can she hear me?"

"Most definitely, young Sexton," Daisy replied. "Do you wish words with me?"

"I'm sorry," he said straight out. "My entire life I believed the story that you killed Randolph St. Croix. To learn it was a lie was hard to accept. Ramsay and Harlan deceived so many people."

Daisy's image wavered. "Forgive them, as I have now

forgiven them. I have peace in my heart. My love for Randolph will live forever."

Sex stared unblinkingly at Daisy Alton, trying hard to keep her in focus. "I wish there was more I could do."

"You can love Bree Emery," Daisy said simply.

His throat thickened. "That I can manage."

"Had I lived, young Sexton, I would have been your great-great aunt. Even without the St. Croix name, I will always look upon you fondly. You have won Bree's heart."

Sex squeezed Bree tightly. "I've no plans of letting her go."

"Lifetimes can be shortened without warning." Daisy's voice softened. "Love and care for each other. Find freedom in the shelter of each other's arms."

The flapper drifted, her image fainter still. "Young Sexton's goofy for you, Bree," she managed, her voice fading away. "In so many ways, he reminds me of Randolph. Sexton is the real McCoy."

Just before she disappeared, Daisy brushed Bree's cheek with a cosmic kiss. "You believed in me. Freed me from my past. I will always be grateful. Should you ever need me, I will be there."

The warmth of Daisy's presence was swept away by a strong breeze. Bree stood for a long time, staring out over the water. She'd grown attached to the flapper and would miss her greatly.

"Are you all right?" Sex asked.

Bree nodded. "It's hard to say good-bye to Daisy."

He turned slightly, tilted her chin up with his finger until their eyes met. "She'll be with you in spirit."

A smile played at the corner of her mouth. "She'll come to our wedding, attend the baptisms of our children, *appear* to whichever child inherits my metaphysical powers."

Clairsentient children?
A ghostly godmother?

At the onset of the cruise, Sexton St. Croix would have crossed his eyes in disbelief. Yet at that moment, he held a great fondness for a special psychic and a Jazz Age flapper.

Life with Bree Emery would never be dull. She would give him a family and countless memories.

And introduce him to the occasional ghost.

He'd never had it so good.

Jazz Age Glossary

Balled up: Confused or messed up
Bee's knees: Great idea or ultimate person
Bluenose: Puritanical person; prude
Bubs: Breasts
Bum's rush: The ejection by force from an establishment
Bump off: To kill
Bushwa!: Bullshit
Butt me: I'll take a cigarette
Carry a torch: To have a crush on someone
Cash or check?: Kiss now or later?
Cast a kitten: To have a fit
Cat with balloon lungs: A musician who never runs out of breath
Chill ya: When something is so outstanding it gives you the goose bumps
Ciggy: Cigarette
Dewdropper: Young man who sleeps all day; doesn't work
Dogs: Feet
Dolled up: Dressed up
Don't know from nothing: Doesn't have any information
Dumb Dora: Absolute fool, idiot
Face stretcher: An older woman trying to look young
Finger zinger: Someone who plays very fast
Fire extinguisher: A chaperone
Flapper: A stylish, brash young woman with short skirts and shorter hair
Flat tire: Dull, boring person
Gams: A woman's legs
Gay: Happy, merry
Get a wiggle on: Get a move on, get going
Get hot! Get hot!: Encouragement for a hot dancer
Giggle water: An intoxicating beverage; alcohol
Go chase yourself: Get lost; scram

Gold digger: A woman who pursues men for their money
Goofy: In love
Handcuff: Engagement ring
Hard-boiled: A tough, strong guy
Heavy sugar: A lot of money
High hat: A snob
Hoof: Dance
Hot sketch: A card or cut-up
Hotsy-totsy: Pleasing
Icy mitt: Rejection
Ironsides: Girdle
Jake/Everything's Jake: Everything's great
Killjoy: Solemn person
Let's ankle: Take a walk
Live wire: Lively person
Milquetoast: A very timid person; hen-pecked male
Nookie: Sex
Off one's nuts: Crazy
Pos-i-lute-ly: Affirmative; positively
Pull up your socks!: Stand tall; get a grip
Real McCoy: A genuine item or person
Rhatz!: How disappointing
Scratch: Money
Silver-tongued darb: Sweet-talker (man)
Smarty: A cute flapper
Stilts: Legs
Stuck on: In love
Swanky: Elegant
Sweet kisser: Sweet mouth
Swell: Wonderful
Tell it to Sweeny: Tell it to someone who'll believe it
Toot: Drunken binge
Torpedo: Hired thug or hit man
Twitted: Dumped or rejected
Vamp: A seducer of men
Water-proof: A face that doesn't require makeup

Turn the page
for a special sneak
preview of

A Connecticut Fashionista In King Arthur's Court

by

MARIANNE MANCUSI

One

If Mr. Blahnik could see me now, he'd be royally pissed off. Not that I'd blame the guy. After all, dragging his kitten heels through upstate New York mud is not exactly the reverent treatment four hundred-dollar shoes deserve.

To be fair, it really isn't my fault. It's not like I volunteered for the assignment. If anyone deserves Manolo's full wrath, it's my editor. She's the one who decided that spending my Saturday with a bunch of no-life weirdos would be a positive career move.

I originally planned a full day of shopping in The Village, lunch with Lucy, more shopping, then a relaxing train ride back home to my Connecticut condo where I would lounge by the pool for the remainder of the afternoon.

Instead, I am on assignment at King Arthur's Faire. My mission? To write 500 words on the emerging trend of medieval garb in today's fashions.

I'm Katherine Jones, by the way. But pretty much everyone calls me Kat. Why, I don't know—maybe it's my eyes. I've got big, green cat-like eyes that turn up at the corners. As a kid growing up in Brooklyn, they were my ticket to fame. The guys couldn't stay away. Even the ones I wished would.

I've moved up in the world since then. Now, as the twenty-nine-year old associate fashion editor at *La Style,* it's my job to claw through the hype and sniff out the trends. I'm good at it, too. Remember that Louis Vuitton cherry blossom purse craze? I broke that story before *Vogue* laid their Chanel-shaded eyes on it.

But does my editor recognize my talent? Uh, that would be a no. In fact, half the time I don't think she even recognizes *me,* though I've been working for the fashion rag for nearly four years.

And so, instead of jetting off to Milan to write cover stories on the beautiful people, I usually get stuck doing back end blurbs that lie lost between tampon ads.

This time it's medieval gear, which I'm sorry, but I think is ridiculous. I can hardly see J. Lo sporting a pointy veiled headdress and am quite positive Brad Pitt would not be caught dead in tunic and tights.

My photographer, Chrissie Haywood, seems to have none of these doubts. She's currently traipsing through the mud in a Chrissie Haywood original—a royal blue velour gown with lace-up corset and cap sleeves. She told me earlier that she made it from a pattern she'd bought off eBay, confirming my suspicions that the Internet really is an evil empire where freaks come together to rejoice in their freakiness. In BI (before Internet) days, if you had an odd quirk, you kept it to yourself. Now you form email loops with thousands of others, bonding together through your common idiosyncrasy.

Growing up, my family couldn't afford a computer.

But I didn't care. All I needed were magazines. Glossy, glamorous, advice filled pages just waiting to transport me to a world of beauty, majesty, and anorexia—for the bargain price of $3.99. Why waste a grand or more on a plastic box only good for downloading porn?

"Here ye, here ye," a barker announces as we walk by his stand. "Whoso shall lift this sword from the stone, the same is rightly born King of England." Or, in this case, will rightly win a plastic Excalibur of his very own. The toy sword emits a piercing scream when slammed against trees, rocks, people—whatever the little brats decide to use as their unwitting target. I know this not because I'd tried my luck at the sword-in-stone thing (I have no burning desire to become British royalty) but because every kid here seems to have already won one and has made it his or her mission to see that I achieve the headache of a lifetime.

I know the story of King Arthur and the Knights of the Round Table as well as anyone, I suppose. Dude pulls sword from stone, becomes king. Marries a total tart named Guenevere who goes off and shags his best friend Lancelot. What I don't get is why people think it's so damned romantic. Having been a victim of an ex-boyfriend's infidelity, I can tell you for a fact, there's nothing beautiful about being cheated on and lied to.

We walk past Ye Locale Eatery where for $5.95 you can get a cup of mead (aka Bud Lite) with your King's Royale Chicken Bites (courtesy of King Ronald Mc-Donald, if I'm not mistaken). They also feature what I'm sure was a Medieval delicacy—Pepperoni Pizza of the Round Table.

"Here, wear this." To my horror, Chrissie plops a tall dunce cap thing—complete with lavender polyester veil—over my head. She must have bought it while I wasn't looking. "Now you fit in," she proclaims, as if that had been my goal—rather than my nightmare—all along.

"Gee, thanks," I reply, pulling the hat from my head and examining it with a critical eye. Could Gucci really be planning this kind of kitsch for the fall runway? Chrissie looks hurt as I pick at the hat's seams, investigating the quality or, in this case, lack of it. I could have sewn better during first year Home Ec at the Brooklyn Community College I went to—and that was the year I accidentally blew up the kitchen! Okay, so I'm a better seamstress than cook.

"You know," Chrissie whines, "you could at least try to have a good time." She twirls around, velour gown flapping in the breeze, taking it all in. "It's not exactly torture, you know. Hanging out in a medieval village. Could be much worse."

It could, and suddenly is, as the skies open up and rain starts gushing down. Super. We duck into the nearest tent for cover.

"May I read thy palm, milady?"

Oh great. The tent we pick just happens to be inhabited by King Arthur's very own Miss Cleo. A tiny, wrinkled gypsy type addresses us from behind her crystal bowling ball. She wears a bright, mauve-colored robe, bordered with intricate gold embroidery. Gotta give her some props—her costume, at least, looks authentic enough, even though I'm pretty sure I've seen that same crystal ball at Spencer Gifts for $19.99.

I motion for Chrissie to take a photo. "Ooh, yes. Kat, get your fortune read," she replies, misunderstanding my pointing hand.

"No thanks. I don't believe any of that psychic mumbo jumbo." Sure, I check my horoscope once in a while—what magazine diva doesn't? But anything that forces me to fork over good money for worthless prophecies that could apply to anyone, I steer clear.

The old crone glares at me with beady eyes, possibly not appreciating the fact that I used the words "mumbo jumbo" and "psychic" in the same sentence. But come on! She must be used to nonbelievers at this point in her career. She looks about eighty. Still, her rather rude stare gives me the creeps and I contemplate leaving the tent, rain be damned. After a second analysis, I decide the cost of dry-cleaning $600 Armani trousers that I borrowed from the props closet at work outweighs being stuck with an annoying old woman who thinks she knows my future.

"Come on, Kat. I'll pay for it and everything." Did I mention Chrissie is persistent as well as enthusiastic? I give in. What else are we going to do while waiting for the rain to end?

Plopping down on the chair, I stick out my arm. A strange chill trips down my spine as the ancient crone takes my palm in her gnarled hands. She traces my lifeline with a long bony finger as I wonder if I should ask her if she's ever heard of hand lotion. I mean her hands are pretty far gone, but it's never too late for moisturizing.

"Let me guess," I say with a sigh. "Long life. Success in love. Great career." These fortune-tellers always tell you what you want to hear. After all, spreading doom and gloom isn't going to get them many customers.

"Thou does not believe." The woman scowls, dropping my hand immediately. "Why would I bother?"

"Look. Chrissie's going to fork over your five bucks," I reply, a little pissed off at this point. Who is this woman to cop an attitude with me? She's a lame medieval fair fortune-teller. Probably doesn't even have her own 900-number. "Just tell me about my illustrious future or whatever it is you do."

The woman sighs (she's really one for drama, let me tell you) and takes my hand again. A sudden fear washes over her crinkly face. "Thou shouldst not be here," she says in an urgent whisper.

"No shit. I should be at Bloomingdale's. Doesn't take a psychic to figure out *that* one."

Chrissie swats me from behind and I giggle.

"No." The woman looks suddenly fierce. "That is not what I am meaning. I mean thou art out of time."

"Already? I just sat down. You haven't even told me my future yet."

"Not out of time with me. Out of time with life. Thy destiny—it is lying in another era."

You'd think with everyone paying twenty bucks admission, the fair organizers could have found a better psychic than this. "All I want to know," I say, glancing back at Chrissie with a wink, "is whether I'm going to be rich, successful, and score a really cute boyfriend. Tell me that and I'll be on my merry way."

"Pay attention!" the woman shrieks, and I nearly jump out of my skin.

I try to pull my hand away, but she clutches it tight, digging her long fingernails into my palm. Her beady eyes are wide open now, but clouded over, her nose scrunched, and her lips curl into a snarl. Okay, this is getting a tad bit freaky for me!

"The lines of tragedy are clearly written on thy hand. If thou does not take heed, *thou will surely die today!*"

That's it! I manage to rip my hand from her claws and stand up. "Yeah, sure, whatever, psychic psycho," I spit out. I'd much rather be caught in the rain than listen to this bull. Who does this crackpot think she is, trying to scare me like this? "Chrissie, I'm so out of here."

Chrissie looks from me to the psychic and back again. "Maybe you shouldn't piss her off, Kat," she says in a low voice. "What if she puts a spell on you?"

I can't help but laugh at that one. "Oh, please, Chris," I whisper back. "She couldn't put a spell on a paper bag."

"That is where thou art wrong, my friend," the gypsy interjects, eavesdropping on our private conversation.

"Oh, really?" I ask, in my best skeptical voice. "Then go for it. If you've got so much power, give it your best shot."

"ABU-SOLSTICE-EXCALIBUR!" The woman suddenly recites her best Harry Potterism at the top of her lungs, following the "magic words" with a rather disturbing cackle. Thunder cracks as she waves her hands with a dramatic whoosh.

OMG! What a freak!

The moment passes. I don't turn into a toad. I'm not suddenly sporting donkey ears. In fact, I'm exactly the same Katherine "just call me Kat" Jones I was before she shouted her crazy curse. Except now perhaps a little less mad and a little more amused.

"Good try, sweetie." I pat the gypsy on her embroidered sleeve. "Maybe a few more years at Hogwarts will do the trick." I turn to Chrissie, who still looks petrified. "What now?"

"I—I think the rain has let up," she mumbles. "I want to get photos of the jousters."

Jousters, huh? As in sexy men dressed in armor and riding horses? That doesn't sound half bad. A lot better than crazy fortune-tellers uttering curses, anyway. Determined to change my attitude and show Chrissie a good time, I amicably set the pointy hat on my head and take my photographer by the arm.

"Bring on the jousting!"

The jousting arena is at the far end of the fairgrounds. The organizers set up bleachers on either side, kind of like a high school football field. We're a few minutes early and are able to snag front row seats.

I steal a glance over at the end of the field where the men are suiting up. Maybe it's due to my recent guy drought, but boy do they look good. One in particular sports flowing black hair and a body to die for. He wears a crimson red crest on his breastplate in the shape of a dragon. Yum, yum, double-yum. I squint to get a better look and wish I brought my glasses.

"The guy in the dragon armor is playing Lancelot," Chrissie informs me, after glancing at her program.

"I'd be his Guenevere any day," I remark, taking in his broad shoulders and arrogant swagger. "I'm definitely digging his whole alpha male vibe." He looks over, and I flash him a smile, then nudge Chrissie. "Get his picture."

She complies, snapping a few shots using her telephoto lens. "Wow, he looks even better up close," she murmurs. "Maybe you should go talk to him."

I laugh. "No way am I going to lower myself to knight-in-shining-armor-groupie level. Besides, I bet he's dumb as a rock. All brawn, no brains."

"You're such a snob. He could be a rocket scientist on his day off for all you know."

"Okay fine." I rip the camera from her grasp and look into the lens. Unfortunately Lancey Boy simultaneously picks that moment to place his helmet over his head so I don't get much of a view. "Oh well," I say, passing the camera back to Chrissie. "Guess it wasn't meant to be." I sigh dramatically. "Though I'll tell you what. *Something's* gotta be 'meant to be' pretty soon. I'm like literally a born-again virgin at this point."

Chrissie giggles at my declaration. Easy for her to laugh. She's married to some Jersey-born beatnik and living a happy, hippie vegetarian existence in The Village. She met the poet in high school and has absolutely no idea what the rest of us go through trying to find a decent man in the Tri-State Area.

It's not that guys don't hit on me from time to time. It's only that lately there hasn't been anything worth hitting back. One would think in Manhattan there'd be cute guys up the yin-yang but no, only on "Sex and the City" reruns. In real life, the scene is a lot more depressing.

Trumpets sound, presumably to mark the start of the tournament. Men and women dressed in silly costumes like Chrissie's scramble to find last minute seats.

"Hear ye, hear ye!" A young man wearing a very fake gray beard, wizard cap, and star-covered gown walks into the center of the field. "Welcome, one and all to King Arthur's Faire. I am Merlin, wizard of Camelot."

Oh, he's supposed to be Merlin, is he? I snicker, wondering who on earth did the casting for this place. First, there was the scary old bag who takes herself way too seriously, and now this teenager posing as an ancient magician.

"Today, you will witness feats of wonder that will amaze and entertain. Valiant knights, brave and bold, fiercely fighting to win the favor of their Lady, Queen Guenevere."

"Yeah, yeah, we get it. In the name of chivalry and all that jazz," I mumble to Chrissie. "Enough intro. Bring on the jousters."

As Merlin keeps talking, I find myself drifting off, unable to concentrate on his long-winded ramblings, his voice lulling me into a strange trance-like state. My eyes blur, and I start to get dizzy. I waver a bit, almost feeling as if I'm going faint. Odd.

I shake my head to try to wake up, get orientated.

"Are you okay?" Chrissie studies me with concerned eyes. "You look pale."

"I'm fine." The dizziness fades as quickly as it began. "Maybe I'm dehydrated or something. Too many buy-one-get-one-free margaritas last night."

"Let me get you some water." Chrissie rises from her seat and walks toward the refreshment stand. After a moment's contemplation of her extreme niceness, I turn back to the ring.

Merlin's endless speech has somehow miraculously ended, and knights on the sidelines mount their trusty steeds. As they gallop into the ring, the front row seems like it might have been a bad idea. I'm not a big fan of horses and find myself far too close to crashing hooves for comfort.

Two knights line up on either side of the field, grasping long, wooden lances capped with steel tips. Each knight is covered in heavy plates of armor from head to toe, offering protection, though not much maneuverability. Even the horses wear armor over their heads, making them look like metal monsters.

A bell rings, and the horses charge, their thundering hooves echoing through my already pounding head. The knights lower their lances, each preparing to bash his weapon into the other, in an attempt to knock him off his horse.

Slam! The lances whack against the shields, splinters

flying everywhere. The green crested knight falls from his horse. He runs to the sidelines and grabs a stick with a chained spiked metal ball on the end. He swings it, guarding his space, while the blue knight, still on horseback but now wielding a sword, circles him. Gotta admit, the whole thing is rather exciting.

The green knight manages to hook his chain around the blue knight's sword and wrenches the weapon from his grasp, sending it flying. The blue knight jumps off the horse and somersaults to his blade, grabbing it mid-roll, and stands ready to face his opponent. I lean forward in my seat. I know it's all fake, but it really is a pretty good show.

Where's Chrissie? I look around. Must be a long line at the concession stand. Too bad, 'cause she's missing everything.

After much clashing and bashing of weapons, sparks flying as metal slams against metal, the blue knight succeeds in cornering the green knight, sword to his throat. The first joust is over, the blue knight victorious. High on a far platform, the woman playing Guenevere, wearing a green velour gown and heavy gold metal crown, claps and tosses daisies to honor her champion.

"Blue knight, thou art brave," Merlin declares, this time riding into the ring on a white horse. "But art thou willing to challenge the realm's most gifted sportsman? A knight above all others? I give you, Lancelot!"

The crowd cheers and whistles and whoops as the red dragon knight gallops into the ring, waving a flag with a matching crest. From the starry-eyed gazes of the other women in the audience, it's obvious I'm not the only one who finds him hot.

The blue knight accepts the challenge, mounting his

horse and acquiring a new lance from his squire. Another helper hands Lancelot his lance and they line up, ready to charge.

At that moment, pain stabs behind my eyes and my vision blurs again, right as the two men are set to run. I want to watch, but instead I'm forced to squeeze my eyes shut, desperate to get rid of the dizziness. The roar of the crowd only makes it worse. I press my fingers against my temples and try to stand. The pain is nearly unbearable. I've got to find Chrissie.

Once on my feet, nausea overtakes me, and I stumble forward, not sure whether I'll throw up or faint. I close my eyes, willing myself to stay conscious. What is wrong with me? All I can think of is the gypsy curse. Her words.

You shall surely die this day!

That's so stupid. This is just a major coincidence. I've got a migraine. I'm not dying. I take a few more steps to clear my head.

"Get back!" a man yells, and I open my eyes, only to realize he's talking to me. In my delirious walk, I've somehow wandered halfway onto the field, right as the jousters have come together for their first run. Suddenly, a huge chunk of wood—splintered from one of the lances—flies through the air like a javelin, directly toward my head. I put up my arms to cover my face, but I'm too late. The lance hits me square in the forehead and I see stars, then blackness.

"Milady?"

A sexy, deep voice prompts me to open my eyes. I'm lying on my back, on the ground, staring up at the most gorgeous blue eyes I have ever seen. I mean, lots of people have blue eyes, but this particular pair is quite literally the color of sapphires, sparkling in the sunshine. Mmmm.

"How do you fare?" the man asks. His callused fingertips brush against my forehead as he lifts a wisp of hair from my face. The sensation sends a shiver down to my toes. I drop my gaze and notice the Adonis is wearing a suit of armor with a red dragon crest emblazoned on it. Ah, the guy playing Lancelot. His medieval garb looks a lot more real close up. My very own knight-in-shining-armor. Maybe this whole getting hit on the head thing could work out in my favor after all. If only it didn't hurt so much.

I force my focus away from those eyes to better assess my current situation. I try to sit, but a stabbing pain at the back of my head causes me to rethink that notion. I lay my head back down and moan. That flying wood must have hit me harder than I thought. Just great. I'm a real damsel in distress now.

"Ow," I cry, closing my eyes in agony. "My head kills. I think I might need a doctor."

"Page, send for Lord Merlin, immediately," a concerned female voice commands in a bad British accent. I open my eyes. Behind the blue-eyed man stands a petite blond woman, wearing an authentic-looking purple silk gown and a sparkly tiara. Probably the one playing Guenevere, though I could have sworn she was wearing a different outfit before.

But never mind her. I turn back to my hero, Lancelot. Chrissie was right; he does look a lot cuter up close. His long black hair, blowing in the slight breeze, makes my stomach do flip-flops, despite my headache.

Where is Chrissie, anyway? I try to turn my head to

get a better look at my surroundings, but the pain proves too great.

"Rest, Lady. The Lord Merlin will attend to your wounds shortly," insists the woman.

I frown. What's this about Merlin? Don't they have a first aid tent or something? I'm certainly not getting medical treatment from the fifteen-year-old who introduced the jousting.

"Hey," I protest. "I don't want to be treated by some kid." Then again, maybe they have two guys playing Merlin today. One who in his spare time serves as a NYC EMT, hopefully?

"I am not sure what you speak of, Lady," the Guenevere wannabe says, furrowing her brow. "Lord Merlin is certainly no baby goat. He is the most powerful druid in all of Camelot and well versed in the ways of magic."

"Goat? What are you talking about? Oh, I get it. Kid. Goat. You're still doing the role-playing thing." These people really take this stuff way too seriously. You'd think it'd be all fun and games until someone loses an eye—or gets hit in the head with a flying lance. I hope they have good insurance, because if I've sustained any serious injuries, I am so suing this place.

"Could we cut the medieval crap for one second?" I ask, starting to get annoyed. "I'm hurt. I need a doctor. A real one, not a magic one. Maybe even an ambulance." I scan the crowd. No reaction. Only blank stares. The Lancelot guy has risen, and I see him whispering with Guenevere.

I fumble for my purse and manage to pull out my cell phone. Screw them, I'm calling 911 myself.

No reception. I forgot we're out in the Boonies. They must not even have cell phone towers here. My day is getting better and better. I close my eyes, succumbing to my fate, at least until Chrissie returns. Voices whisper furiously around me, perhaps assuming I'm unconscious and unable to hear.

"Where did she come from?"

"Out of thin air, I should think."

"She is dressed more like man than female."

"What would Bishop Mallory say?"

"Could she be one of the Fey Folk, caught between the worlds?"

"Don't be daft; she is as human as you or I."

"Then with what strange talk does she go on about?"

"Perhaps she's mad?"

Sick of the conversation, I open one eye, then the other. A crowd of medieval garbed folk has gathered around me. I check for any non-freaks, but don't see a single normal looking soul. Just great.

"Can we go back to the twenty-first century for like one minute so I can get help?" I suggest, the pain in my head throbbing. "Then you can go on with your little fantasy world?"

They stare at me as if I'm the village idiot. "Aye, it definitely appears she may be addled," whispers Guenevere to Lance. "Poor child."

I open my mouth to protest, but suddenly the sea of people parts, and an ancient man with a long gray beard and gnarled cane approaches me. Is this the Merlin guy they were talking about? Well, at least he's not fifteen. Maybe they have different Merlins like Disney has different Mickeys. I hope this one isn't as crazy as everyone else seems to be.

He studies me with an odd look in his piercing green eyes. "Where did this woman come from?" Okay, not a good sign.

"She appeared from nowhere," Lancelot informs

him, evidently not ready to take the blame for his lance's wayward actions.

"Actually," I interrupt, "I was hanging quite nicely on the sidelines when his big lance thing splintered and came flying at my head." No need to admit to my walking out onto the field in case of future lawsuit. Had I signed any kind of waiver? I hope not.

Lancelot's eyes narrow. He reaches beside him and picks up his lance. Not a splinter on it. Running his hand up and down the smooth shaft, he says, "I know not what the lady is going on about, sire. But she was hit by no lance. As I said before, she appeared out of nowhere, already bleeding when she collapsed onto the field."

My face heats in anger. "That's such a lie. You're only saying that so you won't get sued." I meet Merlin's eyes. Will he believe me? "He probably did a lance switcheroo while I was out cold." What a jerk that Lancelot guy is. Forget the whole knight in shining armor thing, the beautiful blue eyes. Underneath it all, he's exactly like the rest of the sorry male race—from Mars!

"Hmm." Merlin's eyes fall on my abandoned cell phone. He reaches down and picks it up, turning it over and around his fingers, a look of wonder and surprise clearly written on his face. He presses a button. The responding beep makes him jump a little, dropping the mobile on the hard ground.

"Do you mind? That's a four hundred dollar phone," I protest, to no avail. The old man's claw-like hands grab the handset off the ground and stuff it into his robe's pocket. "Hey! That's mine. You can't—"

"What is the trouble here?" A rich baritone voice demands. The crowd parts again, this time also bowing their heads in reverence. A blond, bearded man, probably in his late thirties, dressed in red robes and wearing a large golden crown approaches. He looks down at me and then to Merlin with questioning eyes.

Merlin shoots me a suspicious glare, then turns back to the crowned man with a sly smile. "We've caught an intruder, Your Majesty. A spy from another land."

"Oh, give me a break," I moan, unable to take much more. I'm in pain—physically *and* mentally at this point. All I want to do is go back to Connecticut. Where the hell is Chrissie?

"She certainly does not have the voice of one born in Camelot," the king guy agrees, though his tone is cautious. "And her clothing is very strange, indeed."

"She is not a spy, Arthur," Guenevere pipes in. "She is just a girl. I will admit, she may be a bit odd. Perhaps simple—or mad, even. But I think not—"

"Spies can come in all shapes and forms, Your Majesty," Merlin interrupts. "You cannot be too careful these days. Many outside the civilized lands of Camelot wish to do you harm. What better plan than to send in an innocent looking girl to win your heart and gain your trust, all the while feeding back your intimate secrets to her barbarian Saxon lover?"

Oh yeah, whatever, loser. I can tell Guen doesn't like the guy either, from the dirty look she shoots him behind his back. Not that Arthur notices. It's obvious he respects the opinion of Merlin more than that of his "wife." Men. If he's acting anything like the real Arthur did, well, it's no wonder Guenny ends up finding solace in the arms of Lancelot.

"Indeed, we should practice caution," Arthur admits. "Lord Merlin, what do you suggest we do with her?"

"Take me to a hospital. Please!" I beg, starting to get

a little worried at this point. Blood's been trickling from the gash in my forehead for at least ten minutes now, and I'm feeling more than a little faint. The throbbing pain at the back of my head hasn't let up either. I might have a concussion. And they're all standing around—acting! It's like a nightmare, but I can't wake up. "Chrissie!" I call, a lump forming in my throat. *Don't cry, Kat. Don't let these losers see you cry.* "Chrissie, please help!"

But Chrissie is nowhere to be found. The only answer I get to my calls is from Merlin, who folds his arms across his chest, a smug expression on his wrinkled face. "I think we should lock the infidel in the tower."

KATE ANGELL
DRIVE ME CRAZY

Cade Nyland doesn't think that anything good can come of the new dent in his classic black Sting Ray, even if it does happen at the hands of a sexy young woman. He is determined to win his twelfth road rally race of the year.

TZ Blake only enters Chugger Charlie's tight butt competition to win enough money to keep her auto repair shop open. What she ends up with is a position as navigator in a rally race. All she has to do is pretend she knows where she is going. All factors indicate that the unlikely duo is in for a bumpy ride . . . and each eagerly anticipates the jostling that will bring them closer together.